The Furnace

Michael Stevens

Published by Strategic Writing, 2022.

THE FURNACE

First edition. November 21, 2022.

ISBN: 978-0578502700

Written by Michael Stevens.

The Furnace

by

Michael R. Stevens

Michael R. Stevens

There would be no false gold if real gold didn't exist somewhere.
Sufi saying

Do not seek to follow in the footsteps of the wise. Seek what they sought.
Matsuo Basho

Prologue

Berlin, 4 May, 1924

Adam Luce skidded his powerful black bike to a stop in front of the columned portico of the von Schwerin mansion, painfully aware of the inappropriate racket that announced his arrival. As German motorcycles went, the 1922 edition of the Megola Sport he had managed to get his hands on was fast and trustworthy, but loud. For the grueling nine hour ride up from Munich, he had needed a bike he could trust, loud or not. And this wasn't the end of the journey. He had four more hours ahead of him before he reached the harbor in Hamburg and, if he made it, the safety of the open seas.

He dismounted and hung his helmet on the bike's handlebars. Then, after attempting to comb his thick blonde hair with his fingers as best he could, he climbed the stairs to the mansion's massive front door, noting with a pang of nostalgia the wrought iron stanchions on either side where the torches had burned so brightly on the night of his first visit. He felt a little shaky and he knew he needed to rest, even if it meant completing the last leg of his journey in darkness. More importantly, he needed to be with Charlotte one last time.

He pressed the doorbell and waited. A stiff, perfectly groomed Prussian in his mid-fifties opened the door and regarded Adam coldly. The servant saw a sturdy young man of unquestionable Teutonic stock, dressed in the leathers of a ruffian, possibly a Bolshevik, possibly armed.

"*Ich bin hier um Fraulein von Schwerin zu besuchen*," said Adam in his flawless German. *I'm here to visit Fraulein von Schwerin.* At that moment, Charlotte appeared behind the servant. She was dressed in black silk from head to toe, with a vermillion gemstone suspended from her neck by a delicate golden chain.

Her face was as he had held it in his memory, brow pale as the moon, dark eyes that hid more than they revealed, lips painted into a Cupid's bow with bright red lipstick, all framed by fine black hair cut short in the provocative style of the day. But now, that face projected a warmth he had never felt before, even in their most intimate moments.

"Welcome," she said, opening her arms in invitation. He walked past the servant to embrace her.

"You have no business coming here," she whispered once they were close. "This is the first place they'll look for you."

"I don't think so. And if I'm wrong, well, there's no vehicle I can't outrun."

"You can't outrun bullets, *Liebchen*." She pressed against him, paying no attention to the film of grime that had formed on his leather jacket. After a long moment, she pulled away.

"I'm so happy you came. You did what had to be done. I understand."

He thought, *She knows!*

"I had no choice," he began, but she put a finger to his lips.

"How much time do we have?" she asked.

He glanced at the dial of his Breitling that had stood by him through thick and thin. "My ship sails in seventeen hours."

"Then come," she said, taking his hand and leading him down the hall that bordered the grand ballroom and then skirted the kitchen to bring them to the solarium, where glass windows presented a view of the estate's garden, bordered by tall hedges that extended out of view. A small round table near one of the windows had been set for tea. Charlotte seated him and then went over to the back corner of the room to put a kettle on a small gas stove.

"I'm going to make the tea myself," she announced. "With special herbs for you."

Adam stared out at the carefully pruned shrubs, letting himself relax as best he could while Charlotte clattered behind him. Soon the tea arrived. Its aroma was vaguely familiar. He searched his memory, and when he managed to place it his whole body stiffened. It was the hallucinatory brew she had given him once before, at the tea house.

"Charlotte, I can't!"

"You must," she said, sitting down across from him and pouring the amber liquid into their cups.

Adam struggled to think clearly, but even the vapor seemed to be twisting his thoughts. For all he knew, she could summon a host of armed guards at the snap of a finger and... what? That line of thought was preposterous. She loved him. He had to believe that. Her insistence was an entreaty, not an ultimatum.

She leaned over and took his hands in hers. "You must trust me. We have to be together. In all things. In all ways."

A hot wave of desire suddenly washed over him, threatening to dissolve his sense of purpose. What he *must* do was get the diaries in his possession out of the country. *The Berlin Diaries*, as he had come to think of them—his own, the two he had stolen, copies of letters he's sent and received, and of course, the book. If he could only study this material more deeply, he was certain everything would be explained, even the role of The Lodge.

"I came only to say good-bye," he said. "I can't...." He glanced down at his cup.

"There are no good-byes for us, Darling. The two of us are one." She picked up her cup and put it to her lips. "Be brave. Drink."

He couldn't bring himself to walk away from her. He drank.

After a moment she stood and extended her hand. "Let's go into the garden."

They walked out of the solarium onto a freshly cut lawn. On the opposite side, a gravel path beckoned. For Adam, the leaves and branches had already taken on a sharper edge and begun to form patterns that weren't really there, the forerunners of real hallucinations.

Charlotte took his arm. "I'm not sure of anything anymore," she said. "Not how to spend my time, or how to spend all this money, or how to think about what's going to happen next. I don't understand what's real and what's not anymore."

Her voice reminded him of coins spilling out of a purse onto the cobblestones of a small, dark alley, gold and silver, like little suns and moons. The path they were on had become a dark alley. The hedges were tall and dense, precluding vision in any direction, and the path was geometrical, with sharp turns leading them deeper into what Adam now realized was a labyrinth. Charlotte clung to his arm, seemingly a little weak from the drugs and leaning on him for support, yet at the same time in total control.

Nothing here is what it seems, he thought. Charlotte was a depraved slut... and his one true love. The alchemical convictions of The Lodge were rubbish... and yet the source of limitless power. The labyrinth was a geometrical planting of hedges... and his life.

The path came to a fork. Adam perceived a glimmer of filtered sunlight coming from the left fork and he took a step in that direction. Charlotte didn't resist. Soon they came to a clearing in the center of which stood what Adam could only understand as a vision his mind had conjured into the reality of the labyrinth: a huge, round-bottomed volumetric flask at least twice his height. Inside of it was a bed.

Only the Germans could produce a glass vessel of that size, he thought. Or had he and Charlotte somehow shrunk? What did it matter? There it was, and he had to accept it. Charlotte smiled, approached the vision, and then produced a key. She slid it into the steel lock of a glass door set into the curved belly of the flask, and the door swung silently open. Once inside, she tugged at the shoulders of her gown and let it slip off her body onto the glass so that she was completely naked. She beckoned Adam to enter. He thought, *This is really happening*. And there was no turning back.

He stepped into the giant flask and stood silently while she locked the door. Still smiling, she began to undress him, tossing his road jacket, his shirt, his pants and all the rest onto the floor next to her discarded robe. Then, she dangled the key before his eyes for just a moment... and tossed it straight up and out of the great vessel's mouth. It struck the outside of the vessel once as it fell and landed, hopelessly out of reach.

The Berlin Diaries

Diary of Adam Luce

Berlin, 31 October, 1923

The economic chaos here in Berlin is unimaginable. *Hausfrauen* hurry off to the market with wheelbarrows full of banknotes... yes, I have seen this. And when money isn't enough, it is said they offer themselves. Who has need of a cabaret when decadence is available in the back room of the nearest butcher shop? And yet, I find myself sitting near the stage at the Rio Rita or *Die Weiße Maus* all too often. I tell myself I am studying the complexities of Weimar politics, and I am. But I must confess, I am also lonely, and a couple of glasses of Mosel among a crowd of smartly dressed men and women who aren't shy about sharing their opinions with an American brings comfort.

The other night at the *Maus* one of the girls in the review kept staring at me. I'm certain of it.

I cannot free myself from distraction. The blaring headlines, the daily marches along *Unter den Linden*, the noise of the trains, the gunshots, the talkative shop girls with their short, *Herrenschnit* hair styles (a sign that they are willing, some say), the lure of alcohol, of the cabarets, of experimentation.... In this atmosphere I am supposed to bore into the laboratories of the world's most sophisticated chemical company like some abject worm, digest its secrets, and then crawl home and take my place in the Luce "empire" my father and uncle have built.

My father congratulated me after the graduation ceremony with these immortal words: "You're going to make a fine asset to the company, Adam." And so I am. I could have majored in anything and been successful at Yale. That's not arrogance. It's just a fact. For some unknown reason, my mind works like a gramophone. Once I've heard a lecture I can play it back verbatim, which comes in quite handy at exam time. I chose chemistry over philosophy and literature because it was the right thing to do... because chemistry would best equip me to contribute to the family business – mighty Luce Chemical, Inc.

It was a mistake. There, I've admitted it.

Chemistry is the science of boring inevitability. When so many milliliters of sulfuric acid react with so many grams of sodium chloride, the result is always sodium sulfate and hydrochloric acid, and always in precisely predictable quantities.

$$H_2SO_4 + 2NaCl = 2HCl + Na_2SO_4$$

This inevitability is a mirror of my life. When I return home to Margaret we'll marry, we'll "react" (if I can call it that) and the result will be children and a mansion on the hill, no doubt with a tennis court. She'd love that.

Many would envy a life of such promise. But at times, I must confess, I feel as if I am preparing to enter a prison from which there will be no escape. Yes, I came here to advance the fortunes of Luce Chemicals Inc., and turn the company to a more noble purpose, a purpose that will evoke respect among my peers instead of sniggers behind my back. Supplanting the suspicious concoctions we sell with legitimate medicines is a fine goal indeed, and learning the secrets of how to manufacture aspirin, the one drug that gave hope and comfort during the epidemic of 1918, will without question further that mission. But surely there must be more to life. Where are the mysteries? Beneath the surface of things I sense hidden possibilities of which I know nothing. One thing is certain. I will never discover them unless I abandon myself to the streets and clubs of Berlin. If that means putting my personal safety at risk, so be it.

Diary of Adam Luce
Berlin, 1 November, 1923

Sitting alone at this old oak desk and staring out at the deserted alley beneath the second story window that is at times my small room's sole source of light, I wait while my mind replays again and again the events of my graduation party that got me here in the first place. Knowing what I know now, would my words and actions have been different? Of course not.

Uncle Wyn insisted that the party be held at the Waldorf. My father grumbled, but my mother wouldn't hear of Dad's alternative plan, which involved renting one of the local halls. So, we packed into our new Buick – I should remind myself more often that we're hardly poor – and made our way down the coast to the city, my father at the wheel, my mother by his side, me in the back seat, wishing Kate were there too, and not somewhere west of Laramie doing God knows what, and most likely never to return. I have sent her two letters. Why hasn't she replied? But that's my sister for you. No squeezing her into a mold.

Uncle Wyn and my cousin Brad had raced down ahead of us in the Bearcat, and Brad was there in the lobby to greet us when we arrived, drink in hand, flaunting the rules as usual. "Prohibition is better than no liquor at all," he quipped.

I remember thinking that the both of us looked more like models in a magazine ad than newly-minted Yale grads prepared to save the world with brain power alone. We were both dressed in dark pinstriped suits with starched white shirts, perfectly knotted ties and highly polished wing tips. I was the taller, Teutonic-looking cousin, with the stereotypical blond hair and blue eyes, he the southern European-looking one, with curly dark hair and a compact body. We were both fit to pose for the next Brooks Brothers catalogue. Now, as I think about it, all the people standing under the chandeliers in the ballroom that night looked more like mannequins than living, breathing human beings.

Well, not Margaret. But I'm getting ahead of myself.

I was feeling depressed at the prospect of working in the small, dreary office my father had arranged for me so as not to imply favoritism, and worse, living every day from nine to five under his thumb. I drank several glasses of well-spiked punch as quickly as I could, wishing it were scotch – or even gin, for that matter. Given my mood and state of intoxication, I was ready for anything, and I think Uncle Wyn knew it. That's his genius: reading people. When he approached me, I didn't stand a chance....

He looked his jovial self, robust, pink-cheeked, moustache gradually turning gray to match his salt-and-pepper hair. But when he took me aside into a curtained alcove, he showed me an Uncle Wyn I had never seen before, steely-eyed and driven. It was then that he first used the word "mission."

He started off innocently enough, asking about my German. I told him it was fine, *ganz gut*. How could it not be? Ilsa and I have spoken German every day since she was changing my diapers, and I got all the way through advanced German grammar at Choate. I even took some German lit courses at Yale. He knew that when he asked. It was only his opening gambit. Soon enough he was onto the subject of the "damnable" directors of the German consortium from whom we bought the Rensselaer plant across the river. I wasn't surprised to learn that it's barely operational – the processes are just too advanced for our workers, and once the Germans running the plant took the boat back home to Germany it was only a matter of time before things went down hill. Predictably, the technical teams they've promised to send are encountering one delay after another. Uncle Wyn expressed fear that they want it to fail, that they'd rather renounce the profits than let the secrets of making aspirin, the pinnacle of pharmacology, fall into American hands.

All in all, the Rensselaer situation appears grave. If Uncle Wyn was telling me the truth, our very livelihood will be threatened if we can't figure out how to make the damned plant run. But if we can, we'll challenge DuPont, and with medically-proven products instead of the crap we foist off on our customers now.

We sat in hand-rubbed leather chairs as we talked – as he talked – a small round table between us where two tumblers of fine scotch had been poured before I entered the room. There's no doubt that Uncle Wyn has a way with words, and his story was very convincing. All the plot needed was a hero, someone who would be willing to take a temporary position at the KDE[1] pilot plant in Berlin where all the processes for the Rensselaer facility were first developed and refined. Someone who could "keep his eyes open," "get the lay of the land," and either figure out why the Germans were dragging their feet or, if that failed, simply steal their secrets. He didn't use those words, but I'm certain that's what he meant. It seemed a daring plan, and in that privileged, cigar-scented atmosphere, the idea of a year in Berlin captivated me, particularly when it involved inside access to the world's most advanced chemical company. I asked him if he had talked to my father about all this, and of course he hadn't because it didn't directly involve money. Besides, Dad would go along with anything so long as it was for the good of the company.

When I thought the conversation with Uncle Wyn had ended, I drained my glass and prepared to stand up, but he reached across the table and put his big hand on my shoulder to restrain me.

"There's something important you need to know," he said gravely, "something that may affect your decision." I smiled inwardly. He knew which way I was leaning. But he nonetheless pressed on in a low voice.

"I know how your dad feels about you earning your own way in the world and proving yourself. He'll want you on the lowest salary in the company. But you need to spend what you need to spend over there. Do your job, but have some fun too. I'll figure out a way for you to put things on the company tab. That's just between you and me. And if you help get Rensselaer back on track, it'll be worth every dime – and you'll have more green than you know what to do with, even if it has to come out of my own pockets."

When I left Uncle Wyn my head was spinning. It wasn't the whiskey. Or the possibility of earning a lot of money. It was the fact that somebody important was putting his trust in me. Suddenly, the future didn't seem so gray. In fact, it shone bright. And then, across the room, in conversation with Brad, I saw Margaret.

I know I must set down at least some of what happened next, but not tonight. I'm tired, and the delicacy of the subject matter deserves my best attention.

✠

Diary of Adam Luce
Berlin, 2 November, 1923

My first reaction when my eyes fell on Margaret was shock. She wore a black flapper-style dress. Her shiny blond hair was carefully drawn back and pinned. A single strand of white pearls dangled from her neck. I was amazed she would dress so provocatively in front of her parents – but I would soon learn that her parents had elected not to come to the party.

By the time she arrived there was quite a crowd, and it took a moment for us to reach one another in the middle of the room. When we did, she grabbed my tie, pulled me close to her and astonished me with a passionate kiss. She finally pulled away and held me at arms length.

"Congratulations, Adam," she said. "You're my hero, and I don't care who sees us kissing."

Then we fell into that easy banter we have developed over the past two the years. (I miss it more than I care to admit.)

"Have you been drinking?" I said.

"I think you've had enough for the both of us."

"Three glasses. You see? I can still count."

"Perhaps I should have at least one to catch up with you. Or perhaps one-point-five. Will you calculate it for me, my Master Chemist?"

I plucked her a glass of champagne from a passing waiter's tray and we talked casually for a while, but I was more than somewhat distracted by the thought of my Berlin mission, and of course she noticed.

"Let's go someplace quiet and talk about it," she said, "whatever the 'it' is that's on your mind. This room is so noisy I can't think." She put her hands to her ears in one of those theatrical gestures she's so good at.

I looked around the ballroom, mentally checking off the relatives and friends who would feel obliged to congratulate me. I had shaken hands or received a peck on the cheek from all of them. No one would miss me.

When I asked her where she would like to go, she answered me by dangling the key to her room in front of my eyes.

I experienced a moment of panic and told her in no uncertain terms to put the key back in her pocket. I was afraid someone would see us! But on another level, I was afraid of what her unprecedented invitation implied, and what it might mean for the future. If I followed her to her room, it would be with steps I couldn't take back. And then, there was the looming reality of my mission to Berlin.

As always, chemistry prevailed, and before I knew it, we were headed up to the twelfth floor in an ornate elevator, whose smartly uniformed operator leered at us the whole way.

Once inside the suite her parents had taken, she astonished me again by producing a flask. She put it down on the low table positioned in front of the sitting room's dark velvet sofa, fetched a couple of glasses and poured us each a shot of brandy, which she informed me was stolen from her father's private stock. We sat down, not too close, and nervously clinked glasses.

"Talk," she said. "I'm ready for anything."

I tried hard to ignore her double entendre and started to explain Uncle Wyn's offer. Before I could even finish, she was urging me to accept.

"Of course I shall miss you terribly, but I shall wait for your return. You must say yes. It's your chance to change the company, Adam, from 'Pills for Your Ills' to something noble. Think of it! Real medicine."

Real medicine. She was right. I was in a position to put the manufacture of the drug of drugs on a firm footing in America – with Luce Chemicals taking the lead! It would transform the company from a collection of super salesmen who preyed on human frailty to a legitimate source of... real medicine. When I saw Uncle Wyn's mission from Margaret's point of view the die was cast, and I told her so. Suddenly, it seemed that a career in chemistry might not be so bad.

I will not set down in writing what transpired next. Suffice it to say that she was generous, at least to a point. I respect her reserve in regard to intimacy, and I must admit that at times I wish she wouldn't speak so freely about what's in store for me once we've tied the knot.

✠

Address to the Yale College of Chemistry

Dr. Arnold Hastings, Chairman

As we begin the new semester I want to take a few moments to invite you to look beyond what every new semester brings – beyond the lectures, the textbooks, the laboratory work, and, of course, the exams. I want to invite you to broaden your horizons and think about the role of chemistry in the modern world.

In 1898, Sir William Crookes threw down the gauntlet in an address to the British Association for the Advancement of Science in Bristol, England. He was a chemist, gentlemen. He began his speech by apologizing to the audience for the quantity of statistics he was about to present. But he promised that these figures would tell a tale of monumental importance, and he came through. His message was nothing less than this: England, and for that matter, the whole Caucasian race, was in danger of starvation – not at some theoretical time in the distant future, but in as short a time span as twenty years.

Unlike the political economist Malthus, who based his concerns about the food supply of the human race on generalities, Crookes documented every aspect of his argument. The crux of his message was that, for lack of nitrogen to enrich the world's arable land, crop yields would plummet, famine would ensue, and millions would quite simply die.

This impending catastrophe was not without irony. As I hope all of you know, nitrogen is one of the most abundant elements on Earth, comprising approximately seventy-eight percent of the atmosphere. I did a brief calculation this morning and determined that this very hall contains 13 tons of nitrogen. But the nitrogen in the atmosphere is free, not fixed, and it is fixed nitrogen upon which the world's wheat crop depends. At the time of Crookes' speech, the chief source of fertilizer for England, northern Europe, America, Australia and South Africa was nitrate of soda, also known as Chile salt peter. It was imported in huge quantities from that nation, chiefly but not exclusively by the Germans. Crookes had calculated that this source would be exhausted within twenty to forty years... and there would be no substitute to replace it.

In brief, Crookes had determined that the very foundation of Western civilization, its food, was predicated on a resource that was not sustainable. Permit me to quote him.

England and all civilized nations stand in deadly peril of not having enough to eat. As mouths multiply, food resources dwindle.... It is the chemist who must come to the rescue of the threatened communities. It is through the laboratory that starvation may ultimately be turned into plenty. The fixation of atmospheric nitrogen is one of the great discoveries that awaits the genius of chemists.

That was the challenge.

And the science of chemistry rose to meet it.

Haber and Bosch, two leaders of Germany's I.G. Farben chemical cartel, devised the process that saved the day. By synthesizing ammonia from atmospheric nitrogen combined with hydrogen under pressures exceeding two hundred atmospheres, they saved countless millions of lives from destruction, and arguably Western civilization as well.

That is the power of chemistry in action.

Yes, they were Germans. And there's no question that they were driven, at least in part, by the German war machine's need for explosives, which are also based on fixed nitrogen. But that fact merely serves to underscore the pivotal importance of chemistry in the modern world. No other discipline – not political economics, not jurisprudence, not clinical medicine, not the liberal arts – will have such an impact on the societies of the twentieth century as will chemistry.

Do not think for a moment, gentlemen, that there is a dearth of challenges. Whether it's your goal to bring the mantle of scientific leadership to our country once and for all, or advance the needs of our military in future wars, or protect the world from the scourge of diseases like influenza and poliomyelitis, or to synthesize macromolecules to fuel the automobiles and airplanes of the future, or merely to achieve great personal wealth, the study of chemistry will take you there.

✠

Diary of Adam Luce

Berlin, 4 November, 1923

What a joke. Here I sit, Adam Luce, a trained chemist possessed of a keen intellect and the degree to prove it, ready and able to work the long hours chemical research demands under harsh conditions... and the Germans won't so much as let me sweep the laboratory floors, much less teach me something of value. They state, in a formal letter delivered by a courier no less, that my "potential employment is under careful consideration."

Damn it! What is there to consider? I'm the ideal man for the job – if they're serious about helping us with Rensselaer. This was all to have been arranged before I boarded the Polonia in New York. And manufacturing aspirin can't be that much of a mystery. St. Joseph's seems to be managing well enough. But I doubt that even Uncle Wyn could lure somebody from that fine company to work for us.

I've sent a cable to apprise him of my situation. I've politely responded to the letter from the KDE personnel department expressing my enthusiasm at the prospect of obtaining a position. I've alerted my landlady, the sweet Frau Schumann, to be on the lookout for any new communications that may arrive for me. Now, there is nothing left for me to do but wander aimlessly in this vast city, the world capital, say some, of depravity.

Germany is a scarred nation, and the evidence is on every street corner. I'm learning to walk by the whores, the beggars, the amputees, the monstrously burned... they are part of my life and I have to accept it. I can't rewrite history, only witness its results.

There is an abundance of fine architecture here. The German monarchs were ever the ones for the grand gesture, and thus huge public squares, imposing façades and monumental arches are the rule. But what goes on underneath those arches is a horse of a different color. I have never seen so many women in distress, brazenly offering what they once guarded so carefully. Yesterday I encountered a mother offering herself and her daughter as a pair. I gave the woman a dozen silver dollars from my stash and sent her home. It's a drop in the bucket. Perhaps it will tide her over until someone in her family finds work, but who can say in this chaos?

Hardly a day goes by without a march on one of the main boulevards, complete with band music and, all too frequently, gunfire as well. The cafés are full from morning to night, many with a class of people whom my fellow Yalies would view with scorn, but in no other type of establishment can one feel the pulse of the city while avoiding the temptations of clubs like the Maus.

Last night was my third at the Romanische Café. It's a huge neoclassical structure, well known to all, and Berliners never fail to point out how ironic it is that such a monument to the past should have become the meeting place for the most ardent proponents of the "new reality" or *Neue Sachlichkeit*, as they call it – those who would replace the waltz with their harsh "atonal" music and tear down grand old stone buildings in favor of more functional structures of steel and glass. But there they are, night after night, sipping at endless cups of coffee in a run-down structure built in Bismarck's time as they plan the future of the world.

The crowd is a little intimidating: left wing journalists of every shade, playwrights, novelists, painters, architects, all segregated by unspoken rules into their own designated rooms. There are women as well, actresses and artists' models looking for work, a smattering of "companions" with gents who have obviously purchased their services for the night, and not a few bold feminists who take part, and apparently hold their own, in the unending political and philosophical debates.

I had no trouble talking my way past the doorman. They love Americans at the Romanische, with the exception of the military. I chose a room at random, ordered a coffee and fetched a *Tageblatt* from the wooden rack of newspapers which are there for all to share. Within a few minutes, I was engaged in animated conversation with a rather arrogant fellow about something called the Dawes plan, which would apparently lead to a dramatic reduction in reparations.

From my experience, every German who frequents one of these cafés fancies himself a deep thinker. Politics is a favorite topic of discussion, but by no means the only one. The patrons will talk about modern architecture or classical music or the play they saw the previous evening, and they know their stuff. A German factory manager spends as much of his time thinking about literature and the arts as he does about efficiency and throughput, or so it seems. I never imagined there was a place in the world where an argument about the merits Brahms vs. Wagner could lead to fisticuffs, but here such confrontations are not uncommon.

Frankly, I often find myself in quite over my head. I wish I had studied more philosophy back in school. When I hear references to Goethe or Nietzsche or other such figures I recognize the names, but I have no familiarity with their works.

I sometimes wish Margaret could be here to help me out until I get my feet on the ground. She's more than just another smashing blond. She has brains, and a natural enthusiasm for the sort of talk I encounter. Margaret at the Romanische. That's a fantasy if there ever was one. She'd hardly approve of the crowd!

At moments I do pine for her, and not only for the release she has found ways to grant me. I would be proud to have her on my arm while strolling down Friederich Straße. I've no doubt the fine shops would delight her. She's not really money hungry, though. She's just following in her mother's footsteps, as I'm following in those of my father.

I wonder whether she ever asks herself if there's more to life than what we know. So far as I can tell, she has no interest in philosophy, or even science. But I'm wandering from the events I'm here to record... as if there were in fact any events to record. I've more than once entertained the thought of booking a short trip to Paris, but with my luck, the day I left would be the day KDE sent a man with notification that a position had finally been found for me.

Wolfgang Austerlitz

Überlegungen,[2] *4 November, 1923*

The purity we seek in our chemical reactors is a microcosm of what we must extend to the vessel that is German society. This is the essence of The Great Work: purification; and most certainly not the preposterous and doomed search for an elixir that will transform literal lead into literal gold.

But purity must come in its time and sequence. *Separatio. Purificatio. Conjunctio*. The chaos in our streets is sufficient evidence for anyone who has eyes that a separation is still in progress. And until it comes to completion we must rein in our impatience. Restraint will not be easy. I hear every day that there are too many Jews in Berlin, and in all of Germany for that matter. They divert the path of our intentions, infect our workplaces, subvert our politics with their communistic ideas, and even take our women as brides.

It's all too true. They must be dealt with, and they will be, but at this moment we must focus our attention outward, on the Americans. Their industries are gaining strength year by year, and their military will inevitably profit from this growing industrial power. If we are to prevail when the time comes, we will need a weapon against which there is no defense. In this regard, the Joachimsthal project is showing great promise, but in order to achieve production scale, we need money. Here, once again, we must focus on the Americans. Reparations are draining our lifeblood! We can recover none of this money from the French or the British, but the Americans are vulnerable. If we can penetrate their markets with our superior products, we can extract more than enough capital to finance Joachimsthal to completion.

The Luce organization could do that for us. They're a company of salesmen and they don't care who their business partners are so long as there's profit in the deal. With Luce acting as our proxy, we can bypass the laws the Americans put in place to block German ventures. It would be a perfect arrangement, if only the Luce people had the chemical skills to manufacture sophisticated drugs. But even aspirin befuddles them. That's our central problem right now, because the percentage of quarterly aspirin sales they've agreed to pay us is worthless if there's no aspirin to sell.

The Rensselaer plant must be put in order, and the only way to do it is to send a team of workers back to America. Much as I hate to lose them, there's no other choice. The plant won't run itself with American caretakers as I'd hoped, and the idea of giving chemistry lessons to some business novice they've sent here so he can take charge is absurd. Beyond that, sharing our secrets with an American involves serious risks. To be honest, I don't quite know what to do with this young man, or why the KDE directorate decided to make him my responsibility, but teaching him how to make aspirin is not an option.

Diary of Adam Luce
Berlin, 6 November, 1923

To profitably pass the time while others decide my fate, I'm attempting to educate myself and fill in its gaps that resulted from my exclusive focus on the sciences while at Yale. When a name comes up in conversation at the Romanische, I surreptitiously jot it down in a notebook I now carry, and the next day I'm at a book shop to purchase an appropriate volume—the thinner the better, I might add, as I have a great many names on my list.

There's no dearth of bookshops in Berlin. Indeed, it seems new ones have sprouted up like mushrooms in every nook and cranny of the city since I've begun frequenting the Romanische.. Of course that's hardly true. Most have been in their place for decades. I simply didn't have eyes to see them. Now, they beckon to me like street girls.

In the windows and on the display tables are books that follow the fads of the day: vegetarian diets, nudism, Nordic mythology, the *Wandervögle* movement that has so many Germans my age hiking every weekend and saluting one another with extended arms, and so on. But a little searching almost always reveals a nook or two where the books by the thinkers that influence the Romanische crowd may be found.

When night falls, I am following a new maxim: Avoid any club where the dancers wait tables after the show while still in costume, or lack thereof! I hold the theatrical reviews harmless, however, and it appears I'm in good company in my attraction to Berlin's racy shows. Last night I visited a notorious cabaret in the Russian district called Die Blaue Vogel, and who should I spot in the crowd but Einstein, seated at a ring side table just down from mine! He was dressed rather unfashionably in a wrinkled dark jacket and a plain white shirt, but there is nonetheless an air of genius about him. One sees it in his eyes.

I actually exchanged a few words with his companion, one Leo Zsvilárd. He's an intense fellow with dark, curly hair and a distant look in his eyes. A Jew he is, like Einstein, but that doesn't seem to matter here if you have the right connections. We met because, of all things, the girl who checked our coats mixed them up. We easily found one another in the lobby struggling with the ill-fitting garments and made a quick exchange.

By that time, Einstein had disappeared into the cold night, and I lost the opportunity to meet the great man. What would I have said? Do his theories tell us that our futures are indeed pre-ordained? Or is there hope of escape?

In any case, Zsvilárd and I shook hands before we put on our gloves, and he even recommended a club he thought I might enjoy. It's called Heaven and Hell, right across from the Romanische. As it was early by the standards of Berlin, I boldly suggested we might head over there for a nightcap. Since we had met at what amounted to a strip club, I felt there was no risk he'd interpret my approach as the prelude to a homosexual advance.

"Just don't ask me anything about Einstein," he said. Apparently, being the companion of a world-renowned physicist has its drawbacks. Zsvilárd is quite opinionated, and I got the impression that he doesn't enjoy sharing the spotlight. He needn't have worried. Once at the club, I was quite content to sit back and sip my brandy as he expounded on one topic after another.

His political opinions aren't extraordinary or complex – he's a socialist plain and simple—but scientifically, he thinks on another plane than I. He's deeply involved in nuclear chemistry, and I found his theories about the phenomena of radiation and elementary particles exhilarating. To tell the truth, he intimidates me. He's only a year older – two at best – and he's not only a professor with full teaching privileges at the University of Berlin. The man chats with Einstein. I wish I were in a position to attend his lectures, but conversations at clubs like Heaven and Hell may be all I can hope for.

He does have a human side – a fatal attraction for the opposite sex, as he expresses it. For him, many nights are a struggle, as he put it, between Physic und Fotze – between physics and a delicate aspect of the female anatomy I need not translate here. I have the feeling we'll meet again. he seemed to enjoy the company of someone outside his circle of scientific luminaries, and we do have common interests, low as they may be.

Wolfgang Austerlitz
Überlegungen, 7 November, 1923

Treatises too numerous to count hold that the image of the Green Lion devouring the sun represents the extraction of gold from *aqua regia* using green vitriol.

$$AuCl_3 + FeSO_4 = Au + Fe_2(SO_4)_3 + FeCl_3$$

I think it refers to a much more important chemical reaction.

$$6CO_2 + 6H_2O = C_6H_{12}O_6 = 6O_2$$

In photosynthesis, green plants absorb the energy of sunlight to combine CO_2 from the air with water from the ground to produce the sugar molecule at the foundation of every leaf, branch and root in the vegetable kingdom. Once our tradition's obsession with gold is abandoned, this new interpretation of the Green Lion becomes obvious.

The image first appeared in the *Rosarium Philosophorum* in 1550, almost one hundred years before photosynthesis was even suspected, and more than two hundred before it was fully understood.

There's a lesson here. It is both our heritage and our duty to extend our knowledge of the physical world beyond the boundaries of contemporary science. The Joachimsthal project is proof we've been true to our heritage, but we're not two centuries ahead of the world anymore. Two decades would be more like it.

Diary of Adam Luce
Berlin, 10 November, 1923

It's hours past midnight, yet sleep is the farthest thing from my mind. My hands are so stiff from the cold I can barely write, and my head is spinning... but not so badly now, thanks to the long walk back from the *keller*.

"Du mußt mir hilfen."

That's how it began, shortly after five o'clock this afternoon. The sky was a flat gray that promised snow, and Unter den Linden was crowded with Berliners in their dark wool coats and scarves, a mix of hopeful shoppers – more and more goods are appearing in the stores these days – and others, walking with more purpose, who had finished with their day at the office and were headed to catch their train home for some beer and dark bread, perhaps with a little cheese or, if they were lucky, cold meats. I was out for an early dinner, dressed in one of my more fashionable suits, when I heard the voice.

It emerged from the shadows of an arched doorway. I peered in and met the dark, haunted eyes of a girl about my age, dressed in nothing but a sheer party frock and a pair of open-toed summer shoes. She was terribly thin, doubtless a cocaine addict, and she had heavily rouged her cheeks to hide the pallor inevitably produced by that drug. I was caught by the intensity of her plea. It was as though all the pain and confusion of the city were focused through the lenses of those eyes.

"Du mußt mir hilfen."

"You must help me."

When I didn't immediately respond, she approached me boldly and put her arm through mine as though I were her escort. I shied away slightly, but she was persistent. I remember thinking, just what I need. An ugly scene with a prostitute on one of the city's major boulevards.

"I'm cold," she said, now in accented English, as though her plight weren't obvious. "Will you buy me a coat?"

These were not at all the words I expected from her red lips.

"It would be nothing for you," she continued. "One dinner at the Adlon with an important customer. For me, maybe the difference between life and death."

She clutched my arm and looked up hopefully. For a moment I thought she was putting me on, pleading as she was, like a gypsy. But the story about sleeping in doorways some nights was plausible. And what she said about the money was true.

She glanced to her right and when my eyes followed hers they fell on – what a surprise – a furrier's shop. I felt somewhat the dupe, but I could think of no reason to refuse her.

Inside the shop we were greeted by a stooped fellow wearing a yellowing shirt who glowered for a moment at my companion's slutty make-up. He quickly caught himself, however, when he took stock of my expensive clothes. "How may I help you?" he asked, raising gray eyebrows above thick round spectacles.

"We're on our way to a costume party," I said, an obvious lie for it was far too early. "It's much colder than we thought, and since Madame requires a new winter coat anyway we thought we'd have a look. Do you have anything in stock? Nothing too flashy. She doesn't want to be a target for the Bolsheviks."

The man nodded, ignoring my feeble attempt at humor. "I may have something in her size." He disappeared into the back of the shop, which was separated from the sales area by an aging velvet curtain. When he returned, he was carrying a calf-length mink coat with dark, silky fur, which he had no doubt purchased from some ruined burgher for a tenth of its worth. This is the irony of the postwar economy: Luxuries are available at every street corner, while butter is in short supply.

My companion extended her arms as the old furrier helped her don the coat. It fit perfectly.

"It seems it was made just for me, *Liebchen*," she said. Then she spun around in front of the mirror, somewhat unsteadily I thought.

As I expected, the price in rentenmarks was excessive. I drew the furrier aside, and when I explained that I was an American – not obvious because my German is so good – his eyes brightened. For five silver dollars the coat was ours.

Out on the street again, we stood facing one another in the harsh electric light. "Thank you," she said. "I was very cold."

I was about to respond with something like, "It was the least I could do," but I didn't want to admit how easily she had played on my guilt. When all is said and done, I am as much a part of the occupying army as the strutting French, and much of the economic chaos is the result of the harsh reparations we have imposed. We should all simply decamp and let the Germans put their country back together. Our policies are forcing honest women into the streets!

After an uncomfortable silence, she eyed me seductively. "May I thank you for this gift by offering the pleasure of my company as a dinner companion?"

I said nothing, but my expression must have conveyed my concern.

"Don't worry, *Liebchen*, she said. "I know a wonderful place where you needn't fear being seen with me. The clientele is top drawer. Even ministers! And they have a marvelous *canard a l'orange*. You have it with a light Mosel... or better yet, *Sekt*. The beef is also divine" She squeezed my arm ever so slightly.

Just at that moment, one of those old-fashioned horse-drawn taxi one sees from time to time in Berlin came clopping by, and I hailed it. What did I have to lose? We climbed inside, and I was struck by how she unconsciously used her new coat to block my view of her legs as she swung them around into the cab. She is no street urchin, that is certain. And her accent, if not exactly aristocratic, is far from the earthy Berliner *sprache* I have become accustomed to.

She alarmed me once again with the address she gave, a street not far from the Tier Garten, which is notorious for its sleazy hotels where one can rent a room for an hour, or, as a Berliner might put it, "long enough."

"Will you relax?" she said, resting her hand briefly on my thigh. "I know my way around." The seats of the cab were leather, well polished, and carried a light scent of lanolin. I wondered where the money to outfit such a luxurious anachronism as this coach had come from, but I have learned that in Berlin, it is better not to ask. As we bumped along, she produced a small mirror from somewhere and adjusted her make-up so that, when we emerged from the coach, she no longer looked whorish, but in fact rather respectable, in a flapperish sort of way.

Soon I found myself descending the stairs of a dimly-lit *keller* restaurant that sought to replicate a hunting lodge. There was a mounted deer head with impressive antlers at each end of the bar, and the walls were graced with hunting scenes. After we checked our coats, a waiter seated us in a booth that offered a clear view of the small stage where a three-piece jazz band was playing without much enthusiasm. Most of the men at the other tables had at least twenty years on me. The girls with them were young, and quite attractive.

"We'll both use *du* when we talk to each other," she declared as she scanned the menu. "Why pretend?"

I thought, pretend what? but agreed to share the use of the more intimate *du*. As an American, it didn't really matter to me. A German male would no doubt have been insulted. He would have used *du*, but insisted on the more formal *Sie* from her.

She is not at all stupid. In between forkfuls of rich beef, she carried on a running commentary about the recent developments in the Ruhr Valley, mentioning by name several factories that are finally starting up now that the resistance there has crumbled. As if by unspoken agreement, neither of us made any mention of our personal situations. (This is not uncommon among Europeans. We Americans tend to be much more open about things like that.)

The food really was terrific, and so was the wine, of which I consumed more than my share. But in spite of my intoxicated state, I was unprepared for the show that began some time after midnight. I won't dignify its contents with a detailed description. Suffice it to say that New York has never seen such a display of human anatomy in all its potential states, and most likely never will. I must admit that I was shocked, but my companion seemed a little bored, not even laughing at the jokes, which I thought were the best part of the show.

When it was over, the waiter brought the bill in an elegant leather folder, and I inserted enough rentenmarks to cover the meal and half a month's lodging for him as well. A moment later, we were standing outdoors in the bitter cold, white light pouring down on us from the new street lamps of which the Berliners are so proud. This was the moment of truth.

"I have a room for the night not far from here," she said. "Will you escort me? I'm sure you can find a cab once we've arrived at the hotel."

And that was that. She didn't invite me in, and to tell the truth, I can't say with certainty that I would have declined had she done so. They say there's some sort of alkaloid in the air here that encourages licentiousness. But with her, I think I have nothing to worry about. She is not one of "those girls."

In any case, we shall meet again, that's been agreed upon. The day after tomorrow, at the Adlon.

Diary of Adam Luce
Berlin, 12 November, 1923

A second encounter with Charlotte. That's the name of my mystery girl. I wasn't sure she would even keep our date, but the opportunity for late afternoon *kaffe mit schlag* and *küchen* at the city's finest new hotel won her over. Or so I imagine. Frankly, I don't think that I'm the main attraction for her. It's my money. Still, I find her intriguing. And saucy.

She was standing in the fine lobby, wearing the mink I bought for her the other day. After a rather formal handshake, she suggested that we try the café bar that looks out onto Unter den Linden, the boulevard that leads into the park. We sat in chairs with soft, embroidered cushions, elbows resting on the polished dark wood of the table between us. I found myself at a loss for words, and finally asked her if she wanted to take off her coat. It was hardly cold in the café.

"I would," she said, "but there's nothing underneath it." She waited a moment, enjoying my confused reaction, and then added, "except this."

She pulled out a box about the length of a folded cravat, wrapped in black paper and tied with a lavender ribbon.

She invited me to open it and I obeyed. A carton of Lucky Strike cigarettes. My brand! We both lit up, our smoky exhalations mixing with those of the other customers, who were mostly Berliners, with a sprinkling of Bavarians – I can usually recognize them now – and a few Russians.

"How did you know?" I asked.

"Know what?"

"That Luckies are my brand?"

"It was a lucky guess," she said in her sexy broken English.

"How did you manage to find them?"

She gave me a half smile and replied in German. "You don't want to know the answer to that question."

An image passed through my mind, Charlotte coupling with a dark figure against a wall in some alley. Then the waiter arrived to take our order, bringing me back to the present moment. I ordered an Italian coffee, Charlotte a simple pot of house coffee and a huge chocolate creation whose name I didn't catch. I have revised my opinion that she is a cocaine addict. She is apparently just one of those girls who can eat and eat and yet remain slim.

In contrast to the other night, she didn't wolf the thing down. She savored it... but not as much as she savored her ability to keep me off balance.

She began with an innocuous personal question.

"Tell me, what are you doing here in Berlin?"

At that point, I saw no reason to lie. "I'm seeking work at a chemical company."

"Oh," she said in a light tone, "Here to steal our secrets?"

My whole body stiffened at this, and it must have been obvious to her that she had hit a nerve.

"Perhaps it would be more precise to say that I'm here to get a better understanding of how German companies do business," I added. "If that's stealing secrets, I'm guilty as charged."

"Will you wear a white coat and special gloves? Will you have a stainless steel work bench with racks of test tubes?"

"Actually, I have no idea how things will turn out."

"But you love chemistry."

There are times, I'm learning, when Charlotte can seem as innocent as a child, while probing like a lawyer on cross examination. What was I to say?

"Not really. My family owns a chemical company, so I'm bound to take some interest in molecules and such."

She pursued her theme relentlessly. "You're interested in their properties? Or perhaps the different ways they combine?" The sexual allusion was obvious. I pursued it, hoping to turn the conversation away from my reasons for being in Berlin.

"I am interested in what's under that coat," I said,

"I'm sure you are," she replied, linking her fingers and resting her chin on them. "But first, you must tell me the truth about why you're here."

The word escape came to mind. That was the truth, but also a sentiment I couldn't bring myself to share.

She reached across the table and put her hand on mine, as though she understood that her question might involve a painful admission. She gave it a friendly squeeze.

"No need to give me an answer," she said. "I already know it. This is Berlin. We're all here to have fun."

Was that an invitation? I can't say. The rest of our conversation was about the various theaters and cabarets here, which ones were the most intellectual, the most entertaining, the most likely to be frequented by the Right, the Left, the Russians, the homosexuals, the tourists... there is something for everyone in this city.

I suggested it might be fun if we went to a play over the weekend, but she was non-committal. And I have as yet to coax an address or telephone number out of her. She would only say that she often frequents the well-known Café Josty on Potzdammerplatz in the late afternoons.

We shook hands in the street and walked briskly off in opposite directions under the dimming sky, like two charged particles repelling each another. On the way home I was thinking of excuses to leave the office a little early on the following day when something strange occurred. A weather-beaten old woman seated on the sidewalk called out my name as I passed.

I stopped and turned. It was hard to tell how old she was. She had bundled herself into a red and black blanket. In spite of the cold she seemed quite comfortable and – the only word that comes to mind is 'peaceful.' Next to her was a stack of old books.

"Do I know you?" I asked rather stupidly.

"I don't think so" she replied.

"But you called my name."

"I did not, sir. You are mistaken."

It turned out she was a street astrologer. On an impulse, I paid her for her guidance. Could she tell me the most propitious day and hour in the coming week to meet with – and here I hesitated for a word – with "*meine freundin*," my female friend? That's hardly precise, but what precise term exists for such a girl?

The old astrologer told me that since she didn't know the date and hour of my birth, she could only answer in the most general terms. With some reluctance I provided this information, and after consulting a table in one of her well-worn tomes, she informed me that the stars favored a meeting on Tuesday around four o'clock. I will try my luck at that time.

Diary of Adam Luce
Berlin, 13 November, 1923

Charlotte planned what happened today. That is the only explanation I can find for what transpired this afternoon at Café Josty. She paid the gypsy astrologer to accost me – how else could the hag have known my name? – and then enrolled her in a clever deception.

"He's tall and blue-eyed – an American, but not a soldier. If you watch the entrance to the Adlon, the one with the awning, you'll see me saying good-bye to him. His name is Luce. Herr Luce. Tell him to come to Potzdammerplatz on Tuesday at four in the afternoon"

Or so I reconstruct the imagined conversation. And I fell for it, knotting my tie with extra care this morning, catching the U-Bahn to Potzdammerplatz earlier than necessary, glancing at my Breitling constantly for the time, like a freshman on the first date he'd ever had with a girl who might promise more than a kiss.

And then I was there at the station, clattering down the stairs to the street, the railing icy to my touch because, in my haste, I had forgotten my gloves. I walked with long, quick strides towards the Josty, but what greeted my eyes when I approached the entrance stopped me in my tracks.

Charlotte was there all right, sitting in plain view at a table by one of the large windows that face the street, but she was not alone. Sitting across from her was a "gentleman," as they say, with silver hair and a monocle. As I watch, far enough away not to be noticed, I saw her lean forward and whisper in his ear, as though her communication might shock other patrons in the café if overheard. Then, she threw back her head in laughter.

She lured me to Josty to view this scene. She thinks me a plaything. And, I must ask myself, why should this matter? She's one of those Berlin girls whose greatest joy in life is play-acting. Yes, I was attracted to her. I admit it. That can happen when you're in a strange country where there seem to be no rules. But in fact she's nothing to me, and our paths shall never cross again. If they do, I'll offer a polite greeting and a smile, and nothing more.

As I walked back to the station, I passed an officer in full uniform, seated on the street with his back against the wall of a building, cap in hand, crutches propped against the wall next to him. He had but one leg. That man has lost something of value. I have lost nothing.

Wolfgang Austerlitz
Überlegungen, 15 November, 1923

The Raven has planted a strange idea in my head. What if we could win this American over, and lead him to the point where he shares our vision? What if we should see him as one who has been sent to us, a gift from the gods, as it were, instead of a business problem to be solved?

Some will recoil at the thought of inviting an American into our midst, even if I keep him far removed from the actual process chemistry at KDE. But the decision is mine alone. The Lodge does not operate by consensus.

This idea has merit. Within our doors we could observe this American, test his will and intellect, while holding out aspirin as the prize. Perhaps we will never be able to trust him with the secrets of its manufacture, much less those we have unearthed in Joachimsthal, but I think we can control him. And if things go wrong, then one more unlucky visitor to Berlin will die from a stray bullet during a street battle.

Diary of Adam Luce
Berlin, 16 November, 1923
Margaret asks in a letter how democracy can function in a society that's inherently autocratic. The answer is, it can't. The Reds want everything to be run by workers councils. The Whites think such people ought to be shot – and they often are. *Das System*, as the ruling coalition is known, coaxes the two sides to compromise in the middle somewhere, the result being a course of action to no one's liking.

But for once the universally despised System has struck a consequential blow for order. Their leader, Stresemann, has by fiat promulgated a new currency called the rentenmark, and overnight he's managed to put the brakes on inflation. Indeed, he's vanquished the beast. There's only one way to rule this country, and that's by decree. The rentenmark is a case in point. If it hadn't been forced on the country, the poor Hausfrauen would need hay wagons to carry their money to market by now.

Gefreiter[3] *Helmut Schreck (1887 – 1924)*
Field Notes, 16 November 1923

Another day of infamy. With one sweep of the pen, Stresemann wipes out the savings of millions of honest Germans in the name of stability. What kind of stability is that? The old strategy in the Ruhr was good. The Frenchies show up, the good German workers go home, the mines and factories shut down and we just wait it out until they give up and go back to France. They've already proved they can't run our factories. We've got all the cards. We should say, "You want our coal? You want our steel? Go home, get off our soil, and we'll sell it to you." If we did it that way, the old Mark would rise and people's pensions would mean something again, and we'd have no need for his asinine rentenmarks.

I shouldn't complain. In my line of business, you get paid in dollars or gold, so why should I care? It's just the damned stupid System in action once again. What else should I expect?

Diary of Adam Luce
Berlin, 17 November, 1923

I would be lying to myself if I didn't admit that Charlotte is constantly in my thoughts. No amount of reasoning will banish her, nor any quantity of spirits. I've been by the Josty dozens of times, lingered for hours near the alley where I first encountered her, and even searched – fruitlessly – for the street astrologer with whom she most likely conspired.

I thought she had begun to care for me and I was ready to follow any path I might find to nurture that sentiment, the cost be damned. For any man with his wits about him, her vanishing act would be a blessing, but for me, it's a curse. Or perhaps both. She brought a quality into my life that's been missing for as long as I can remember: mystery.

My mind tells me that these wild and uncontrollable feelings are transient, and will pass as certainly as night follows day. But what do they teach me about the strength and quality of my bond with Margaret, or for that matter, of love itself? I'm not the sort of man who "chases anything that wears a skirt," as my mother once described Uncle Wyn in an unguarded moment. Nor am I prone to stray beyond the bounds of convention. I'm not like Zsvilárd. The whores don't even tempt me. Nor do the drug peddlers. Charlotte is my cocaine.

Brecon Hall No.1
Bryn Mawr College
Bryn Mawr, Penn.
November 4, 1923

My Dearest Adam,

Your letters pile gloom upon gloom. I can't picture the people you're meeting in these "intellectual cafés," you mentioned, but I think you should avoid them! Don't forget that these Germans you find so clever and sophisticated are the race that gave us poison gas for the battlefield as well as Beethoven and Bach. So I don't hold their ethical opinions in particularly high regard, and I don't think you should do so either.

Oh dear, listen how I berate you. Am I becoming too much of a feminist? I don't think so. I most certainly intend to vote in the election next year – and not for Coolidge! But I draw the line at smashing stills.

I'm afraid I don't have much to say about my boring life at the moment. It's quiet here on campus. As a senior, I have a room to myself, and there's nothing I enjoy more than curling up with a book in front of the fireplace. I only wish you could be here with me. I have chosen The Odyssey as the topic for my senior thesis, with emphasis on the character of Penelope.

Do you remember anything of your humanities classes? Penelope was the wife who fought off all those suitors while waiting for her Odysseus to return. You are my Odysseus, my dear Adam, and I do hope there's no Calypso over there attempting to cast a spell on you and hold you in her clutches.

Please take care. Are there sporting clubs in Berlin? Perhaps some exercise and friendly competition would cheer you up. Do write soon. I await your triumphant return.

All my love,

Margaret

Diary of Adam Luce
Berlin, 19 November, 1923

An official offer of employment arrived this afternoon, "effective immediately" no less, and I of course signed it and sent it back with the courier who brought it. I am to report for duty tomorrow morning at the KDE building on Friederichstraße. Not bad! I must admit, with Charlotte in absentia, the offer now seems like Berlin's consolation prize, but is it not consolation that I'm most in need of at the moment? I'll not be attending any shows tonight. I shall go to bed early, and hope I can sleep.

Diary of Adam Luce
Berlin, 24 November, 1923

My job involves, of all things, matching purchase orders with bills of lading, so that the company can be certain that it indeed obtained so many liters of sodium sulfate before it pays the supplier so many rentenmarks. A shop girl could do this work! And the head of my section, one Herr Habermeyer would no doubt prefer that. Particularly one with large breasts who could spend lots of time in his office with the door closed and locked. Indeed, I've no idea how he spends his time, only that he seems to be constantly on the telephone.

Perhaps I exaggerate the simplicity of my work. In fact, it can be complex, as every vendor seems to have a slightly different discount schedule that has to be verified. But at the end of the day I still have to wash blue-black carbon stains off my fingers like a common secretary.

There are six men with the title of reconciliation clerk (including myself), two female filing clerks, Frau Penke and Fraulein Strietzel, and one runner who fetches our documents from the mail room and distributes them among the six of us based on what seems to be an arbitrary judgment of who has the least work in his inbox. He calls himself Johnny – American names are in style here among people my age – but his real name is probably Hans or something like that. The reconciliation clerks inevitably complain when Johnny delivers a new batch of invoices to be cleared, and this is virtually the only repartee that takes place in the office. The rest of the time we sit quietly, rustling our papers, three of us on each side of a polished oak trestle table with modernistic goose neck lamps to light our work.

Johnny has what Berliners call *die Schnauze*, a sarcastic and somewhat crude style of speaking that the other clerks seem to enjoy. Yesterday, as he dropped a stack of invoices into one of the clerk's in boxes, I heard him whisper, "Six opportunities to summon Fraulein Strietzel and have her tits in your face while you instruct her on which back-up documents you require. You'll never get any closer to Paradise, Herr Meinigin." There is a semblance of order here, but in fact, the lowest lackey in the section is running things, controlling the work load, and probably engaging in more mischief than I know.

Because I'm an American, he assumes I'm rich, which I suppose I am, at least by the standards of post-war Berlin. "You should build a cocaine factory, *mein Freund*, he has suggested more than once. "I'll be your director of sales." He's not serious about building a factory, but I do think he believes I could fund him as a full-time drug dealer.

At times I'm almost tempted by his suggestion. My job is hardly challenging, and often boring.

But of course my true job – dare I commit this to writing? – is espionage. What else can I call it? But sometimes I feel like a common thief.

Enough of this grumbling. When you're down two touchdowns in the fourth quarter, you don't complain. You buckle down. And you don't let your mind wander off to thoughts about some girl you'll never see again in your lifetime. Damn! I daresay she *was* the girl of a lifetime. There are no other words for it. And we never so much as kissed.

Rural Route 7
Albany, N.Y.
November 12, 1923

Dear Adam,

I've been going back and forth with the Germans, and I wouldn't be surprised if you were hopping mad at me by now. I'm sure it appears that I've sold you a bill of goods with this Berlin deal. But I want you to stick it out.

The KDE big shots are watching you from a distance right now. They're big believers in patience. I think that's why they gave you this job as a paper pusher. If you show them you can stick with it and don't make any mistakes, they'll eventually move you over to the factory. Right now, I think they're afraid if they let you in you might blow something up!

I don't have any way to pressure them on this end, but you can be sure that none of their people are going to see any of our customer lists or anything else like that until you get a look at some lab notebooks.

While we wait, if there's a way you could get me some intelligence on exactly what they're buying and what they're paying for it, that would be a big help. You can send it by diplomatic pouch. Just get in touch with Al Houghton. He's our legate in Berlin. I contributed to his campaign when he was in Congress, so he'll play ball. As a matter of fact, he already knows who you are. He set up your bank account for me.

Good luck, and get me that info if you can.

Fondly,

Uncle Wyn

Wolfgang Austerlitz
Überlegungen, 27 November, 1923

As if I didn't have enough problems already, I heard rumors today of a plot somewhere within the KDE hierarchy to assassinate the American. I'm not sure I can block it, if indeed it's anything more than a beer hall fantasy. As yet, I don't even know the conspirators' names, but no matter who they are, I can't just tell them to stop. I don't outrank them. As far as they're concerned, I'm simply a brilliant chemist whose word they had better take for law on technical matters if they know what's good for them. They know nothing of the Lodge.

I need to find a way to smoke them out. I want that American alive. He is ours to exploit, and we would be fools not to make use of him.

Beyond that, I need to return to Joachimsthal. There is nothing like a walk in the forest after a fresh snow to calm the mind. Here in Berlin, it's all too easy to forget the primordial source of our power.

There, one is reminded of it with every twist and turn in one's path. Wagner understood this. So did our predecessors. It's easy to see why so many of them chose to live in the woods.

But, back to the problem at hand. The list of those who could be behind this plot isn't all that long. I need to create conditions where they'll reveal themselves. Perhaps I should feign sympathy to their cause and offer to engineer the American's death myself. That would at least give me some control in the short term.

Diary of Adam Luce

Berlin, 29 November, 1923

Thievery! There is no other word for the despicable subterfuges that I am now contemplating. Uncle Wyn wants "intelligence on exactly what they're buying and what they're paying for it." I couldn't be better positioned to obtain that data, could I? Did he plan this? Was his whole story about penetrating the pilot plant's secrets just a ploy to place me in a situation where I could get a peek at the books? I wouldn't put it past him. My father has complained about his deviousness for years. But then, it takes a devious streak to win the day in the world of business. Anyone knows that. What I don't understand is, if I'm not the man to get Rensselaer running, who is?

In any case, at least for now, Uncle Wyn's game is the only game in town, but getting the numbers I'm charged to obtain won't be easy. I wish I could think of a way to steal the log book that summarizes the daily transactions I've approved. If I were to stay half an hour late, could I sneak it out in my briefcase, copy my entries, and sneak it back the next morning?

Why am I even thinking these thoughts? This is not why I stayed in the lab while my friends played poker or quaffed beers at Mory's. The answer is obvious. The thought of coming back home a failure is intolerable. I have to hold on to Uncle Wyn's idea that this is a test. I *will* eventually get access to the labs and – why not say it? – come home a hero.

Margaret deserves that. I've for all practical purposes abandoned her for this so-called mission in Berlin, and she remains faithful while I entertain lascivious thoughts night and day.

For now, I think the best remedy for my problems would be a couple of brandies at the *Maus*. It's amazing how chemicals affect the human body. Two liters of Löwenbrau and you're happy. Two grams of arsenic and you're dead. There are moments when the latter seems more appealing than the former. But not tonight.

Gefreiter Helmut Schreck
Field Notes, 29 November, 1923

I'm not ashamed of my work. Why should I be? These days, a man has to do what he can with the skills God gave him, and God gave me the skills of a marksman. So I put them to use. The Buffalo Bill of Berlin, that's me. Except, of course, my targets are men instead of animals.

In my line of work, you can't be overly picky. You have to take the jobs as they come. Otherwise, you get the wrong kind of reputation, and before you know it, you're out of work.

But I do draw the line.

A few weeks ago Rudi wanted me to take out a colonel who had already lost an arm and one eye leading a charge at Verdun. A colonel – leading a charge! I never saw anything like that in all my time at the front. The colonels I knew drank cognac and drew lines on maps – and anything else they could do to keep their asses out of the line of fire.

The idea was to shoot this particular colonel during a demonstration and then pin it on the Reds.

I said no, straight out. Rudi tried to explain the psychological effects – that's what he called them – but I just told him to shut up. I mean, maybe he's right. Maybe it would "enflame the masses against the Reds" if they saw a "beloved hero" cut down by what they thought was a Red bullet. But I don't shoot my brothers in arms. And the fact is, Rudi was just trying to get rid of one of his rivals. Anyway, that's what I think. Not that anybody cares what I think.

Usually, I just take the job. These days it's easy. And, to tell the truth, the Berlin police don't investigate a crime too thoroughly if the so-called victim is a Red.

If the Reds were in power, they'd act the same way. People are people. You take care of your own. And if you're lucky, you make a decent living.

Diary of Adam Luce

Berlin, 1 December, 1923

I've hit on an idea. At the office, there's an ample supply of carbon paper. Original documents go to the Chief Disbursement Officer, but we also make a carbon copy for Receiving, another for Purchasing, and a third that stays in our own files. Given that abundance and high degree of usage, an extra sheet taken from the stack now and then would certainly not be missed.

That sheet will go into my personal log book, backed by a clean white sheet of paper, upon which every transaction for the day will be copied. At the end of the day, the extra carbon will go into the burning bin along with all the others. The copy of my transactions will go home with me in my briefcase... and the next day by diplomatic pouch to Uncle Wyn back in the States.

If I'm caught, I can say I'm simply taking my work home to review it for mistakes. Would the Germans believe a flimsy story like that? Not for a minute – so I had damned well better not get caught! I'd as well end my life as be sent home to America in shame. But that's fantasy. If caught, my home will be a Plözensee prison cell at best.

Diary of Adam Luce

Berlin, 7 December, 1923

I met Mr. Houghton today, at the Adlon per his insistence. When we talked on the telephone it was my distinct impression he didn't want us to be seen together at the embassy. What manner of skullduggery is going on behind the scenes is beyond me, but there's clearly more of it than I know. In any case, the lunch was pleasant enough. I had a *wurst* with *knödeln*, he took fish, and we shared a good bottle of Austrian white. His manner is a bit more polished than Uncle Wyn's, his phrases measured and often inflated with erudite references, but he and Uncle Wyn are definitely birds of a feather.

When we finished our meal, he asked for the package, whose guilty contents I gladly handed over. I don't like this one bit.

Now the day is over, and I have nothing to await but a dreary repetition of it tomorrow, sans lunch at Berlin's finest hotel. The winter seems endless. Although the sky was clear today, the dim, hazy sun was powerless to bring warmth to the city. I understand why people light candles at this time of year, even when electricity is plentiful. It's the craving for a primitive source of energy: fire.

I can't stand another night alone like this. I'm going to go find a boot girl. If I'm living in the world's capitol of depravity, I might as well experience it first hand.

Wolfgang Austerlitz

Überlegungen, 7 December, 1923

Will the troubles with this American never end? This afternoon I was told that he lunched at the Adlon with a high-level official from his embassy, the legate himself. It could mean nothing. The boy's father apparently has some political connections with the legate. The lunch could have simply been a gesture of thanks for past contributions. But it is disturbing that the meeting should coincide so neatly with the boy's hiring. It looks suspicious, and now I'm put in the position of defending him if I want to keep him around. Damn it! Doesn't he understand how dangerous this city can be?

Here's some advice, boy. This is Berlin, and in Berlin life is cheap. If you want to save your skin, you had better stop acting like a spy.

Diary of Adam Luce
Berlin, 9 December, 1923

The boot girls in Tauentzienstraße gather around improvised stoves made of discarded oil drums, and they burn whatever they can: coal when it's available, old newspapers and broken furniture if necessary. The arc lamps cast a harsh and unflattering light on the wrinkled faces of the older whores, and make the younger ones look even more worn-out and frail.

Curiosity drew me there, the tales of how the color of the boots indicates the specialty of the girl who pulled them on, but it's the last place in the world you should go seeking comfort on a dark night, and I can't truly say what I expected to find.

I certainly didn't expect to find Charlotte.

At first, I couldn't believe my eyes, but there she was, bundled up in the dark fur of the coat I bought for her. She had been lavish with her eye make-up and had painted her lips bright red so that she looked almost like a china doll. Our eyes met, and an expression of bemused detachment played across her face as she sauntered over and addressed me in her imperfect English.

"What a naughty boy that you come here on a night like this! Do you need to be punished?"

I almost said yes. There's something about my *mission* here that has never felt right. But instead I answered with my own question.

"Were you waiting for me?"

"Yes," she said, and this response sent a chill through my body that was more profound than anything the icy night air could produce.

"Come with me," she said, switching to German and linking her arm in mine. "I can't punish you properly here in public."

"I don't want *that,"* I said quickly, but she just laughed.

"I know what you want more than you know yourself."

Soon we were climbing a cold, dimly-lit stone staircase that led to a hallway where all the doors were painted black. She produced a key that let us into room 9. It was furnished with a black velvet couch, a couple of cloth-covered chairs, and a dark wooden coffee table where someone had fanned out half a dozen sex magazines. Off to one side there was a tiny cooking area – you could hardly call it a kitchen. Directly ahead, a half-open door led to a second room where I could see chains that terminated in metal shackles hanging down from heavy wall mounts.

Charlotte's gaze followed mine. "It's a metaphor for life, *mein liebchen*. We are all trapped in the prison of our ambitions and desires. Some of us are unwilling to admit it. Others submit. I don't let my clients fuck me," she added. "I just punish them a little to make them feel better.

At her use of the word *client*, I could only wonder if that were to be my role for the evening. I didn't for a moment believe that she had any actual "clients." In fact, I was thinking that she had staged this whole scene and I said so. She took off her coat and tossed it onto one of the chairs.

"Well then, if this is a play, do you like my costume?"

She was dressed in black, thigh-high *Stiefelmädchen* boots that had been polished to a glossy shine, a black leather corset with chrome eyelets, and nothing else. We sat down on the couch and she favored me with a coy smile.

"Shall we have some coffee while you think about what you want in your heart of hearts?"

"Coffee?" I said, wondering if in fact there was any coffee to be had.

"To help you think," she said. With that, she got up off the couch and set about boiling water. It was an incongruous sight to say the least. She served the coffee in porcelain cups on a tarnished tray that was nonetheless genuine silver, placing it in the center of the couch so that it separated us. Then she sat down, cross-legged, displaying a few curly hairs at the juncture of her thighs that her corset didn't quite manage to conceal.

Needless to say, I had difficulty concentrating, but I was determined to... what? To put some boundaries on our liaison, I suppose.

"What were you doing out there tonight among those whores?" I asked, attempting to affect a casual tone.

"I could ask you the same question," she said with an air of righteousness. "My family gives me nothing. I have to make a little money somehow."

"Nonsense."

"Think what you will."

"What if someone had come along before I arrived and made you an offer? Would you have accepted?"

"That would depend on who made the offer."

"How about a middle-aged gentleman with thick silver hair who frequents Café Jospy in the late afternoons?"

To my chagrin, she broke out laughing. "You're jealous!" she said finally, putting her hand to her mouth as though to stifle another outburst.

"Answer the question," I said. "What if I hadn't come along?" I was getting a little hot under the collar at that point.

"But you did."

"By accident."

"There are no accidents," she said sharply. "You of all people should know that."

That stopped me cold. Did the cruel laws of inevitable causality extend even into situations like this? Or did she somehow engage a troop of beggars and n'ere do wells to spy on me. In these times it would cost nothing to post observers on the streets where I most frequently pass, observers who could quickly find a public telephone kiosk and report my location so that she could encounter me *by chance.*

"Am I being followed?"

"It wouldn't surprise me."

"Why do you insist on being so evasive?"

"I am hardly trying to evade you, *Liebchen*," she said, toying with the strings of her corset.

I reached out to put my hands on her bare shoulders but she caught them and pushed me away and glared at me. "About that 'silver-haired gentleman?'" she said.

"Yes?"

"Sometimes you are so stupid. How the Hell do you think I'm going to get you in front of important people? That's what you really want, isn't it? To come to the attention of someone who has the power get you out of that stupid office?"

She was practically shouting.

"I'm trying to help you," she continued. "Can't you see that? If you want to become a chemist who can save the world, don't you think you ought to take a few lessons from some people who actually know what they're doing?" Again, she hit a nerve. The knowledge I needed to elevate Luce Chemical from the muck was indeed to be found only here in Germany. In Berlin.

But how did she know I was working in a 'stupid office?' I was sure I'd never mentioned the fact to her. To be truthful it's been a point of embarrassment I've been careful to conceal.

I decided to be direct. "Are *you* having me followed?"

"It was my twin sister who arranged it," she replied. "She thinks you're stealing company secrets to take back home with you."

I think she sensed my guilt, and was probing blindly for something tangible, information she could pass on perhaps sell to someone for whom it might have value. She couldn't possibly know what I was up to.

I decided to counter attack with my own stab in the dark.

"You don't have a sister."

"Do you want me to go downstairs and call her on the telephone? Did you want to have us both at once? I didn't realize you were that adventurous."

"No!" I replied emphatically, although I confess that the images her words evoked had a certain sordid appeal.

"Some other night, perhaps. Right now, I want you all to myself."

With that, she got up and walked into the other room. I followed. The room was dark, and had the air of a dungeon. The only piece of furniture, if you could grace it with that name, was a rough-hewn bench.

"Take down your pants and bend over," she said. Somehow, a riding crop had materialized in her hand. "I am going to punish you."

Our eyes met.

"Do you deny that you deserve to be punished for what you're planning to do? You're no better than a common thief."

I cringed at this accusation. How could she know? She couldn't! And yet... she did. I unbuckled my belt. Her demeanor softened just a bit. "The pain will assuage your guilt, Adam," she said. "Each stroke is a stroke of love."

There is no need to further set forth what took place last night. I shall never forget those moments. But I must note that although I confessed to no specifics, I feel as if I had told all, and in doing so healed my conscience.

✠

Gefreiter Helmut Schreck
Field Notes, 12 December, 1923

I never once put any pressure on Marguerite to do it with me. The first time, to be honest, we were both drunk. But she wanted it. She told me that. It had nothing to do with the money I'm giving her. It's my duty to take care of her, and little Heinz too. If it wasn't for her husband, I'd be dead. But instead, he's dead, and I'm still here. They'll have a roof over their heads as long as I'm around. But I'm not moving in. Too dangerous – for me *and* them. The way my place is rigged, I'd have a fighting chance to get out alive if somebody tried to come after me. But you can't have booby traps and trip wires with a three-year-old kid running around. Marguerite understands, but she doesn't like it. Neither do I. I wish we could live like a normal German family. But a man has to do what he has to do. At least she's not parading herself around on Tauentziehenstraße in thigh- high boots to get money for the rent.

She did make a weird suggestion the last time I slept over. I guess that's why those boot girls are on my mind. I told her I didn't want that kind of thing from her – or any woman – and she said she was just making sure I was getting what I needed.

What kind of society is it when you have that kind of conversation with a housewife who has a kid? A decadent God-damned society. I say, leave that kind of crap back in France where it belongs. That's what's wrong with our so-called leadership. They talk about tolerance and respect for the individual, but what they're really doing is flushing all our moral values down the toilet.

Somebody has to put a stop to this, and whoever that man is, he's my leader. For now, I'm helping where I can to eliminate the worst offenders, and put some bread on Marguerite's table while I do it.

Diary of Adam Luce
Berlin, 16 December, 1923

Frau Schumann tells me this is the first Christmas season in several when she's been able to buy presents in the shops. After the war and during the economic collapse, all the "fine things" were to be had only from so-called *schiebers* – young men who sell goods of suspicious origin in back alleys where a decent woman wouldn't care to be seen. The rentenmark, it seems, has changed things overnight, and a measure of normalcy has returned to the season.

In spite of rather heavy snow, I walked over to the KaDeWe yesterday. It's Berlin's best-known department store, like Gimbel's or Macy's in New York, and once I was inside I almost felt as if I were back home in the States. I bought a fine hairbrush with a matching set of silver combs for Mom, a leather desk set for Dad, a German-made fountain pen for Uncle Wyn and a silk scarf from Paris for Kate, if she ever decides to come back home. I still need to find something for Margaret, but I'm at a loss. I suppose there's no hurry. None of my gifts will arrive at their destination before New Year's anyway.

Writing out the cards at the shipping desk was a sad moment. Having no real friends here, I felt lonely, and the walk back only made it worse. I passed through an outdoor Christmas market and several of the stalls had fresh *pfeffernüsse* like Mom used to bring home from Germantown.

A coffee or a schnapps with Charlotte would cure all this homesickness in an instant, but predictably, the girl has disappeared from view.

Diary of Adam Luce

Berlin, 17 December, 1923

How quickly one's spirits can be revived! This morning Johnny entered the office with a smirk on his face and deposited a gilt-edged envelope in my basket instead of the usual stack of invoices. It was sealed with red wax, into which a family crest had been pressed – the von Schwerin crest. I recognized it instantly. How could I not? I walk under it every morning as I enter the KDE building.

I broke the seal and extracted an invitation to a formal dinner the following Friday.

What can this mean? Did Uncle Wyn finally manage to pull some strings for me? I'll send a telegram today to inform him and ask for instructions. This coming Friday I'll be rubbing shoulders with KDE directors at the von Schwerin mansion on the Wannsee.

Diary of Adam Luce

Berlin, 18 December, 1923

Frau Schumann has gotten a Christmas tree. I first saw it yesterday on my way out to buy some cigarettes before all the stores closed. It was standing by itself in the center of the downstairs parlor, looking a bit naked in its unadorned state. But when I returned, delicate glass ornaments of every color were hanging from its boughs and Frau Schumann was perched on a small wooden step ladder clipping candle holders to the higher branches. She looked down at me with a sad smile. "Günter used to do this," she said. "I'm not very good at it. Do you think the candles will be safe?"

The trick, I realized was to position them so that the wicks were nowhere near the higher branches, which wasn't all that difficult. She had in fact done a good job, and I told her so. There was a long hesitation and then she invited me to join her and her sixteen-year-old son for "the celebrations" – if I didn't have "other plans," as she put it.

My plans, such as they were, had involved a lonely dinner at the Adlon, one of the few establishments that doesn't shut down for the holiday, perhaps in the company of a few other stranded Americans. I gladly accepted her invitation. We'll have carp and potato salad, of course, and I'll furnish the wine. Damn it, the truth is that the whole scene nearly got to me, tears and all. I think she noticed.

Diary of Adam Luce
Berlin, 19 December 1923

I am lucky to be sitting in this dark room of mine instead of a prison cell.

My mind has been unsettled by the holiday season, and after dinner I decided to take a walk in the snow, followed by a visit to my favorite local *kneibe*. My intention was to record an experience stemming from the political divisions here in Berlin while enjoying a Pilsner or two. Instead, I let myself get dragged into a conversation about said subject with a group of Whites. They couldn't stop railing against the "foreign influences" that were ruining the Fatherland, by which they meant the Jews, of course. I didn't write a word... but thank God this diary was on my person. That's the point here.

Upon my return, when I opened the front door, a troubling sound from the parlor caught my attention. I went in to investigate and found Frau Schumann sitting beside the Christmas tree in the room's only upholstered chair, dabbing tears from her cheeks. I assumed that she was caught up in a remembrance of Christmases past, but when she looked up at me I saw not sadness in her eyes, but fear.

I approached her, and in a gesture that both surprised and touched me, she took my hands in hers.

I was perplexed, and asked her what had upset her. Her answer sent ice through my veins. Two men had come by the house asking for me. When she told them I was out, they declared themselves to be friends of mine and said they would wait in my room. Without making explicit threats, they made it very clear that she had no option but to unlock my door. From their accents she could tell they were Berliners, but she doubted they were friends, a surmise which I could confirm.

I can still hear the tremor in her voice. "I had to let them in, Herr Luce. My son...." At that, she trailed off, leaving me to imagine the details of this intimidation. They remained for about an hour and then left.

"They spoke politely, Herr Luce, but I think they were up to no good."

I wanted more than anything to calm her. I told her I understood that she had done what she had to do, and added that there was no reason to be alarmed, a necessary but obvious lie. I thanked her for sharing her information with me and then ascended the staircase, braced for the worst.

My room had been searched alright, but quite carefully. The objects the searchers moved had been returned, at least approximately, to their rightful place. I might not have noticed had I not been on the lookout. Thank God there was no evidence of my espionage to be found. It's sheer luck that I decided to record the day's events in a bar. Or was it? At times it seems that the city is guiding my steps, opening the doors to its secrets one by one and, I daresay, keeping me safe.

Spending too many hours with the bohemian crowd at the Romanische invites this sort of speculation, and speculation it is. But one thing is beyond question. I have to be more careful. If I'm found out, it's certain death.

Wolfgang Austerlitz
Überlegungen, 19 December, 1923

The boldness with which the true flag of the German empire prefigures both the future of our nation and the essence of natural law never fails to inspire me, and these days I seek inspiration anywhere I can find it. At times, bridging the gap between the spiritual vision of those who went before us and the realities of life in a defeated nation seems an impossible task... and then I see our flag, proclaiming with its black, red and white bands the eternal threefold nature of all chemical processes, as well as the political drama that is playing itself out in the streets at this very moment. The black root of dissolution from which spring the red and white branches of spiritual mercury and sulfur... the black moment of Kaiser Wilhelm's abdication in which is rooted the rise of the Reds, the communists, and the Whites, the *Freikorps* loyalists who defend us against them.

What mastery on the part of our departed brothers of the Great Work to hide the truth in plain sight! The riddles and ciphers most of our predecessors used to disguise their discoveries seem like children's games in comparison to our one true flag. The new flag that has been proclaimed by Stresemann and his crew of back-stabbers is an abomination. In place of the pure white, a yellow band the color of chicken shit. Every one of those flags should be burned, and shall be. But I must not indulge these reveries right now. I must ponder the place of the American in all of this. That ridiculous company of his could be a gold mine for us, if I can put it that way. How interesting. Figurative gold was once the endpoint and reward we sought in our long and diligent Work. Now, literal gold is just the beginning.

Diary of Adam Luce
Berlin, 20 December, 1923

I feel like I'm peering at Berlin through a keyhole, one which affords me but a partial view of those who can influence my circumstances. My need for information is acute. Who arranged for my room to be searched, and why? I would like to believe the search indicates that I'm under serious consideration for a transfer to the lab, that those who would make that decision want assurances my room isn't full of contraband, or illegal drugs, or some other indication that I've fallen prey to Berlin's cornucopia of temptations, not the least of which is industrial espionage. That's my hope, but in fact I have no idea what's going on, and without a clear sense of the lay of the land, I'm sure to blunder at the von Schwerin soirée this coming Saturday.

I suspect the prime source of the inside dope I need has been in front of my eyes for weeks. It's Johnny. Beneath his coarse exterior I detect a man whom I can trust, at least to a degree. He keeps his eyes open, he puts two and two together, and he has every reason to help me. Who else is going to fund his cocaine empire?

Diary of Adam Luce
Berlin, 21 December, 1923

Johnny instantly accepted my invitation to get together for a beer or two after work today, but not at the establishment I proposed.

"Do you want to be seen drinking with a messenger boy?" he asked in a whisper. "It's below your station! They'll all think you're queer. Why else go out with me?" Suitably warned, I agreed to his suggestion, a small *kneibe* just off Hermannplatz at the north edge of Neuköln, the Communist stronghold. I feared I'd be overdressed in that neighborhood, but Johnny had picked a place frequented by men who wore suits to work, and not a few young women who were clearly making themselves available, for a price.

"How can I help you," said Johnny after we were seated with a couple of heavy tankards on the table. He used the phrase the shop girls use when they approach you in department stores. I had to laugh.

"Tell me what you know about the von Schwerins."

He spread his hands as though I had asked for an item that was sold out. "I know what everybody knows. That they are Germany's prime source of dyes, drugs and some other chemicals they don't like to discuss. There are rumors that they're about to join forces with Farben and their competitors so Deutschland can a united front to the rest of the world in the chemical market.

"They need a foothold in the American market. I think that's where you come in."

I attempted a noncommittal shrug, and I think I carried it off, but Johnny's conjecture shook me. It suggested a larger game, one in which Rensselaer was but a pawn.

We moved on to what appear to be his favorite subjects, drugs and women. I don't know how much better prepared I am to meet the KDE brass, but my list of must-visit clubs is quite a bit longer now.

Diary of Adam Luce
Berlin, 23 December, 1923

I didn't take a taxi to the Wannsee, as the invitation had stated a car would be sent, and in fact one was. The snow that now covers everything had already begun to fall when, at precisely seven o'clock, two bright headlamps appeared at the end of my street, creating cones of light as the car approached, a black Mercedes. The chauffeur left the motor running as he trotted around the front of the car and opened the door for me, greeting me by name. He was in his mid-forties and had a dueling scar on his cheek. Another fallen aristocrat, no doubt bitter about his lowly station but at the same time aware that he is lucky to have work at all.

As we wended our way through the dark streets of Kreuzberg towards the now-frozen Wannsee, the fantastical thought went through my mind that I was being kidnapped, that somehow my ruse with the carbon paper had been discovered after all, that I was about to become a pawn in the much larger chess game being played by the industrialists of Germany and their American counterparts. But of course, we were merely avoiding the heavy traffic of the Kufürstendamm. Who in Kreuzberg could afford an automobile?

Large torches burned brightly on stone pillars that stood on each side of the von Schwerin mansion's massive iron gate as we entered the long, curved drive that lead to the front portal. A liveried servant took my hat and coat at the door and gestured towards the grand salon. When I entered I felt as if I had stepped into another century. Carved, gilt-framed paintings of military officers on horseback and women in elaborate gowns hung on the walls, which were covered with pale golden wall paper that had a subtle vertical stripe.

The waiters and maids were all dressed in strict black and white with red trim, the colors that are held by most upper class Germans to be the *true* colors of the Fatherland. They moved among women who were resplendent in brightly colored silk gowns and men who, if they were much over thirty, sported monocles. Underneath the muted cacophony of polite conversation I heard music – Beethoven, if I'm not mistaken – and sure enough, when I looked around I saw that a string quartet had installed itself in one corner of the room on a small, triangular dais: three young men in tuxedos and a striking platinum-haired woman in a floor-length black gown. It crossed my mind that Margaret would have been in Heaven had she been at my side at that moment.

Within seconds I was offered a glass of champagne—they call it *Sekt*—which I gratefully accepted. There was not one familiar face in the crowd. How could there be? But one thing was certain: at least half a dozen of the men in the room knew the tricks of manufacturing pure aspirin. I must admit that I was quite intimidated by this gathering, and tempted to quickly down quite a bit more *Sekt*, but I resolutely paced myself.

Halfway through the second glass I was approached by a man in his mid-fifties who looked like he had descended from one of the gravely formal paintings on the walls.

"Allow me to introduce myself," he said rather stiffly. "I am Ernst Graf von Schwerin. Welcome to my home."

"It is a pleasure and an honor to meet you, sir," I replied, using my best formal German. I hadn't expected to come face-to-face with KDE's managing director. High level chemists, yes, but not the grandson of the founder. Thank God I hadn't indulged with the hooch.

"I hope you are enjoying your time in Berlin. I know it may seem difficult to be posted as a clerk, given your degree in economics from such a prestigious American university. But it's our belief that everyone must understand our business from the ground up. My own son held a post such as yours when he began his career."

I remember thinking that I must have somehow misheard. I searched for a polite response.

"These days, I think a degree in economics would be of great value," is what I came up with. Then I added, "Unfortunately, mine is in chemistry."

"Chemistry?" he repeated. "Then I've been misinformed."

I could see that he was both embarrassed and angry. But he quickly recovered.

"Nonetheless, I'm told you've done quite well in your role as a finance clerk."

This time I knew how to respond. "It's only a question of paying close attention to every detail."

He gave me a long look, then shook his head. "Chemistry," he muttered again. Then we shook hands and he disappeared into the crowd.

I told myself the worst was over, and I hadn't done so badly with the leader of KDE. Then, gradually, the implications of his misinformation about my studies began to sink in. That "misinformation" could have but one source: Uncle Wyn!

There is much more to record – Acts Two and Three, as it were, but not tonight. I need to clear my head and come to an understanding of what this all means. Why didn't Uncle Wyn simply tell me about his ruse? Did he think I would decline an offer unrelated to chemical operations? If so, he doesn't know me very well.

When the oriental gong was rung to announce dinner I was still on my second *Sekt* and by no means inebriated. My seat was at the head table, but not close to the host. To my left was a colonel's wife with obviously dyed blond hair and a lot of gold jewelry who *was* inebriated. This Frau Oberst Henkel talked a blue streak, assuring me she felt no hatred towards the Americans – she adored Wilson and greatly admired our boxers as well, "even the negroes," she whispered.

The seat to my right was still empty, and my new "friend," Frau Henkel, volunteered that the Fraulein von Schwerin, the host's daughter, was always late, "but worth waiting for." She said this with what she must have fancied was a sly wink. I felt a pang and thought again of Margaret. What was going on here? Von Schwerin's daughter! Was I being set up? An American beau for one of the von Schwerin family's ugly ducklings? Or an innocent pairing of two young people at a gathering where most of the guests were quite a bit older?

The servants were preparing to serve the first course, a simple consommé, and I was beginning to wonder if this *fraulein* would even make an appearance. At that moment, who should walk through the door but Charlotte! She wore a fitted black gown with a single strand of black pearls at her neck and gold earrings.

Frau Henkel squeezed my arm. "There, I told you, didn't I? Isn't she fine?"

I was distraught, and it showed. In fact, I was having trouble believing my own eyes. Charlotte walked to her place beside me with cool, almost masculine confidence, stopping briefly to kiss her father on the cheek and whisper what I took to be an apology for her tardiness, although I couldn't actually hear what she said.

I stood up as she approached, extending her hand with strict politeness. "Portia von Schwerin," she said.

I felt an involuntary flush spread across my cheeks as I shook her hand, which only added to my discomfort. I had always held the suspicion that the woman I knew as Charlotte was somehow play-acting, and this confirmed it.

"It's a pleasure to make your acquaintance," I responded. I used the same polite formula I had used with her father.

"The pleasure is mine," she replied.

Upon seating herself she turned to me with a look in her eyes that approached anger. "So you've met her," she said under her breath.

I gave her a questioning look. "Her?"

"My twin sister. Charlotte. She has a penchant for Americans. Did she bump into you on the Ku'damm and enquire about English lessons?"

I began to offer a vague answer but she cut me off sharply. "I don't want to know the details."

There was a moment of awkward silence and then our soup arrived. She ate hers staring straight ahead, ignoring me. I had quite lost my appetite but went through the motions. Frau Henkel observed us as though we were putting on a show for her personal benefit. I glanced around and it seemed that no one else was paying us the least attention.

When the dishes were removed to make room for the next course, it was as though some one had switched on an electric lamp behind Portia's eyes. She turned to me with a wry smile I had seen more than once on her sister's lips.

"We got off to a bad start. I'm sorry. My sister is prone to indiscretion, and because of our special relationship that's troubling in ways I can't even explain." She paused to let me ponder these words and then continued, now using the familiar *du* to address me. "Forgive me – perhaps I have a streak of indiscretion myself – but in some ways it's as if I already know you."

A waiter came by to fill our glasses with a sparkling white. Von Schwerin stood to offer an initial toast.

"To the Fatherland," he said, and then, looking in my direction, "and all true friends of the German People."

I touched glasses with everyone within reach: Frau Henkel, her husband the colonel, who was seated opposite his wife (and who until then had given his attention exclusively to the attractive woman sitting on his right), the pale young man directly across from me – a painter, I was to learn later on—and "Portia."

Frau Henkel had tears in her eyes from the toast. If you don't live here, it's impossible to understand how deeply many of the Germans feel about what they call "The November Betrayal" (the Versailles treaty). In my own way, I'm with them. I wish Wilson's plan for a just peace had won the day.

When I touched glasses with Portia, she said, "to friendship."

Platters of a white fish I couldn't identify arrived next. In contrast to Charlotte, Portia ate tentatively, as though she weren't really hungry but merely joining the crowd to be polite. Still, as much as her mannerisms differ from Charlotte's, on a purely physical basis I'm not certain I could tell them apart.

When the last course had been consumed, a few of the men, including the colonel, adjourned to a small, oak-paneled room adjacent to the grand salon – I presume for cigars and brandy, and perhaps some serious business talk. The rest of the party returned to the grand salon, where a dance band consisting entirely of strings save for the drummer had installed itself. The music was hardly what we're accustomed to back home!

Frau Henkel insisted that I dance with her. I couldn't very well say no, but I kept a nervous eye on the hallway, imagining the colonel would emerge at any moment to see his wife pressed against me like some dance hall girl. It was obvious that she wanted to go to bed with me, and under the cumulative influence of the evening's strong wines, the thought had some appeal. She wasn't that old. And she was persistent!

"Won't you let me show you the rest of the villa? I know it well, all the secret rooms." A pause. "They have good locks. No one can just barge in." Another pause. "German women like exotic things, you know." (I can't bring myself to put down in writing what she actually said.)

I felt myself getting excited and she noticed, which gave encouragement I hadn't intended. But in the end, the thought of Portia (Charlotte?) seeing me sneak off with the woman kept me in check – and Portia didn't take her eyes off me for a minute. In fact, she seemed to be enjoying my discomfort.

I had just managed to extricate myself from Frau Henkel's clutches when the contingent of older men who had left the salon earlier rejoined the party. To my enormous shock, Charlotte's companion at the café was among them. Portia approached him immediately, favoring him with an enthusiastic hug and a kiss on the cheek that left a residue of bright red lipstick, which she solicitously rubbed away. A moment later they were on the dance floor.

To say that I was puzzled would be an understatement. I wondered, are Portia and Charlotte sharing this "gentleman" in some debauched ménage à trois? Was it Portia and not Charlotte I saw at Café Josty? I still do not know, despite the evening's subsequent events.

Abandoned by both Portia and Frau Henkel, I naturally drifted over to the bar that had been set up, where I sipped cognac with an older KDE chemist named Beckman, who reminded me a bit of my father. He had a singleness of purpose that rubbed me the wrong way, and I had to struggle to remain polite and stick to the point as he bombarded me with endless questions. At first they were general, looking back, I see that he was setting me up.

"Do you have any familiarity with the transformation of benzene rings?" He asked out of the blue. "Acetylation, for example?"

This was a loaded question if there ever was one, acetylation being the process by which the corrosive properties of salicylic acid are mediated to produce aspirin. I hadn't prepared to be thusly interrogated, but my training and my memory stood me in good stead.

"There's no mystery to the theory," I said. Then, borrowing a pen and a scrap of paper from the bartender, I wrote out the relevant equations. He studied them briefly and nodded. "But as you must know better than I, achieving practical results is not so easy." I paused, then added, "We in America are painfully aware of this truth."

He offered me an enigmatic smile. "Nothing is easy in these terrible times. We must all do our best."

The fact that Portia kept drifting by in the arms of one dance partner after another didn't help matters in the concentration department. But looking back, I'm glad that I stuck with Beckman. I think he was a plant, deliberately sent over to the bar to evaluate me. And in fact, at the end of our conversation, he said that my skills seemed well suited to the challenges KDE was facing.

I can't remember speaking to anyone else. I was very tired by that time, and when Frau von Schwerin offered a bedroom for the night I gladly accepted. As I recall, she made some reference to Berlin's dangers for "people like us" who had to travel through "certain neighborhoods" late at night.

And now, the difficult part. My visitor. She arrived somewhere around three in the morning – I can't really be sure, nor do I know how long she stood beside the bed before she put her hand on my forehead and woke me up.

It was Charlotte.

"I'm glad to see you're still alive. From my sister's report, I feared alcohol poisoning." Then she slid her hand down to rub my thigh. "Apparently, you have quite the hollow leg."

I recalled the scene I witnessed at the café, and with that, my resolution to end our relationship came flooding back.

"What are you doing here?" I whispered.

"What would you like me to do?" she responded in her most coquettish voice.

"Charlotte – " I began, but she put her finger on my lips.

"Shush. I'm Portia."

"No you're not."

"Are you sure?"

I was stymied. Charlotte always seems to find a way to take control of the situation. And last night, she did it again. If indeed it was her, and not Portia under the influence of too much wine.

"Would you like me to take my clothes off?" she whispered.

She didn't wait for an answer.

A dull glow from the distant lights of the city center passed through my bedroom window and fell on her pale white skin in such a way that she seemed to glow, as if dusted by radium.

While my body responded as would any man's, my mind was in distress. I demanded that she tell me her true identity.

"I am your secret bride," she replied.

She had brought with her a special white rose soaked in ether, which is quite in fashion here. I took only a couple of small bites, but it was enough to make me uncertain of what happened next – uncertain, indeed, of the whole affair. I shall write no more of last evening save to say that, given my state upon awakening and the condition of the linen, I can safely conjecture that no intimate act was consummated.

A servant came to my room around nine o'clock with a silver tray bearing a small pot of hot coffee and two *brötchen*, which I devoured immediately. To my surprise, I felt swell, if a bit confused. I dressed in my evening clothes – that felt strange – and then went downstairs to find my driver awaiting me in a fresh uniform and highly polished boots. And so I made my unceremonious departure.

Now, as noon approaches, I'm feeling strangely detached. Everything is white outside. The whole city feels like it is locked up against the cold, and here I am with no place to go.

I wish I could recall exactly what happened! What am I to do? If I were Uncle Wyn I suppose I'd just charge ahead armed with roses and chocolates and whatever else it might take to win her over and manipulate her delicate sentiments to my advantage. After all, I'm here to ferret out the mysteries of aspirin, and she's a direct link to the man in charge. That seems so low. But, on the other hand , this Charlotte is not exactly a girl of delicate sentiments. She's practically a drug addict. And what am I to make of this "sister" she has conjured up? Is it possible that I am indeed I dealing with twins?

I must think clearly. The greater good is to transform Luce into an honest company. But does that end justify the means? This is all too complicated. I wish I had thrown the woman out of the bedroom and not indulged one moment in her concupiscence. But nothing in this city is simple. Portia and Charlotte are identical twins, and it's common knowledge that such twins communicate in ways science can't understand. I can't rule out the possibility that Charlotte was behind my invitation to the fête in the first place. It's hard to believe her sister was seated next to me by chance.

Wolfgang Austerlitz
Überlegungen, 25 December, 1923

I cannot find a way to master the emotions I feel on this day, remembering past Christmases that can never return. To lose a son in a war is unbearable. Otto's death put Elsa in decline before her years, and now she knows nothing but suffering and confusion. Her will to live left her when he died. That's all there is to say. My wife is gone, though she still breathes. If I have my way, no German youth will ever again fall victim to an enemy shell in defense of our flag. No country will dare challenge us, not in industry, not in the sciences, not in the arts, and not on the field of battle.

Diary of Adam Luce
Berlin, 25 December 1923

I am gradually regaining my bearings. Upon analysis, whatever took place in the bedroom last Friday night is of no real consequence. I'm through with Charlotte and her sister and that's that. What's important about the evening was my opportunity to correct von Schwerin's misunderstanding concerning my training and to speak with a senior chemist who might have some influence in determining my fate at KDE.

I must confess to a touch of homesickness this Christmas day. America seems so far away. Football season is over and done, and I don't have any idea how the Yale eleven fared this year. I miss those Saturdays, and I miss Margaret's company. She could be a swell companion at a post-game party, or in the back seat of a Buick. I can't deny that's part of her charm.

I thought of her last night as I sat by the Christmas tree with Frau Schumann sipping hot chocolate, a treat that's once again available. She misses her son, who's studying engineering in Stuttgart and didn't have the train fare to come home for the holiday. He's apparently close to obtaining a degree, and she hopes a good job will soon follow. But with the hoards of unemployed, one must wonder if there will be work available h3n he complete his studies.

The Germans open their presents on Christmas Eve instead of in the morning, and last night there was a present under the tree for me, a small box wrapped in dark blue cloth and tied with a red ribbon that had obviously been saved from prior years. When Frau Schumann handed it to me I noticed that her hands were trembling slightly. I unwrapped the box and opened it to discover a silver amulet linked to a very fine chain. It turns out that Frau Schumann's husband had worn this device for almost two years during the war as a good luck charm – this was apparently very common among soldiers – but on a visit home from the front he had given it to her to keep. Shortly thereafter, he was killed by a shell that exploded in his trench.

"I think maybe you need it now," she said, making reference to the shooting of an American during a demonstration on *Unter den Linden* last week that was headlined in all the daily *blatts*.

It's an odd piece of work – a plus sign with each bar bent to the right to form a square shape. I know I've seen it somewhere before, but I can't place where. I think it's connected to a political party. In any case, she told me I needn't wear it, but should keep it in a pocket for safety when I went out. She said she had always believed that if her husband had continue to wear it instead of giving it to her, he would still be alive.

I'll take her advice.

Wolfgang Austerlitz
Überlegungen, 26 December, 1923

One can see that the American is intelligent. According to Beckmann his German is perfect and his knowledge of chemistry is impressive. That was the word he used, and Beckmann isn't easily impressed. In short, this young man is far more useful than I had imagined, and therefore far more dangerous. After the Christmas fête, his potential will be common knowledge among the higher echelons at KDE. That's not good. There's clearly a faction that wants to get rid of him. It's same faction that opposed the Luce deal from the beginning. What's worse, they're the ones ultimately control the purse strings for the Rurhleben project. They love the Fatherland, but that love makes them blind to what must be done.

I just don't know how long I can keep protecting him. I've let it be known that his room was clean, and that helps. No stolen documents from KDE, not even any notes on his work. I've also hinted that Herr Doktor Austerlitz has plans for him that could re-open the American market for us, and that will buy me some time.

The Raven has been his advocate since the beginning, and will be pleased with these developments. This American may indeed become 'our secret weapon,' but not yet. He needs to be tested.

Diary of Adam Luce

Berlin, 28 December 1923

Johnny has sent me an invitation to join him at a cabaret this coming Monday to celebrate *Silvester* – New Year's Eve, as we would call it. I don't know how in Hell he found out my address, but actually I don't mind. It's a casual invitation with no strings attached. "If you show up, you show up." (I translate his slangy German as best I can.) The club, *Die Rote Fux*, is a notorious left-wing dance club "full of tasty red cherries," he says, promising that I can "have my pick."

The problem is, if I go, he'll have something he can hold against me: consorting with Bolsheviks! Can I trust him? Would he try to blackmail me? It's not out of the question. If he does, I'll plead the ignorance of a foreigner. Better yet, I'll say I'm gathering intelligence on "the enemy."

The Reds are indeed a real threat here. They can mobilize thousands at will. And if the economy doesn't improve soon, they could succeed in turning Germany into the next Russia. In my opinion, their views are simply stupid. You can't gather everybody in the factory together to vote on what to do when a pipe's about to burst or a chemical reactor's ready to explode. And the idea that the state will eventually "wither away" and everybody will live in some sort of workers' paradise is nonsense. Laws are needed, and a means to enforce them. Anyone can see the truth of that. But people believe what they want to believe. This new playwright everybody's quoting – Brecht is his name – has it right. Truth isn't so important when bread is in short supply.

Not a bad line, if I do say so myself. Maybe I'll use it at the *Fux*. I'm going, and damn the consequences!

Diary of Adam Luce

Berlin, 1 January, 1924

I wasn't prepared for what happened last night. No one could be prepared for such a thing, no matter what the Berliners may say about their New Reality.

I arrived at the *Fux* around ten o'clock. It's in the Wedding district, "Red Wedding" as it's called, because it's such a Bolshevik stronghold. It seems like there are hammer-and-sickle posters on every bare wall, and many of the stores are decorated with red banners. I felt out of place before I even reached the cabaret. My expensive clothes attracted hostile stares from the workers on the tram, and I heard the words "White Pig" (*weiße Sau*) more than once. There are no neutrals in Wedding. You are either a Red or a *Freikorps* "White." I should have taken a taxi.

The manager of The *Fux* is a short, stocky man with sparkling blue eyes and the gnome-like features you often see in older Berliners. He took my coat and handed it with care to the hat check girl, who wore a man's tuxedo, and then led me down a hallway to a smoky, crowded room filled with stylishly-dressed city types gathered around small tables and engaged in animated conversation. Most of them were about my age, and obviously not of the working class. A light-skinned negro with close-cropped hair and a carefully trimmed moustache played jazz tunes on an upright piano next to the cabaret's small stage.

Johnny was seated near the piano, and he had apparently convinced a couple of girls to join us. Both had heavy mascara and dark, curly hair cut short in the *herrenschnitt* style. He introduced us, and then called out to a waiter for a bottle of champagne and two brandies, which he knew I would pay for. I could already feel a headache coming on. Thank God for aspirin!

The girls excused themselves after one glass and drifted off. "Don't worry," said Johnny. "They'll come back later. And if they don't, there are plenty of others."

He pulled out a pack of cigarettes and offered me one, which I declined. He lit up, inhaled deeply and smiled. "To understand Berlin, you must begin with the people," he said, gesturing towards the crowded tables, the lit cigarette extending from his hand like a sixth finger. "Behold the future of Berlin!"

"Do you really think so?" I asked, wondering if Johnny was about to confide to me that he was really a Red.

"Who knows?" he responded. "But it sounds good, don't you think?"

That's Berlin. People say what seems right at the moment, because they never know what tomorrow will bring. Not Johnny with his complicated left-leaning network, and not the old aristocratic families that live in mansions in Zehlendorf, no one. Of course, everybody knows in their *mind* that it's impossible to predict the future. Here, you feel it in your *body*.

Before long, our waiter was hovering at our table with a second bottle of champagne, which he uncorked and poured with great ceremony.

Johnny raised his glass. "To Lenin," he said, rather loudly, while favoring me with a wry smile.

"To the health of The People," I responded. I didn't quite know what to make of the whole situation. It seemed strange to toast The People with champagne and brandy, but we were hardly the only ones in the cabaret who could afford a step up from beer and schnapps. A lot of people in this city flirt with Communism. Perhaps they hope to make friends... just in case the Reds prevail. Maybe that's what I'm doing.

Johnny set his glass down on the table as though the now absent girls and the toast had been a preamble to our main business. "So, my friend," he said, "What are you really up to here?"

I wanted to answer that I didn't know, that I was on a fool's errand. That's the thing about Johnny. You want to tell him what's on your mind. But I held my tongue. "I could ask you the same question."

He nodded and thought for a moment. "My goal in life is to bring the spirit of Communism to the KDE Accounts Payable department." He lowered his voice. "You know, the true Red girls believe it's their duty to spread their legs for their comrades. My ultimate desire is to fuck Fraulein Strietzel. Chocolates and lace won't work with her. She needs ideology."

I had to laugh, although I don't think he was entirely joking. Fraulein Strietzel does seem to have an idealistic streak. She just might fall for a communist. Johnny smiled as though acknowledging my laughter, but then fell serious. "I've shared my true aspirations with you. Now you must share yours with me."

I felt trapped. I couldn't match his Berlin wit, and I certainly couldn't reveal my true purposes. And refusing to answer would tip him off that I had something to hide. After hesitating too long, I told him that I was simply here to study German business from the inside.

He seemed to accept this for what it was: half-truth.

At that moment, the negro pianist broke into a sort of fanfare and a young, swarthy-skinned man in a tuxedo and top hat leapt onto the stage. The evening's *conférencier*, a sort of master of ceremonies. He may have been a Jew. I'm not sure, but his delivery had the nervous quickness that people here talk about so much, the

"Jewish haste" that sets the pace for everything here in Berlin. His jokes reflected the sad state of life on the edge. Jokes about how to keep from getting shot during a demonstration, about how to help your wife get a role in a sex education film. Disturbing as it was, I relaxed into his patter after awhile. The girls had come back, and one of them – Greta was her name – had linked her arm inside mine as we listened. She had started to use *du* with me without even asking.

Suddenly, there was a loud crash that came from the front of the cabaret. I heard a male voice yell "Nein!" and then a uniformed *Freikorps* trooper appeared at the rear of the room, revolver in hand. He advanced unsteadily, obviously drunk.

"Russian scum!" he yelled, leveling his weapon at two male customers seated near the stage. "Traitors! My brother is dead!"

The *conférencier* spoke then, still on the stage, microphone in hand, leaning forward slightly towards the trooper. "Your brother is our brother too, my friend. All Germans are brothers... and sisters." I was astonished at the man's courage.

The trooper spun to face the *conférencier* and pointed the pistol at his heart. "You're no brother of mine," he said in his thick Bavarian accent. And then, he farted loudly.

A girl seated at the table next to ours started giggling – out of sheer nervousness, I'm sure – and the trooper wheeled around, arm extended. For a moment the pistol was pointed directly at me, but he corrected his aim and managed to shoot the poor girl.

Screams. Bright red blood. The trooper turned on his heel and walked towards the exit with drunken concentration. No one tried to stop him. A man pushed his way towards the wounded woman yelling for some clean cloth. He had apparently been in the medical corps during the war, and he quickly fashioned a field dressing out of dish towels. In less than five minutes, the woman was being aided out by two male companions, their shirts red with her blood. She had been hit in the shoulder and she looked very pale, but she could walk.

The crowd began to settle down. The negro pianist started playing again. A couple of waiters came out, replaced the bloody tablecloth, cleaned the floor and brought new chairs. For a moment, it was as if nothing had happened. Then, a *Freikorps* colonel appeared, accompanied by a small retinue of troopers, two with rifles. For a moment, I thought I was in genuine danger of losing my life. And I wasn't alone. Greta was trembling, digging her fingernails into my arm, and even Johnny had lost some of his habitual nonchalance. The colonel strode up to the stage, took the microphone in hand, and surveyed the audience with cold Prussian eyes.

The room fell deadly silent. I'm ashamed to say that I reached into my coat to assure myself that I had my American passport with me. Johnny noticed and, reading my mind, winked. Greta clung to me for protection which I was by no means certain I could offer.

"Ladies and gentlemen," the colonel began, "I would like to offer my most heartfelt apology for the despicable behavior of a man who would call himself patriot. It is inexcusable, and will not go unpunished. That is my promise to you."

As he spoke these words, the tension in the room immediately subsided.

"And I have another promise," he continued.

"If we meet in the streets this coming Saturday, we will fight you with every means at our disposal, we will defeat you, and we will cleanse the city of your foreign ideas. But not tonight. Not by shooting a helpless woman in a cabaret."

With that, he leapt off the stage and walked out, followed by his troopers

Greta began to cry. But before long, with the help of more champagne, she was giggling, and before the night was over we were all relaxed and laughing at a comic shadow play in which three women acted out a lesbian *ménage à trois*.

"Looks like fun," Greta whispered in my ear.

When the show was over, the four of us collected our coats and headed out to find a café for an early breakfast. We were all starving, until we saw the trooper.

He was hanging on a lamp post, suspended by a thick rope that ran under his arms and across his chest. He had been shot several times, I imagine by the colonel himself. You could see the oozing holes in his tunic. His eyes were staring straight ahead. And he wasn't yet dead.

I have never seen anything like that.

Johnny spirited the two girls into a taxi, handing them a wad of rentenmarks as they got in. Then he put his arm on my shoulder and guided me down the street to find another club where we could have one last brandy. As we walked away, he delivered the bombshell he had been holding back all evening. He spoke in casual tones, as though he were making a comment about the possibility of snow.

"That trooper back there? He could be *you* one of these days if you don't find a better way to hide the documents you're stealing."

Diary of Adam Luce
Berlin, 3 January, 1924

By pre-arrangement, I met Johnny after work at The El Dorado, a homosexual club that's not far from the office in physical terms, but oceans apart in atmosphere. It was Johnny's idea, and it was a good one. Being seen together in an ordinary social setting would have been difficult for both of us. At The El Dorado, we were unlikely to be seen by anyone we knew, as the crowd is mainly tourists. If we were, whoever saw us would never admit he had been at the El Dorado for fear of being branded as a queer.

Everyone was dressed to the nines. The bar "girl" who served us was a stunning blond. We both ordered brandies. After she left, Johnny commented that being queer might not be so bad, and I had to laugh. You get used to the queers here. It's no big deal. Our brandies soon arrived in large snifters that were warm to the touch. Johnny raised his and offered a toast to life. We locked our arms and drank the first swallow like acquaintances who had finally agreed to say *du* to one another.

"Welcome to the real Berlin," he said, pointing his finger at me with a *ka-pow* as if it were a pistol. "I'm referring to last night," he added, as though his reference weren't painfully clear. *The Real Berlin*, the city where your killer could appear out of nowhere, where, without even being a target, an accidental bullet could end your life on any day at any hour. Johnny put his hand on my arm and stared into my eyes. It occurred to me that we could easily have been taken for a queer couple, but that was the least of my concerns at the moment.

"Adam," he said, indeed using *du*, "What in the devil are you doing?"

This was a turning point, and we both knew it. At the moment, I could only think that Johnny had been in a position to expose me, but had chosen to warn me instead. I told him the truth, and I don't regret it. In fact, the words that came out of my mouth surprised me, and cast my situation in a new light.

"I'm here at my uncle's behest," I said. Then I explained about the problems with the Rensselaer plant, the lack of technical support, and the failed hope that I would be able to get into a lab and either pry some knowledge out of the KDE chemists and managers, or, in the worst case steal it. I explained that my endeavors to obtain KDE purchasing information for my Uncle were merely an attempt to make the best of a bad situation.

"You have no idea how dangerous this is, my friend" he said. "If you're caught, they're not going to give you a spanking and send you home."

I felt a chill no amount of brandy could counteract. If his assessment was correct, I was truly risking death.

"You have not yet been found out," he continued. "If you stop now, you will be safe."

Safe, I remember thinking, *and useless to everyone.*

"I think you should keep your nose clean. Eventually they will let you into a lab. And there you might find something that's really worth stealing."

I asked him what made him believe I'd eventually gain access to what I sought.

"Maybe they think you hold the key to the American market." He paused. "That may not be the case, but they don't know. They have no idea how much influence you may have over it as time passes. Believe me. They're not going to let you get away until they're sure they understand how much you're worth."

Again, he put his hand on my arm, and this time it made me a bit uncomfortable.

"You are playing a dangerous game," he said, rather melodramatically. "Did you ever ask yourself why your Uncle sent you here?"

"Because of my knowledge of chemistry. And my German."

"Let me ask you this. What would happen if you were killed?"

I didn't understand what he was getting at, and told him so.

"If you were *accidentally* killed, who would inherit Luce Chemical?"

I told him that, so far as I knew, my share would revert to my father, and then to the corporation upon his death, with a pension for my mother assuming she survived him.

"In other words," he said slowly, "If you're killed, all those assets would eventually revert to Luce Chemical, which means it comes under the sole control of your Uncle's branch of the family."

I pointed out that this view seemed unreasonably suspicious, given my role in gaining the information we needed to make the plant once again productive. If I were to fail, Luce would lose millions, and perhaps fall into receivership.

"True," he responded, "but are you really the only person who can make the plant operational? In fact, aren't there many with more experience who could do a better job?"

Of course, the answer was yes. There were dozens of senior KDE chemists who could accomplish that, were they but given permission! Unlike me, they wouldn't have to be trained. And beyond that, written documentation of the various processes most certainly exists. The Germans document *everything.*

At that point, I downed the remains of my brandy and ordered another. The blond waiter (waitress?) winked at me when he delivered my new snifter. "Drowning our sorrows tonight, are we?" he said. "I could help."

I wasn't really paying attention. Johnny's words were sinking in. He continued his harangue.

"What if your uncle sweetened the deal he's already struck? He could offer KDE a larger share of the profits once the plant's operational. He could agree to make other KDE products available to the American market through your company. KDE can't legally market in America, you know. With a sweet enough deal, your uncle wouldn't need you. Your primary advantage is that you're the cheapest option, at least in the short term."

"Will you stop!" I yelled.

Johnny held his hands up like a trapped bad guy in a Western. We received nervous glances from several of the nearby tables. In the *New Berlin*, public arguments often ended in gunfire.

"Calm down. I am simply pointing out that anything can happen. I offer myself as an example."

It turns out that Johnny comes from Dachau, where his family owned a small arms factory. He was posted to a garrison during the war and didn't see action. Afterward, he came to Berlin and spent two years studying economics with an eye towards an academic career. But before he could complete his studies, the family business went under in the economic and social chaos of 1919. With the factory's doors shuttered, there was no more money for books, and barely enough for food and lodging. Johnny somehow managed to talk his way into his low-level job at KDE. Beyond that, to use his words, he has "other means" for earning money. He says that most of what he earns goes back to support his parents in Dachau, although I must say that he doesn't skimp on clothes.

I thought he might be putting me on, and still wonder a little. When I asked him why someone with formal training in economics was working as a messenger he first answered that he wanted to be well-positioned when "The People" gained power, meaning the Reds. But when I pressed him he gave a more candid answer.

"A mail runner has access to the entire KDE complex," he said. "A mail runner learns a lot of things that can be useful."

We interrupted our conversation to order some beer and sausages. I looked around, wondering if there were any real girls among the crowd. In some clubs, it's impossible to tell. Johnny was also surveying the crowd, but I suspect he was looking for potential customers to whatever scarce goods he was fronting at the moment.

"I want to go to America some day," he said after awhile. "That's where the future lies."

I didn't reply.

He puffed at his cigarette thoughtfully.

"I'm going to keep your secret," he said at last, and with an air of finality. "I'll even help you. Just tell me what you need to know. I'll find it out. Of course, there will be a price. And when the time comes, you must promise to help me with my new life in America."

All the happy-go-lucky conviviality had drained from his eyes.

"Do we have a deal?" he said in his surprisingly good English.

Did I have a choice? I don't think so. He probably has access to ten times as much information in a week as I could root out in a year. And it didn't escape me that beneath Johnny's ready *bonhomie* lay a veiled threat of blackmail.

I replied in English. "We have a deal."

God help me. What have I gotten myself into?

Wolfgang Austerlitz

Überlegungen, 1 January, 1924

My dear Elsa doesn't know me as her husband anymore, only as the man who brings her the nightly injection that takes her pain away. Heroin. It's been condemned as an international scourge, but that's only because few physicians understand how and when to prescribe it, and too many patients who could be successfully treated come to crave its soporific effects beyond their time of need. Elsa's time of need will never come to an end until she dies, and thank God I control a laboratory that can produce what I need to ease her suffering.

The trips to Joachimsthal are becoming a problem. I must find a nurse I can trust to administer treatment in my absence. It's yet another problem to solve, and one that deserves my urgent attention. That's the trouble. All my problems are urgent. They surround me like a pack of yapping dogs.

I need to talk to Portia about this. She would surely accept the responsibility of caring for Elsa, and although I hate to admit it, I need help.

✠

Diary of Adam Luce

Berlin, 4 January, 1924

Yesterday I bought a pistol and a dozen bullets from a *schieber* recommended by Johnny. (Who else?) I met him in one of the streets off the Alexanderplatz. It's a somewhat dangerous part of town, so I took a cab and made the driver wait for me, which he gladly agreed to do when I flashed a silver dollar. You can get people in this city to do anything for a little money.

I have hidden the bullets in a box of English tea bags on the shelf in my closet where I keep my cigarettes. The pistol itself I will carry on my person when I feel the need. It probably won't do me any good, but at least I'll *feel* safer if I'm armed..

I do suspect I'm being observed.

Item: When I returned home from work yesterday, I found the latch to my mail box half-sprung in an obvious attempt to steal its contents. None of the others had been touched.

Item: when I retrieved my coat and scarf two nights ago at the *Maus*, the pockets had been rifled, and one of the linings turned out.

Item: On two occasions, a taxi I've hired here on Jägerstraße has been followed.

An innocent explanation can easily be found for all these occurrences. My poor landlady tells me that the mail boxes have been broken into in the past on more than one occasions. Any cloakroom girl might search through the pockets of an expensive-looking topcoat in hopes of finding a few extra *groschen*. And to be honest, I can't say that the two cars that appeared to be following my taxi weren't simply headed to the same destination as mine by coincidence. Nonetheless, I'd be a fool not to give these hunches at least some credence. And I must admit Johnny's speculations about Uncle Wyn have set me on edge. I can't believe he would consciously engineer my death. That's preposterous. But I most certainly *can* imagine him tossing me into a situation where death is a possible outcome. As a matter of fact, isn't that exactly what he's done?

Gefreiter Helmut Schreck
Field Notes, 3 January 1924

The first thing Papa wanted me to do when I got to the farm was put on my uniform. I'd just rather forget the whole war, but it makes him feel better so I did it.

He thinks I've turned into a *schieber*. How else would I get all this money? And what else would I be doing in Berlin? I just tell him that business is business, and let him think what he wants. He doesn't turn me down when I put a few gold coins into his pocket, even though I know he suspects they came from a Jew.

Papa's wrong about the Jews. They aren't the problem. There were three of them in my unit, and they were all good soldiers. Of course we can't have Jews commanding troops or anything like that, but they have their place in the trenches, and most of them want to serve the Fatherland.

Would I want one to marry Hanna Lora? Papa would go nuts! I don't know about myself. She's my sister and I want her to be happy, but I don't think it would work out. And there aren't many of them down here anyway. They're all in Berlin – or that's what it seems like.

The thing is, the Jews are smart. They may have crazy political ideas, but when you buy something from a Jew, you know you're not going to get the best price. He'll outsmart you every time. So I say, put the Jews to work selling our chemicals and steel. Bring that money back to Germany where it belongs.

Everybody complains about the foreigners down here – by which they mean the Jews – but the real foreigners they should be worrying about are the Americans. They're already manufacturing dyes over there from our stolen formulas. Those factories ought to be sabotaged! And anybody trying to take secret formulas out of this country ought to be shot. I'd do it for free.

Brecon Hall
Bryn Mawr College
Bryn Mawr, Penn.
28 December, 1923

My Dearest Adam,

It is quite late here, and I imagine that your alarm clock will soon ring. Were I with you, I would bury the thing under a pillow and distract you with kisses.

I'm afraid I am a bit zozzled. Can you tell it from my handwriting? Claire filched two bottles of burgundy from her father's oh-so-precious cellar during Christmas vacation, and tonight we partook, along with her roommate Sally, whom you've met. We read aloud from Iphigenia, and then from Aristophanes' Lysistrata, which is quite racy.

We got to laughing so hard we attracted the floor matron's attention, but by then the bottles had been emptied of their contents and hidden under Claire's bed. It was quite the bee's knees.

Now I am alone, and missing you terribly. I've been picturing you hunched over a bench in your German laboratory with bubbling flasks on all sides as you unlock the mystery of aspirin.

I know you will succeed, and I hope it's soon. The Luce company already has competitors in the miracle drug category, you know. St. Joseph's brand is on all the shelves now. But I shan't worry. I'm sure the Luce sales force will prevail once your company enters the market. So work hard, my genius, and come home soon with the secrets of success.

I think I shall close and go to bed now. I am tempted to simulate your caresses, dear Adam. I have done so in the past. Are you shocked? I personally suspect many of the girls here engage in this "therapy," although no one talks about it.

Oh my! I can't believe what I've just set down on paper. Perhaps I shouldn't post this letter. No, I shall. I shall throw on my robe, tiptoe down the stairs and put it in the mail box this minute before something changes my mind. Live dangerously! That's my motto tonight.

Shamelessly yours,

Margaret

Diary of Adam Luce
Berlin, 6 January, 1924

I must find a way to extricate myself from this situation. It's hopeless, it's stupid and it's damned dangerous. That's no joke. I could lose my life here – and while on a fool's errand at that. Why, then, am I sitting here in my chilly room on this clear February morning, scribbling in a journal no one will ever read, when I could be sitting in that Pariserplatz café next to the travel agent's office, sipping a *mit schlag* and waiting for him to open his doors?

The answer is all too obvious. It's not a potential offer from KDE that's keeping me here on tenterhooks. It's Charlotte. As much as I renounce her, she continues to creep into my thoughts at the slightest provocation. Who is she? How can I find her in this city of millions? And why in God's name do I want to find her in the first place? She's nothing but trouble – and yet I'm undeniably attracted to her. When it comes down to basics, we humans are no better than those Russian dogs trained to salivate at the sound of a bell. Except in my case, instead of a bell, it's the scent of her damned perfume.

For all that, I still hold out hope that she'll appear in my life once again, and that somehow I'll succeed in piercing the veil of theatricality that separates us even when we're together. But the sad truth is, I've no means to seek her out, much less probe her defenses. Visiting her haunts, such as they're known to me, has proved fruitless, and I certainly can't come knocking at her door. That we'll ever be reunited is a faint hope indeed, one that I should abandon.

As though playing the lovelorn suitor weren't trouble enough, I'm failing on the business front as well. Johnny's efforts to augment the meager payables data I was able to glean from my work aren't panning out. It's not that he isn't trying. But for all his guile, he's been unable to gain access to the lab. As he tells it, the closer he gets, the greater the resistance. The purchase orders and bills of lading that he has been able to filch tell a monotonous, repetitive story. I suspect Uncle Wyn still hopes I'll discover some secret ingredient that will convert the sticky pink output they're getting from Rensselaer into pure white crystals of ASA.[4] But no such ingredient exists! Our problems lie in the details of pressure, temperature and timing – the very details that are only to be found in a lab notebook, and they're never going to let me into a lab. Upon reflection, I'm certain that my exchange with that KDE chemist at the Christmas fête was a thinly disguised job interview. I have to accept that I didn't pass muster. It's been ten days since that event, and if they had an offer in mind it would have arrived by now.

The game is over. I'm wasting my time here. I should simply go back home to the swell girl who loves me and let the chips fall where they may. Who was I to think I could remedy the Rensselaer situation? Johnny's right. Uncle Wyn could make a deal with the Germans any day of the week if he really wanted to. So it might cost him a little more than he planned. That's part of business.

I don't have to go back to Luce Chemicals. Yes, I'm relinquishing a huge opportunity, but I can find some other way to make my mark in the world in the world. I'll do it on my own, and Margaret will stand by me. She isn't playing hide-and-seek. She's reaching out to me. Hell, she'd put on leather boots and parade around the bedroom naked for me in a minute if that's what I wanted. She'd probably like it, judging from that last letter.

It's settled. I shall seek out a travel bureau tomorrow and book passage on the next steamer out of Hamburg before something changes my mind. To Hell with this city.

Diary of Adam Luce
Berlin, 7 January, 1924

I easily found a travel agent on Königgrëtzstraße near the train station there, but he couldn't book my passage because the telephones were out. I can't help but take it as an omen. I was already on the fence about going home, which amounts to trading one set of uncertainties for another. Here, at least, the potential reward is well defined. Superstitious as it sounds, I believe the city was sending me a message. To remain in Berlin is my fate, and a difficult one it is. The thought of passing even one more day paging through endless contracts to determine the agreed upon cost of potash is intolerable. But tolerate this dreariness I must if I'm to nourish any hope that Johnny's analysis is correct. He clearly believes the doors to the labs will eventually open to me if I'm patient, and that's my path to a good life. I must admit, I do wonder if he has information he's withholding from me.

Diary of Adam Luce
Berlin, 13 January, 1924

Johnny is a Jew! He revealed this to me last night in the most off-handed manner over a rustic dinner in one of his Wedding beer halls. We had been joking about the cocaine factory he insists we should build. I said that if he was so interested in manufacturing he should go back to Dachau and start up the factory his father had operated successfully for so many years. He himself, I've learned, is quite clever with his hands, and the factory is equipped with precision tools for the manufacture of anything from high pressure valves to gears for automobiles. It would only be a matter of taking the dust covers off the machines and ringing up the workers, assuming they have telephone service down there.

He nodded in agreement when I brought this up. Then he revealed his secret by adding, ever so casually, "It's not the most wonderful place in Germany for a Jew."

My look of astonishment caused him to laugh heartily. "You mean you've never noticed how I'm always in a rush and never short of cash?"

At the mention of these stereotypes, I too had to laugh.

According to Johnny, it is not so bad (*nicht so schlim*) to be a Jew in Northern Germany. In fact, the Jews may have it better here than in other parts of Europe – France, for example, which has a long history of anti-Semitism. Johnny claims that in Berlin he could marry a blonde if he wanted, and he's probably right. One of my landlady's daughters has married a Jew, come to think of it. The only concern she ever expressed had to do with the Jews' "strange customs," by which I'm sure she was referring to circumcision, although her delicate manners prevented her from being explicit. She's no Berliner!

But I should return to Johnny. I think he's genuinely afraid of what might happen to a factory owned by a Jew in Bavaria, even if the workers were all Germans receiving a fair wage for an honest day's work. It was all too likely they'd see themselves as workers whose labor was being exploited by the evil Jewish capitalists, and so on and so forth.

It's evident that mistrust of the Jews runs deep down there, bordering on hatred as Johnny would have it. I just don't understand. Granted, a Jew would never make it into Bones back at Yale, but being prevented from running a business is a horse of a different color.

One thing is certain. Johnny's revelation was a true gesture of confidence, and not to be taken lightly. I would never have anticipated it, but the fact is we're becoming friends, and it's a valuable friendship indeed. His point of view takes me off my romantic high horse, at least for the time we're together. I've held back telling him about my predicament with Charlotte, but perhaps I should come clean. He's practical. He's got connections everywhere. I'll be forced to endure a lecture about how foolish it is to pine away for some girl who's obviously in need of psychoanalytic help, particularly when a replacement is to be found on every street corner. But when he's finished berating me, he'll help me.

Wolfgang Austerlitz
Überlegungen, 13 January, 1924

I must come to a decision about the young Luce, and soon. He's smart, he's industrious, and he seems to be keeping himself under control for the most part. One visit to Tauenzienstraße in two or three months? That's something I can forgive. The truth is, he reminds me more than a little of Jürgen. He doesn't have my departed son's athletic body—Jürgen was like a Greek god—but anyone can tell he's got Aryan blood, and Aryan determination. I don't have any doubts that he could get that Rensselaer plant up and running again. And if his uncle cheats us a little, so what? We need a foothold in the American market.

On the other hand, he's an American, and I don't know where his loyalty really lies. If we teach him what he needs to know and send him back home, what's to prevent his uncle from welching on our deal altogether?

The Raven keeps insisting he's got potential we can develop beyond the aspirin business. Maybe that's not so much of a stretch as it seems. The Joachimsthal project would be much easier to carry to completion with help from an American insider, and I have to admit that I like the picture of Luce leading the charge. No, that's a real stretch. If I question whether or not I can trust him with the details of our ASA chemistry, how can I even think about trusting him with the secrets of Joachimsthal?

Diary of Adam Luce
Berlin, 14 January, 1924

As fate would have it, or the stars for all I know, I had no need of Johnny's help. Charlotte was waiting for me when I left my house this morning, standing in the middle of the sidewalk wearing the fur coat I had bought for her before I knew her family was worth millions. She approached me and took my hands in hers. There was a wild look in her eye, and for once I believe it was no act.

"We have something between us, and it's important," she said without preamble. "I know I'm clumsy. I know I'm difficult. I can't help it, my dear Adam. Please don't leave. I want to spend time with you and at least pretend we're ordinary people, even if we're not."

With that, she pressed a scrap of paper into my hand with a telephone number scribbled onto it. "I'll stop disappearing, or at least I'll try," she said. "Call me at this number and ask for Portia. She can always find me."

Then she squeezed my hands tightly and walked off.

My dear Adam, she said. *Please don't leave*. I can't get her voice out of my head. And I can't help wondering how she knew that leaving Berlin was in my thoughts.

Gefreiter Helmut Schreck
Field Notes, 16 January, 1924

I'm getting soft. It's all the time I'm spending with Marguerite and little Heinz. Sunday dinners. Trips to the Tiergarten. Back massages and special cream for my scars. I never thought I'd have a normal life again. But I could. The factories have started hiring. If I wanted I could just get a job and put my old life behind me. Marguerite would like that.

She's right about one thing. What I do for a living is dangerous. There's no getting around it. Whenever you take somebody around the corner you make enemies, and eventually one of them is going to try to hunt you down. But I have to be honest. It wouldn't be easy for me to take orders from the same boss day after day. With Rudy it's different. I can say no now and then and still keep my job. The other thing is, Rudy and his friends count on me, and they take good care of me in the money department.

The fact is, I'm stuck where I am, at least until things settle down. Until we get a leader who can give us something to believe in.

Diary of Adam Luce
Berlin, 20 January, 1924

I am swimming in deep water.

Yesterday morning I finally got up the courage to telephone the number on the scrap of paper Charlotte gave me the other day. I reached a butler at the von Schwerin mansion and as instructed I asked for Portia. After a series of clicks I was put through.

"Is this Charlotte?" I asked.

"This is Portia," she said rather brusquely. She told me in a tone that precluded further inquiries that Charlotte was not available, Then, to my shock, she invited me to a theatrical performance that very day. "I presume your wardrobe includes evening clothes," she added – a somewhat stinging reminder that I had been a bit under-dressed for the festivities last month at the mansion.

I assured her that I was in possession of a tux, and with that obstacle overcome she told me she would send a car over at seven. Then she hung up without so much as a good bye, much less an apology for the last-minute nature of the invitation. I didn't know what to think. With whom was I to spend the evening? Would I indeed use the formal "Sie" when addressing a girl in front of whom I had recently disrobed?

I was indeed Portia who met me in the ornate lobby of the Kroll Opera House dressed in a stunning black gown that quite literally took my breath away. It was like seeing Charlotte in the costume of an aristocrat. An usher led us up the two flights of stairs to our box, which was furnished with four plush seats facing the stage as well as a small couch. There was a low table carved in the oriental style in front of the couch, and on it was a bottle of *sekt* and two fluted glasses. The usher filled them and then left after accepting a silver coin from Portia.

Still standing, she toasted the Fatherland and U followed her lead. Then we sat down on opposite ends of the couch. Just as we had emptied our glasses the orchestra began tuning. With a quiet rustle of silk Portia took one of the seats, and then patted her hand on the one next to it as if she were inviting a pet to hop up. I chose to accept her gesture as one of friendship and joined her. The orchestra fell silent. Then, the music began and the curtain rose.

The story of Das Kämpferleid revolved around an aging king in search of the elixir of youth. An alchemist succeeds in producing it, but the king's new wife – a young foreigner – adds poison to the elixir before he drinks it. The poison induces madness. In his mind, his own sons are transformed into monsters. He orders them killed, but they escape to the Black Forest where they are schooled by a wizard to become warriors. At the end of the third and final act they set off to recapture the kingdom that is rightfully theirs.

The stagecraft was spectacular from the beginning, and the singing like nothing I have ever heard. I could scarcely take my eyes away from the stage, and when I did I was shocked to see Portia's face bathed in tears. When I put my hand on her bare forearm she slapped it away.

"You understand nothing," she hissed.

After the final curtain fell, she apologized for the affront and suggested we finish off the champagne.

We sat facing one another. Her eyes were downcast. "I know for you what we saw was just a stage play, a somewhat clumsy allegorical one at that, but I lived through it. You can't comprehend how much was lost."

At least I knew what the word "allegory" meant, having struggled through Pilgrim's Progress like every other poor fellow in Dr. Waterbury's frosh English. The king was Germany; the foreign queen, Communism. The sons, Nationalists who had refused to compromise and had withdrawn from "The System." I couldn't think who or what the wizard might represent, but there are candidates enough among the cults here.

In any case, I found her talk of "how much was lost" unconvincing. She must have read my thoughts – that the post-war collapse, whether in its economic or moral aspect, didn't seem to have touched her family.

"It's not about money," she said. "The German people will soon have plenty. Men like my uncle will see to that. It's about a heritage that's in grave danger.

Afterward, as we drank even more *sekt* and nibbled on caviar and toast at the Adlon, she gave me a history lesson, to use her words. Seated across from me in soft electric light augmented by candles, she seemed an astonishingly accurate mirror image of Charlotte as she "instructed" me.

The Kaiser's abdication at the end of the Great War had been an act of despicable cowardice, the Treaty of Versailles a shameful capitulation. The resultant economic collapse had emasculated the German worker. All Germans, rich and poor, had become disconnected from their historical *volkische* roots.

"Americans are a rootless people," she finished, with no small measure of condescension. "I can't expect you to understand."

I took her remark as a challenge, and, considering the amount of *sekt* we had consumed by that point, mustered a decent argument that America had proposed an alternative to the Versailles accords that would have given Germany a fair shake at recovery.

When I had finished, she leaned across the small table and put her hand on my thigh. "I can see why Charlotte likes you so much," she said

At her touch, I experienced a sexual thrill and a sense of panic. The complexity and precariousness of my situation became frighteningly clear at that moment, and I patted her hand in the most brotherly fashion I could manage.

"I think it's time to call for the car," I said, and I could swear a look of disappointment crossed her face.

"Not yet," she said, touching my arm this time. "there's something important I want you to know."

She stared for a moment at the empty glass resting in her hands, perhaps pondering if its contents had influenced her decision to speak.

"You may have the opportunity to take part in something vital to Western civilization. We may need your help, and it could involve staying here in Germany longer than you planned, and not in Berlin.

Portia was playing me like a violin. That developments were afoot in the German chemical industry that would have global ramifications was hardly beyond the bounds of credibility. But I would have scoffed at idea that I might be involved had it not been put forth by the daughter of a powerful aristocrat, a woman who was clearly in the know. At that moment I was ready to agree to anything.

"You must be ready when the time comes," she said."

"Ready for what?"

"She put her finger to my lips, a gesture whose intimacy took me off guard.

"I've said enough. Now it's time to say good night before I get into real trouble."

If the truth be told, I wanted her. She's given signs that she'll offer me what Charlotte always finds a way to withhold at the last moment after long and calculated teasing. But should I fault Charlotte for her chastity, if that word can be applied to one so brazen? She's no slut whom one enjoys and then forgets the next day, without ever learning her name. She's high-minded, if capricious, and... must I admit this? I can see us together strolling down Fifth Avenue.

Diary of Adam Luce

Berlin, 21 January, 1924

I was in the middle of a somewhat complicated calculation this morning involving multiple vendors with multiple discount rates when the room fell silent. It is never noisy, of course. Chatting is frowned upon, and only Johnny gets away with it. But at that moment, even the clicking of the typewriter keys stopped. Herr

Habermeyer had emerged from his office, and everyone held the same thought. *This cannot be good.* He fixed his eyes on me and nodded once. I had been summoned.

I stood up, buttoned my coat, and walked towards his office. All the eyes in the room were on me, and in those eyes I perceived no small measure of relief that it was me, *der Amerikaner*, and not one of them. He motioned me into his office and closed the heavy wooden door behind him. The room reeked of that Balkan tobacco that is so popular here, and of Habermeyer's sweat. He sat down behind his desk in his swanky chair, leaving me standing. Then, after a suitably dramatic pause, he made his announcement.

"You are to proceed to Ruhlebener Straße immediately. A car is waiting for you at the entrance." *Ruhlebener Straße.* I was going to the KDE factory! I tried, unsuccessfully I think, to hide my excitement.

Habermeyer clearly felt a need to comment. "I don't know what this means," he said. "I never know what things mean with you. For what it's worth, I've given you good reviews."

He stood up and, to my surprise, offered his hand. "Good luck with Herr Doktor Austerlitz."

I didn't know who he was talking about, so I simply repeated the name.

"Herr Doktor Wolfgang Austerlitz. You're meeting with the chief chemist of the company. He's a strange bird. It's said his mother was from Bohemia. Perhaps that explains it."

The Germans make exaggerated distinctions among themselves just as we do – among the "passionate" Italians, the "wily" Jews, the "romantic" French and so on. Often, however, the German versions of these references are incomprehensible to me, and I've no idea what he meant.

I said goodbye, feeling a sense of finality as I did so.

By chance – *was* it chance? - I was driven to Ruhlebener Straße by the same man who brought me to the Christmas fête. He showed no sign of recognizing me, and I wondered if he felt that to do so would amount to fraternizing with the enemy. *Ein Amerikaner!* I have never seen such bitterness among the defeated as I have seen among the Whites, who have lost not only their wealth, but their sense of honor as well.

The factory is located near the river Spree since, like any chemical factory, it requires a plentiful source of water. My driver kept a firm grip on the wheel as we made our way over the packed slush that covers Berlin's broad boulevards and back alleys alike. After half an hour or so, we passed through the stone gates of the facility, where *Freikorps* guards in black uniforms stood at attention, rifles at the ready. The architecture of the Ruhlebener factory is classical, or perhaps neo-classical, but whatever the designation, it puts the blockish brick construction of our facility in New York to shame. There is a level of respect for science here in Germany that is unknown in America, even in universities.

I was met in the spacious atrium in front of the main reception desk by a fellow about my age who gave me a suspicious look, offered me a quick handshake, and then led me down a maze of corridors. The first set were spotless, with high ceilings and an abundance of natural light that the Germans consider so fundamental to health. Double paned windows afforded a view of the plant itself with its huge chemical reactor vessels and complicated piping. Workers in white laboratory smocks moved efficiently from gauge to gauge and valve to valve without a moment's hesitation, loading hoppers, monitoring the operation of the shakers and in general tending to the plant's smooth operation. I detected a faint smell of vinegar in the air, and could hear the muffled sound of the huge exhaust fans. Here was knowledge in action!

The second set of corridors, nearer to the center of the building, seemed to be older. They were, like the first set, immaculate, but not to an antiseptic extreme. The floors were of highly polished wood, and there were regularly spaced doors with engraved bronze plates bearing the occupants' names and titles. Then came another transition where we walked on long, narrow oriental carpets under rather elaborate chandeliers. It was as if we were traveling back in time.

At last we arrived at a small anteroom furnished with two couches upholstered in black leather. Over one, the old German flag with its black, white and red bars was displayed. Over the other hung a portrait of a hooded monk seated in front of an old wall furnace with a bellows in his hands. At the far end of the room there was a single wooden door, richly carved with a floral motif. I could make out a lion and a deer hidden among the leaves and flowers, and perhaps a peacock as well.

My guide – I never did learn his name – produced a large, old-fashioned key and inserted it into a lock located just below the door's round knob of a handle, in which a stylized image of the sun had been engraved. The door opened a crack into what appeared to be total darkness.

"Watch your step," said my guide.

Did I detect a *double entendre* in this admonition? In any case, I pushed the door open and stepped inside, feigning a boldness I by no means felt. My guide pulled the door shut behind me, leaving me alone and effectively blind. My eyes quickly adjusted, however, and I realized I was on the top stair of a spiral staircase that led down into impenetrable gloom. I descended, grasping the iron railing and "watching my step" as best I could.

I found myself in a second anteroom, this one with dimly lit stone walls and a small, bubbling fountain in the center. I walked around the fountain to the room's only door. Not knowing what else to do, I knocked... and was bade to enter.

At first I thought my eyes were playing tricks on me. But no. The stocky, square-shouldered man seated behind the weathered desk facing me was none other than Charlotte's companion at the Jospy. He had a ruddy complexion and projected that aura of German good health born of frequent exercise. It was easy to imagine him in his younger days as one of those tireless soccer players who effortlessly run miles during a match. He wore steel rimmed spectacles and had a starched white lab coat over his suit, as though he had recently returned from a tour of the factory and hadn't bothered to take it off. I could hardly conceal my shock. Austerlitz fixed me with a piercing gaze, and without a word gestured to one of two stools next to a workbench that ran along the wall to my left. Set into that wall was a furnace that bore a remarkable resemblance to the one I had just seen in the portrait of the monk, but with modern electrical controls. The opposite wall was filled with old books from floor to ceiling. A second, much smaller desk faced outward from the far wall, upon which was an open volume. Several electric lanterns suspended from the ceiling provided illumination.

There was a long and uncomfortable silence. I felt that Austerlitz was sizing me up, and for a moment I wondered whether he would deign to speak to me at all. Unable to sustain eye contact, I turned my attention to the wall of books. Many were in Latin and some, it appeared, in Arabic.

At last, he broke the silence. "Quite a collection, wouldn't you agree?" he said, addressing me with the familiar *du* that one would use when speaking to a child. He referred to his library with a stiff gesture that appeared to cause him some pain. "It's like no other collection in the world – a rare amalgamation of lies, fantasy and..." he paused, "knowledge of incalculable value." He fixed me once again with that gaze of his, apparently still taking my measure.

"If you're thinking that the formula for the world's next wonder drug is up there, I can assure you that it's not."

I flushed at how easily he had read my thoughts.

"There's more to life than learning how to shut down chills and fever," he continued. "But in any case, that's not why you're here in Berlin, is it?"

He quickly answered his own question. "You're here because you want to become more powerful."

This pronouncement hit me like a bolt of lightening. In his presence, my noble vision of Luce as a source of "real medicine" took on an air of pretension. Was taking up my Uncle Wyn's challenge merely a strategy whose true purpose was to put myself in a position where I could call the shots and eventually direct the course of my own life? Was I merely working to lift myself above his and my father's endless manipulations? Austerlitz waited a moment while I pondered these questions and the meaning of his... shall I call it his accusation? Then he continued.

"KDE isn't a soup kitchen that gives what it has to any poor soul who happens to wander by."

At this point I attempted to express some words of deference, but he cut me off.

"The secret knowledge that's held within these walls can't be bought. The knowledge of how to manufacture aspirin, for example. A man must earn it. He must show himself to be worthy – and able. I have no time to waste on runners who can't finish the race or get lost along the way."

He stared at me with uncomfortable intensity. "Are you ready for a test?"

These words produced a thrill in my spirit that has not diminished with the passing hours. I felt as if his question summarized my entire life. I was stunned that he could be so perceptive. What was Berlin if not a test? What is life if not a test? Sitting on that stool, I no longer felt like a junior partner in a business venture. Rather, I felt like I was on the verge of becoming Austerlitz' apprentice.

"I suppose I am ready," I replied, but my tone betrayed my uncertainty.

"There's no room for indecision in our work," he said sternly. Although I doubt that he had any ill intent, his response was like a slap in the face.

"Yes, Herr Doktor," was all I could say, and somewhat meekly at that. I have never met anyone who commands such instant respect.

"You'll be contacted," he said, "When a problem of a significant scale arises." With that he stood and offered his hand. I noticed for the first time that it was mottled with white scar tissue, and that he had a small tattoo on his inner wrist, a variant of the letter "H" as best as I could make out. We shook, and then I turned and exited what I've come to think of as his *lair*. I am at a loss to understand why he should choose to conduct business from a dimly lit dungeon that would seem more suited to alchemy than modern science. But then again, he intimated that more than business was at stake. What then? Where will this encounter lead me? For now, what I must do, like it or not, is await my test. I dare say it may involve aspirin. He did mention the drug. May it be so! If I were a religious man, I'd be on my knees.

RADIOGRAM

Kopie

Betriebsgesellschaft für drahtlose Telegraphie m.b.H, System Telefunken

RKBEX 4311 4FEB24
MR. WYNFRED LUCE
RURAL ROUTE 7
ALBANY NEWYORK
MAJOR PROGRESS. MET WITH LEAD CHEMIST AT KDE. ACCESS TO FACTORY POSSIBLE. DETAILS TO COME. ADAM

Diary of Adam Luce

Berlin, 22 January, 1924

I'm picking up where I left off. I had no wish to return to the office after my meeting with Austerlitz, nor any need. Herr Habermeyer would hardly question my absence, and in any case he'd have no way of knowing I wasn't still with the august chief chemist. I had my driver take me to the Romanische with the hope that the café's noisy atmosphere might distract my mind from fruitless speculation about what an "appropriate" test might entail.

I took a copy of today's *Vossische Zeitung* from the rack and buried myself in its liberal, if gloomy, interpretation of current events, the most prominent being the upcoming trial of a Bavarian politician named Adolf Hitler who's accused of attempting to overthrow the government. Given the universal disdain for the current government, one would think any such an attempt would win enthusiastic support from all sides. But this Hitler apparently failed to win over the generals, a fatal deficiency in a country where guns rule.

When I finished the newspaper I looked up to scan the crowd, half expecting to find Charlotte among them. I didn't, but emboldened by the strong pilsner I had drunk I decided to again try the telephone number she had pressed into my hand. I left the café and quickly found one of the familiar blue and yellow telephone kiosks at the foot of Kufürstendamm Straße, deposited my coins and dialed the number. Charlotte herself answered on the second ring. I proposed a celebratory dinner, withholding any details about what was to be celebrated, and she accepted in an instant.

We met around seven thirty in one of the endless string of "friend's apartments" to which she has access. She was dressed to the teeth in one of her black, clingy outfits, and at first she was flirtatious, playfully insisting I share a cup of tea that contained an unspecified intoxicant. When I told her about my new situation at KDE and the test with which I was to be presented, she suddenly became quite serious. "You must succeed," she said, grasping my shoulders and staring intently into my eyes. "So much is at stake for you."

I said, "For me, perhaps. But I dare say the most advanced chemical company in the world will survive if I fail."

She gave me a stricken look. "You don't understand," she said, shaking her head. "You really don't."

I was confused and taken aback by her demeanor. In a much more serious tone, I asked her just what it was that I didn't understand.

"You have the possibility of becoming a real chemist. If you knew what that meant, you would have no other goal in life." She put her hands on her hips. In this position, the sheer silk of her blouse pressed against her breasts, which attracted my gaze – and she actually slapped me. There were tears in her eyes.

"Listen to me! I'm telling you this because... I care for you. More than I should." I think she was shocked by her own words. But shocked or not, she continued rapidly.

"It starts...." Here she paused, searching for words. "You have to burn away all your old feelings and ideas. Then, when there's nothing left, you can start over. You can purify yourself. It's like what's happening here in Berlin. All the old ideas are going up in smoke."

Suddenly, she broke off. "I've said too much," echoing her sister's words of two nights past. She` brushed her tears away with the knuckle of her forefinger and smiled wanly. "*Liebchen*, this is such good news. It's so important. No wonder you want to celebrate. And I know just the place."

She eyed me up and down. My clothing was suitable, she said, but she would have to change into something less ostentatious. She disappeared into the bedroom, leaving me to ponder her bizarre outburst. When she emerged, she was wearing a coat that was obviously designed for warmth, not style, and clumsy low-healed shoes. She looked almost frowsy. "We're going to Wedding," she announced, "to have supper with the Reds."

We took the underground to Leopold Platz, which was crowded with street vendors. A Quaker soup wagon parked on one corner of the square had attracted a long line of women wearing dark wool coats not unlike Charlotte's. They looked weary and defeated. We pushed through the crowd towards our destination – a cavernous beer hall situated next door to a brewery which, I suspect, employs many of the workers in the neighborhood. Inside, it was warm, and like the square, quite crowded. The walls were draped with red banners that bore the Russian hammer and sickle, interspersed with paintings of Lenin and Trotsky haranguing crowds of heroic workers.

We found a place at the end of a bench and ordered beer, sausages and potatoes. As usual, Charlotte ate voraciously, while making coarse jokes about the size and shape of the sausages. She seemed completely comfortable among "the people" and somehow managed to look the part of a worker in spite of her delicate features. I received wary looks from a few of the men, but I think most of them took me for one of those rare students sympathetic to their cause.

After two large steins of the strong beer we were both a bit zozzled, a state which accentuated my general confusion about why she had brought me there. I finally came right out and asked her.

As I expected, she didn't give me a straight answer. Instead, she gestured towards the banners and said, "Have you ever seen so much red? It means these people have arrived. They have found what they were looking for. They don't know it, but all this red is what makes them feel so good."

This struck me as yet another example of just how bizarre is Charlotte's universe, but I pursued her theme nonetheless.

"So colors have meaning beyond those special boots the girls wear on Tauenzienstraße?"

She stared down at the table and I could swear I could hear her counting to ten, as my mother taught me to do to help contain my anger.

"Why is it that whenever I tell you something important you try to turn it into a joke?"

"I'm sorry," I said somewhat clumsily.

"I brought you here so you could absorb what success feels like. With all this red. It's simple. Now let's go back and finish what we started.

We managed to find a taxi for the ride back to the apartment that was hers for the night. The streets of Wedding were dark and deserted. It was a sharp and unsettling contrast to the bustling scenes we had encountered only a couple of hours previously. I must admit I felt more comfortable once we reached a fully electrified district with street lamps, although, if the truth be told, no street in this city is truly safe.

When we arrived, Charlotte produced a bottle cognac and two glasses. We sat down at opposite ends of a plush sofa upholstered in red velvet and sipped in silence. After a time she scooted closer put her hand on mine. Her eyes sparkled.

"I think Uncle Wolfie wants you to succeed."

"Uncle Wolfie?"

"Herr Doktor Wolfgang Austerlitz."

I was stunned by her intimate reference to the man who held my fate in his hands. Charlotte slid over to me and rested her head on my shoulder. Then she began talking about Uncle Wolfie.

"I don't see him so much any more," she said. "When I was a girl he took me and Portia to the zoo almost every Sunday He would buy peanuts and let us feed the elephants." She went on in a dreamy fashion for some time as we gradually consumed more and more cognac. Finally, she glanced down at the two glasses we had now emptied thrice.

"I think we've gone far enough," she said, rubbing my thigh again. "If you don't leave now, you're going to want to ravish me, and for my part, I will very much wish to be ravished. So out with you."

She stood, pulled me to my feet, and favored me with a passionate kiss. Then, after cleaning my face of her lipstick with a silk handkerchief, she shoved me towards the door.

"It won't be hard to find a taxi, my dear. Dream of me."

It's becoming clear that, for all her games, Charlotte is not the flighty, play-acting slut she pretends to be. This is the face she presents to the world, and indeed presented to me during our first encounters, but it is like those elaborate masks some of the patrons wear at the *Maus*, whose only purpose is to conceal the wearer's true identity. The truth is, she's an aristocrat, well-educated, and possessed of an incisive intelligence, not to mention connections, I must admit, that could influence my fate. Who else does she know in the KDE hierarchy? I can't shake the impression that when she asserts much is at stake for me, she's not talking about the Luce Company's venture into aspirin.

And what am I to make of her insistent reference to purity? It's hard to say, but I do now question her accounts of what she has witnessed in the private salons of "good Prussians," as she ironically describes the participants in the orgies she sometimes conjures up when we talk. I think she invents these tales to make me jealous. I must confess that on occasion it works, and the more of her true self she reveals, the less comfortable I am learning about her erotic escapades, real or imagined. I think the latter case more likely. Would she freely give to strangers what she insists on withholding from me?

Diary of Adam Luce

Berlin, 25 January, 1924

I had an early dinner with Johnny this evening in a small wine bar just south of Wedding to share the news that there might be a position for me within the factory. For some reason I didn't mention my test.

I expected a slap on the back when I told him of my good fortune, but the first words out of his mouth were, "I'm afraid this isn't good news."

When I asked him what he was talking about, he began by rehashing his "Evil Uncle" theory, but with a new twist. When Uncle Wyn bought Rensselaer, he thought he was purchasing an enterprise that would run itself, and generate a tidy profit in the process. After the Germans decamped, he quickly realized he was in over his head. Dispatching yours truly to Berlin on a mission that was doomed to failure would furnish him with a face-saving exit to the whole affair. He'd have proof that the aspirin business was a bust, and a free hand to convert Rensselaer to the production of the kind of pills he knew how to sell. That accomplished, he'd find some way or other to kill me off to keep the Luce Chemical fortunes all in his side of the family. It never fails to aggravate me when Johnny trots out this fantasy, but he argues that I don't like it because it's all too plausible.

Can he be right? It does appear that Uncle Wyn's intentions are ambiguous. But Johnny's plot line – that I was originally sent here to gather what little data I could before I fell victim to a stray Berlin bullet, if not a paid assassin – is just beyond the pale. I'm no more or less safe than I was the day before Austerlitz summoned me to Ruhlebener Straße. Uncle Wyn has hatched no plot for my death. And for that matter, I'm not fully convinced Uncle Wyn would want my cousin as the one to be minding the store. He's a good fellow, but a bit unstable, and hardly a dominating intellect.

The alternate interpretation Johnny came up with last night is more credible. In it, I have already succeeded beyond Uncle Wyn's wildest dreams, and with the means to manufacture and sell aspirin to the American market once more within his grasp, he's not sure how to proceed, e.g. where to obtain the necessary financing, whom to put in charge of hiring, how to deal with a new set of regulatory bodies, and so on and so forth. (Johnny has quite a head for business, I must say.)

It's also possible that Uncle Wyn may simply be uncomfortable with the responsibility of manufacturing the genuine article now that he's thought about it. At heart, he's a huckster. Selling a product through druggists – men with scientific training who could verify its purity and who had a stake in its efficacy – would transform Luce Chemical into a quite different operation, one that depended more on precision of execution than salesmanship. As the slogan goes, "Your druggist is more than a merchant!"

Uncle Wyn has learned the hard way that aspirin is not some "glandular extract" Luce Chemical can cook up and thereby enjoy growth with no effort. Perhaps he now thinks the whole venture not worth the trouble. But why then did he send me here in the first place? I'm beginning to suspect he saw my mission as a desperate forward pass, one that he felt obliged to attempt, but for which there was virtually no hope of success. Then I succeeded, and now it's a whole new ballgame – one for which he is quite ill prepared. Can it be true that in his heart of hearts he wanted me to fail?

In any case, I must write to Margaret and tell her the good news. It's been days since my last letter.

Diary of Adam Luce
Berlin, 27 January, 1924

I know what's real and what's not. These tricks of vision are the consequence of too many late nights, and nothing more. That bear's head on the floor at the very edge of my field of vision is nothing but a balled-up shirt in need of laundering, and I see it as such if I but turn my head to view it straight on. And that message painted on the wall in the alley last night where I stopped to urinate on my way home. "*Rot über alles.*" Red above all. It wasn't meant for my eyes only, and surely bore no relation to Charlotte's obsession with the color, nor with my earlier encounter today. It was the work of some disgruntled communist who lacked the courage to express his convictions on a more public wall. And yet, there it was. A coincidence? Or a message?

I am at a loss to explain the woman in the red coat. I spotted her late in the day at the Adlon. She was sitting outside at a table by herself, sipping a coffee and reading a copy of *Die Dame*, a signal of availability in itself. It struck me as strange that none of the men around her seemed to pay her any notice. It was as if she were invisible. The brim of her hat shadowed her features, yet somehow I felt that I recognized her, and when she rose to leave, I felt compelled to follow. She walked along Friedrichstraße towards the Victory Column at a brisk pace, moving smoothly through the early evening crowd. Then she turned right onto Puttkamstraße, a much quieter street. Soon, we were the only two souls in sight. I thought she was most likely headed towards Wilhelmstraße, which runs almost parallel, but instead she turned into an alley, which was a dead end. There were no doors and no avenues of escape, only bricks, and yet when I arrived she was nowhere to be seen. What did meet my eye was the slogan painted on the bricks in the same shade as her coat. *Rot über alles.*

I cannot help but entertain the idea that the city is speaking to me, but in a language I cannot understand.

Diary of Adam Luce

Berlin, 1 February, 1924

Another week of waiting. I wish the business world weren't so opaque and filled with devious stratagems. But so it is. Uncle Wyn has not responded to my cable, nor to my most recent letter. On top of that, I'm still officially at my old post in the Finance Department, awaiting transfer documents. I hold the suspicion that these two facts are linked, although for the life of me I can't see how that could be. Are secret negotiations taking place that put conditions on my access to information? It's not such a preposterous thought. And if it's true, may these negotiations come to a speedy conclusion!

Without Charlotte I don't know how I would deal with this uncertainty. She's been there for me almost every night with reassurance, jokes and flirtatious comments that totally dissolve my anxiety. There was a time when I would never have gotten mixed up with a girl like her. But I have, and now I can't banish her from my thoughts. She has kindled within me a flame of desire that cannot be snuffed out like the candles at the end of a dinner party. My God, listen to me! "Flame of desire." But what else shall I call these longings?

Am I a cad? I suppose the very fact that I'm posing the question suggests an answer in the affirmative. But in all fairness to myself, I made no explicit promises to Margaret. Beyond that, the feelings I hold for Charlotte are surely like those one experiences in a dream. Yes, they may linger into the morning, but they fade with every passing hour.

Why then, can I not put her out of my mind? When I'm with her, every sense impression seems heightened, and there is painful meaning in trivial scenes, an old discarded shoe in an alley, a shopkeeper bundled up against the cold sweeping the snow from the sidewalk in front of his store. It's the drugs she plies me with in my weaker moments, or perhaps their residue.

I do sense that she sees more deeply into life's mysteries than does Margaret, for all her classical studies. Well, so it seems.

Berlin has brought out too much of the romantic in me. The fact is, I have a German girlfriend who's a bit debauched, and she's using her family's political connections to help me get what it is I'm here for. It's as simple as that, and it's not half bad, or rather, it's just that: half bad.

I cannot seem to find clarity in all this. Were Charlotte sitting beside me as I write, she would say that nothing made by God can be fundamentally evil. "Not even me," she would probably add.

I need to spend more time with Johnny. He brings me down to Earth.

Diary of Adam Luce
Berlin, 4 February, 1924

I have a new routine to pass the time while I await an assignment from Austerlitz. Each morning after my coffee I head to the Nordic Dawn Athletic Club, where I am now a member in good standing. The other members are to the far right politically speaking, and a bit strange with their stiff-armed salutes, but the club has marvelous facilities and it's close by. As soon as I arrive I pull on my running shorts and put in five kilometers on the cinders. I usually swim ten laps as well. It's a co-ed pool, and on Thursdays everybody goes naked – the women as well as the men. It takes a bit of getting used to, but it's really quite innocent, with none of the flavor of the cabarets.

Every afternoon is like the last, and to speak bluntly it's driving me bananas. To kill some time, I decided to make another visit to the vast public library to see if I could track down the symbol tattooed on Austerlitz' inner wrist. With typical German efficiency, the clerk at the research desk directed me to a dictionary of symbols, just what I needed. I found a free table in the stately reading room and began my search. It didn't take long. I had suspected that the symbol was either of chemical or astronomical origin, and I was correct. It stands for the planet Uranus.

I've no idea how to understand this bit of knowledge. Nothing I have encountered since my arrival is without an aspect of hidden mystery.

Diary of Adam Luce
Berlin, 8 February, 1924

Frau Schumann greeted me at the front door today in a state of extreme agitation, one that I now share, albeit for quite different reasons. Two American soldiers had appeared at the door shortly after nine o'clock in the morning with a letter addressed to me. This mode of transmittal, while hardly unprecedented, has become rare in recent times. The social chaos that led Americans of a certain social rank to mistrust the German postal service has abated.

The poor woman was so distraught that I opened the envelope then and there. I couldn't have been more shocked by its contents: an offer of employment from DuPont, signed by the Director of Research himself. As I scanned the letter, a thousand questions raced through my mind. How did this man even learn of my existence, much less my present location in Berlin? What led him to believe that he could lure me away from a company owned by my own family? What did he want with me?

After assuring Frau Schumann that nothing was amiss, I immediately went up to my room and rang up Johnny. An hour later over coffee and strudel at the Jospy, he put the finger on Margaret, my "woman in reserve in the states," as he insists on calling her. As usual, his theory lay at the edge of plausibility, but not beyond its bounds. Margaret's father is a banker, and a man of many connections. His bank, which counts DuPont among its clients, was also an important intermediary in the transaction by which Luce acquired the Rensselaer facility. My father was quite taken with him, and saw Luce Chemical's connection with one of DuPont's bankers as a sign that we were "moving up in the world." In fact, it was at one of the bank's annual Fourth of July bashes that I first met Margaret.

Margaret's father was Luce Chemical's banker for the Rensselaer transaction, *ergo* he has both the means and the motivation to keep an eye on the company's fortunes, particularly with a potential son-in-law of his involved. He also has contacts within DuPont and could easily find a friendly ear into which he could sing my praises. He might certainly do so were he to learn that the Rensselaer facility was sitting idle, with no prospects for starting up any time soon.

Of course, Johnny knew none of this until I told him. He only knew that, outside the Luce family, Margaret alone is in possession of my address here in Berlin. When I revealed the other relationships, he immediately jumped on them as proof of his theory. In his view, I am quite the prize. I am not only an honors graduate from a rather prestigious university. I am perhaps the only American in the world with the inside dope on German production techniques for the most important new drug of the twentieth century. That's what they think, in any case.

How could Margaret's father know all this? By asking his daughter!

In brief, seeing financial troubles ahead for Luce, he was acting on Margaret's behalf to avert financial trouble for her *beau*. All of which belies the question: How shall I respond to this offer? Is the family business genuinely in trouble? I confess it's more than a bit chilling to realize that if it were, there is no one whom I could trust to tell me the truth. And if there is trouble, am I to abandon all that I've struggled to achieve and become a cog in a wheel of the DuPont chemical engine?

In Margaret's conservative eyes, DuPont would be the safe move. Better the ground floor of a stable edifice than the penthouse of one that's about to topple. And a choice for DuPont would quickly bring me home. The offer is not without its merits. I would have a secure position with access to first-class facilities. And Margaret and I would be able to live in Manhattan, which is her dream.

It would be a stable life, but one built on a the foundation of a father-in-law's patronage, not my own hard work. I would never be my own man. And therefore, I cannot seriously entertain this offer. Its only attractiveness lies in my uncertainty borne of Uncle Wyn's silence.

I'll post a polite refusal tomorrow, or better yet, I'll send it by pouch. In doing so, I'll close a door that will never open again for me, but I've made a commitment and I'm sticking to it. When I'm done, my success will rest on no one's shoulders but my own.

That said, I can't help but ask myself what I'll do if the test I've been promised never materializes. And I can't deny that Charlotte may be playing a role in my decision.

Diary of Adam Luce
Berlin, 10 February, 1924

What happened this afternoon in the Grunewald changes everything, that is, if it really happened. If it didn't, then I must surely add my perceptions to the list of what can't be trusted in this city. And that is a frightening thought.

So here it is: The Earth spoke to me today.

Later, drinking red wine in one of our familiar haunts, Charlotte told me that it wasn't speech *per se,* but rather my "ordinary mind" at work, translating new understanding into a language with which it was familiar. When I challenged this explanation, she gave me her best mocking smile.

"Will Adam only listen when it's an angel who speaks?"

But I'm racing ahead of my narrative.

The day began much as any other, with a light German breakfast followed by a hour of vigorous exercise at the club. When I arrived home, I accepted Frau Schumann's invitation to join her and her nephew for a fine afternoon meal of sausage, spätzel and asparagus, which is highly prized by the Germans.

It turns out that her nephew, Johann, has just been taken on as an apprentice at Siemens, and the meal was in celebration of his first pay check. He was full of questions about America, and particularly the Indians and the "Wild West." Was there any chance of an uprising? Had I ever been buffalo hunting?

Frau Schumann was happy almost to the point of tears. It seems to her that things are finally "settling down," and her nephew's ability to find work isn't the only example. The new availability of meat in the markets and the diminishing violence in the streets also speak to the re-emergence of order – that virtue the Germans esteem above all others. Now, if the Russians would only go home and take their Jewish ideas with them, all would be well. I can't blame her for those opinions, and I didn't express my own: that Berlin is much enriched by Jews' ideas, if not by some of their black market shenanigans.

I grew restless after a time, and as soon as I could I politely excused myself. I went upstairs to my room and quickly telephoned the von Schwerin residence before I could talk myself out of it. When a servant answered, I asked for Portia. To my great surprise, she was on the line in an instant.

Portia – if that's really who it was – greeted me with the German version of, "To what do I owe this honor?" and there was more than a hint of sarcasm in her voice. I explained that I was trying to reach her sister, whom I hadn't seen in more than a week, and that I had no other means to establish communication.

"And I am supposed to know where she is?" she asked dryly.

"I thought perhaps I could leave a message."

"And what might that be?"

I wanted to enquire as to why, after weeks of showing up "by chance" wherever I went, she was suddenly gone from my life, but of course that wouldn't do. There was an awkward silence. Then, Portia came to my rescue.

"There is an oriental tea house called the Pale Moon on Kurfüratenstraße just south of the Technische Hochschule. I think you might find her there in an hour or so. I can't promise, but she enjoys the atmosphere."

I took the S-Bahn to the Hansaplatz station and found the tea house with no difficulty. And, as promised, Charlotte was there, seated under an umbrella in the rear garden, reading a slender volume which I later learned was Graf von Schack's German translation of *The Rubaiyat* of Omar Khayyam. It's one of Margaret's favorite works.

Ever the chameleon, she was dressed in a summery frock and looked every bit the aristocrat that she is. As I approached, she looked up and her face registered (or feigned) surprise. Then she sprang from her chair, ran to me and threw herself into my arms.

"I've missed you so much!" she said, quite to my astonishment.

"I thought you'd been avoiding me."

"The planets weren't aligned," she said. "I didn't want to take the risk." With that, she sat down and invited me to join her.

A moment later an oriental woman approached wearing an extravagant silk kimono with a pattern of blue and white flowers. Being completely unfamiliar with the items on the menu, I asked Charlotte to order for me, which she did.

After my tea had been brought, Charlotte leaned over and whispered, "This is special tea."

I ignored this comment and returned to the question of astrology.

"Are our meetings now to be determined by the position of the planets?" I asked.

"They always have been, Darling," she replied. Then she put her hand on mine. "You don't still believe we met by chance, do you?"

I told her I certainly didn't believe our meeting was foreordained by some conjunction of Jupiter and Saturn. I think – and it is difficult to commit this supposition to writing, as I don't want it to be true –I think she has had me followed since the beginning. But I didn't mention that supposition. Instead, at her encouragement, I drank my tea.

I wish I could remember the events that immediately followed in more detail, but I simply wasn't paying close attention to what at first seemed an ordinary afternoon's encounter, to the extent any encounter with Charlotte could be characterized as ordinary. We sat in silence for awhile, enjoying the fine weather of an unusually early Spring. As always, I paid the bill when it arrived. Then, Charlotte suggested that we walk over to the Tiergarten. I do recall that the noise of the street had a particularly grating edge to it, and I was glad to enter into the calming green of the huge park. Looking back, I realize I was already in a peculiar state of mind.

Soon we were alone in a glade of oaks. The new leaves rustled softly, and the effect of that sound was immensely soothing.

At that moment, Charlotte stepped away from me and put her hands at the hem of her frock, as though to curtsy. Then she asked me a rather bizarre question. Could I see how ridiculous clothing was as compared to nudity? Strange to say, at that moment her comment made perfect sense. The naked swimming on Thursdays at Luna Park and all the other approaches to nudity that I had previously viewed as silly at best were in fact expressions of a legitimate and even laudable striving for a state of harmony with nature.

Charlotte continued to pose before me, and for a moment I feared she was going to suggest we disrobe then and there. But instead she turned and set out walking deeper into the wood. At first, she seemed to be picking her way in a haphazard fashion. After a few hundred yards, however, I realized we were following a deer path. At that moment, the fact that a path had been prepared for us – so I viewed it –was of the utmost importance to me. In a world seemingly created by random accidents, guidance was available! One need but know where to look for it. This was no philosophical proposition expounded in the cigarette smoke and coffee fumes of the Romanische. It was quite literally as solid as the ground under my feet. The words on this page cannot capture the emotion I experienced in that brief moment.

It was shortly thereafter that we came upon the mushrooms. A dozen or so were growing in what my mother used to call a fairy ring in an area of fertile dampness by the path. They were rather large, with mottled gray caps that came almost to a point, creating in my dazed mind the impression of little old men in wizard's hats. It was the eldest who "spoke" to me, although as I sit here in the rational light of the morning, I'm inclined to accept Charlotte's contention that it wasn't speech as such.

In any case, I feel that whatever "he" may have "said" pales in comparison to the demonstration the whole experience provided about the quickness and reach the human intellect can achieve. The wood became a book that taught me how the instruments of knowledge should be put to use. It was as though the relationships between the plants and the animals resolved themselves into equations that would easily yield up their solutions to the efforts of a well-trained mind. In an instant I saw the links between a bird rustling in the brush, its excrement, the minerals therein which would provide nourishment for the sprouting seeds, whose young shoots were in turn food for the insects upon which the next generation of birds would prey.

I struggle to set down these insights. I do believe that whatever Charlotte slipped into my tea gave me a glimpse into the operation of the great minds of science, not least among them the German pathfinders who evolved the art of dye making into the chemical industry that saved the world from starvation.

I can't say how long I was caught up in this extraordinary reverie, but at some point I realized that Charlotte was holding my hand. I looked down and saw a most ordinary cluster of mushrooms arranged in an imperfect circle, and nothing more.

I remember saying to her, "Chemists are pathfinders," words that seem pretentious and a bit stupid now, but at the time I felt she understood at least some of what I was trying to convey.

She squeezed my hand affectionately.

"Did you enjoy your chemistry lesson?"

Diary of Adam Luce

Berlin, 15 February, 1924

I took a long walk this morning in the sunshine the Spring is now providing for us, pondering my extraordinary encounter with The Voice of the Earth, as I've come to call it. That voice was no hallucination, and the insights I experienced remained valid in the cold light of the morning. But for now, I must put these mysteries aside.

When I returned Frau Schumann handed me an envelope that had been delivered in my absence by a messenger from KDE. I had been summoned.

At half past three a black Mercedes appeared in front of my house, driven by a uniformed chauffeur whom I didn't recognize. I was conveyed once again to the Ruhlebener facility, but this time Austerlitz awaited me in an office that was quite conventional save for its high ceilings and elaborate polished woodwork. He sat behind an imposing oak desk that had the affect of distancing him from me, and limiting the intimacy of our exchange. He may be a technocrat, but he's no stranger to theatrics. He's turned each of our meeting places into backdrops that reinforce the points he wishes to communicate. In this case, his unspoken message spoke to the dominance of German chemical know-how.

Austerlitz didn't rise when I entered, nor did he offer his hand. Rather, he gestured stiffly towards an upholstered chair in front of the desk. I sat, and was compelled to endure a rather long and uncomfortable silence.

Finally, he reached into his inner coat pocket and produced two fortune telling cards. I recognized them as belonging to the so-called Tarot deck, which I had seen at a party held by one of Margaret's Bryn Mawr friends where a fortune teller had been one of the attractions. That Austerlitz should have in his possession such questionable items was in itself a shock. His interpretation of their meaning was even more perplexing.

He first set down a card called The Magician, which depicts a young man who stands behind what might well be a chemist's bench. Upon the bench are arrayed the symbols of the four elements of medieval science. Beside that he placed The Fool, a card that portrays a proud young man in a brightly colored jerkin. In one hand he holds a white rose. The other grasps a stick resting on his shoulder to which is tied a small poke. He is about to step off a cliff.

"They are one and the same man," said Austerlitz rather dramatically. "The building blocks of the natural world are available to the Magician, who may do with them what he will. The Fool carries those same elements in his sack" Here, Austerlitz paused for effect. " But he does not know that they are there and that he already owns them. My point is that you may have more knowledge than you think. But somehow you've forgotten where you put it. That state of affairs must change if you want to become a real chemist."

"I understand," I said, hoping to convey the humility I genuinely felt in his presence.

"You understand very little," he replied, as though he were stating an obvious fact, such as the absence of salmon on a menu. "If you want to find secret knowledge, the first thing you have to know is where to look." He glanced down at the two fortune telling cards. The implication was obvious. He was the Magician. I was the Fool.

With that, he reached into his jacket pocket and produced three bottles of aspirin that looked like they had come off the shelf of a nearby druggist, complete with the familiar KDE label. He nodded, indicated I should unscrew one of the caps. The pills inside weren't the familiar white that one would expect. Instead, they were varying shades of brown, ranging from the color of sand to that of excrement, obviously the result of a manufacturing error.

"Oxidation?" I asked.

"You tell me," he replied. "I'll arrange for a lab. You have two weeks."

With that, our interview was over. We stood up, shook hands and then I left, clutching the bottles as though they were filled with precious jewels.

✠

Gefreiter Helmut Schreck
Field Notes, 16 February, 1924

I've been wondering how long it would be before I drew an American. This one lives in Berlin Mitte and works at KDE. Why they would let an American in the door like that is a mystery to me. They're probably training the bastard. Don't they realize what's going to happen if we let German formulas get into the hands of our enemies? They'll blow us up with shells we taught them how to make.

The funny thing is, Rudi said there was foreign money behind this hit. That would usually mean Jewish money, but not in this situation. Rudi would never do any work for a Jew. And besides, the Jews are too busy selling everything we lost after the war back to us at ten times the price. So who is it? Not the Frenchies. He hates them more than he hates the Jews. So that leaves the Brits and the Americans.

I shouldn't think about these things, but I can't help it. I think the Frenchies and the Brits and the Americans are starting to fight among themselves. That's no big surprise. They're only here to grab as much as they can for as long as they can, and if they can't get coal and iron, they'll try to get their hands on our secret formulas.

That's where I come in, because a secret formula doesn't do you any good unless it stays a secret. When I knock off the American spy there's one less hand in the cookie jar. That's capitalism for you. Dog eat dog. The Reds are no better. But at least they stand for something. Stresemann and his cronies are a bunch of pansies.

Rudi *wants* this one to look like a political statement. He says I should make sure I look like a Bavarian, whatever that means. And he wants three shots, including one that misses entirely. This is his brilliant way of making sure nobody thinks the shooter was a professional. Next thing I know he'll want me to just wound the guy. God save us if Rudi ever gets into power. He's got more bad ideas than ten Stresemanns.

Diary of Adam Luce
Berlin, 16 February, 1924

I met Charlotte at the Romanische today to convey my good news. I didn't think it wise to reveal any details with Johnny, and she is my only other friend here in Berlin. Well, she's a bit more than a friend.

At her suggestion we chose the room favored by painters, and more than once she nodded at new arrivals as they entered the smoke-filled room, receiving smiles and winks in return. I did wonder if she had modeled for some of these men, but for some reason the thought of her standing naked in front of them didn't disturb me. Had I asked her about it, she would surely have responded that it wasn't important, and that would be true, at least here in this city.

Something has changed between us. She has let down her guard a bit, and there are moments when I feel that her words have no hidden meaning and no manipulative intent.

On only one point did she seem her old evasive self. Apropos of my upcoming "trial by fire" – those were her words – she said she was thinking of accompanying her sister on a trip for a week or two so she wouldn't be a distraction to me. When I asked her where, her response was vague. "In the south, I think. Perhaps in the mountains." Then she quickly added, "I really don't know. It's not up to me. But I do know I'll miss you."

She has never said anything like that before, and I could see that she relished my surprise.

"Tell me about your test," she said, quickly changing the subject. "Can you talk about it? Is it a secret?"

I thought that an odd question, but chose to ignore it and recounted in some detail my meeting with Austerlitz, including his production of the Tarot cards. It turns out she's quite familiar with the deck. The girl is full of surprises. I asked her why on Earth he would choose to make a point about me using fortune telling cards.

"He probably wanted to see your reaction. He was testing you. You understand that, don't you? Everything is a test now."

Without thinking, I blurted out, "Even you?"

She stared at me, and I could swear she was on the edge of tears. She stared down at her half empty cup of coffee for a moment. Then she said, "Let's have a brandy."

The waiter didn't bat an eye at my order of two brandies in mid-afternoon, and when they arrived she took a healthy swig without even remembering to toast. I followed her example, and felt the immediate effect alcohol gives one on an empty stomach. She seemed to be pondering something, and I waited patiently for her to speak, half wishing I were a painter, to tell the truth, one who could capture the mystery in those dark eyes of hers.

"You're here to learn about aspirin," she said at last, "but there's more to chemistry than aspirin."

"I understand."

"You understand very little," she replied in a suddenly chilling echo of Austerlitz' words. She stared at me silently, and I became aware of the babble of voices around us. It reminded me of the sound water in a stream makes rushing over rocks.

"The human body is a chemical factory, and its whole purpose is to synthesize the chemicals that... let us understand our place in the universe. We can ingest them, but it's not the same as it is when we make them ourselves."

I was yet again taken by surprise. She had never before spoken in this vein and yet her voice had the ring of authority.

"What are you talking about?"

"Your chemistry lesson."

I struggled to comprehend her.

"You're saying that the human body could synthesize the chemicals you put in my tea? But how? None of what goes on in our bodies is under our control.

"Well, you're right to say it's not under *your* control."

"But how could that possibly change?"

"Pain is one catalyst."

I started to object but she held up her hand. "I picked an example you're familiar with. It's but one of many. And you have to understand that I don't know everything there is to know."

Left unspoken was the name of the man who most likely did possess that knowledge.

"We shouldn't be talking about this," she continued. "It's a distraction, and you need to focus on aspirin. You'll be learning how to take away at least a little bit of suffering in the world, Adam. You can have that power. It's enough."

"And what about my chemistry lesson in the park?"

I shouldn't have done that. But I wanted to show you how beautiful the world is when we see things as they are. I did it out of love."

She put her hand to her mouth, too late because the word so long forbidden had already escaped. I nodded slowly, too stunned to speak.

"I had to show you, but please, Adam, don't let yourself be distracted. Just stay here in Berlin. Don't go elsewhere. And when you've learned everything you need, we'll just say good-bye and cherish the time we've had together for the rest of our lives."

I was overcome with emotion. She took my hand and kissed it, leaving a trace of red lipstick. A single tear rolled down her cheek. Then, suddenly, she brightened.

"Do you ride?" she asked. I didn't understand what she meant, and asked for clarification.

"Giddy-up?" she said, raising her hands and arms as though holding imaginary reins.

I had to confess I had never tried it.

"Then let's just go for a long, long walk in the Grunewald."

We took a taxi to the entrance of the huge park and walked in silence for almost two hours. When we said good bye she put her hands on the lapels of my jacket and stared into my eyes.

"Every minute is important to us."

Diary of Adam Luce

Berlin, 17 February, 1924

I've not had feelings like this for any girl in my life, and it would be dishonest not to face them. Dare I use the word "love," as she did? Yes. I love her. There it is. The truth.

When I am with her and for hours thereafter, my thoughts, my vision of life itself is transformed and ennobled. I understand with new clarity that chemistry is no mere branch of science. It is a calling. I feel as if I can see into the future, where there is a place for me among the guardians of mankind... with Charlotte at my side.

Would she come with me to America as my wife? New York city, grand as it may be, is no match for Berlin, but there are enclaves of Bohemianism to be found, I'm sure of it: theater and art and the paths first forged by Emerson and Thoreau. We would not have every diversion we might want, but there would be enough. Our bonds are strong. We would flourish.

I must put these thoughts out of my head now. Or, if they come unbidden as I suspect they will, I must use them as inspiration as I engage in my test. I think I know how Babe Ruth must feel when he steps up to the plate. I'm ready, and I have a plan. As soon as I've put the lab in order I'll be ready to put it into action.

I know from long hours in Dr. Hastings' analytical chemistry lab that in cases like these, the culprit is most often a small quantity of some highly pigmented substance. I shall begin my search for this contaminate by soaking half a dozen of the affected tablets in toluene or perhaps hexane, whichever is at hand. If the color migrates from the solids to the toluene layer, I will instantly know that the villain is the carnuba wax, which would be no surprise, considering its South American origins and its journey here in the holds of filthy ships with God knows what other cargos.

If that fails, I'll dissolve a dozen or so tablets in cold water. That will isolate the ASA, as it's not soluble in H_2O. Nor is carnuba, for that matter. The solute will thus contain cornstarch, and the mystery molecule. At that point, I can simply distill it out. If the distillate is yellow, I'll have to proceed with nitrophenylhydrazine, which is unknown territory for me. It's dangerous stuff, highly explosive and therefore tricky to handle and store. I may have to synthesize my own stock. I think I can get it from an aniline, but I'm not sure.

I have a lot of work ahead of me—more work than time. No carousing tonight. I need to be at the Ruhlebener site when the gates open tomorrow morning for Day One of the fourteen I've been granted.

Diary of Adam Luce
Berlin, 18 February, 1924

My own lab! At last the paperwork that attends any new development here came through, and now there are moments when I quite seriously feel the need to pinch myself to prove it's not a dream. My name isn't painted on the frosted glass, merely the words, *Forschung Nr. 7*, but there's a lock, and I possess the key. When Herr Würtz, the chemist assigned to show me around, first swung the door open to my new work space, I literally gasped.

Along one wall there is a black marble counter top with a built-in sink and two gas valves for Bunsen burners. A stainless steel hood with an electric exhaust fan for evacuating noxious fumes extends the length of the counter. The opposite wall is for storage. It has built-in drawers of light oak that extend from the tile floor to waist height. They're filled with neatly-coiled tubing, containers of one- and two-hole stoppers, filter paper, wooden test tube holders, clamps, rubber-coated tongs for handling hot items, a couple of extra Bunsen burners, protective gloves, a white mortar and pestle – all in all, more items than I can catalog here.

Above the drawers are shelves for glassware – round bottom flasks, Schlenk flasks with glass stopcocks, flat-bottomed Erlenmeyer and bücher flasks, beakers, graduates – and the familiar frosted glass bottles of reagents, all neatly labeled in German handwriting. I have never seen such a collection. My shock was evident, and I think Würtz reveled in it.

He's curt, and somewhat officious in the stain-free lab coat he wears over his suits. But even though he takes every opportunity to remind me that he outranks me, I think the man is a bit intimidated by the way Dr. Austerlitz has singled me out and provided me with what amounts to unlimited resources.

In any case, Würtz quietly let me absorb the implications of what it meant to be in the employ of the world's largest chemical cartel. Then he handed me my key. "Now you can invade us without firing a shot," he said.

I was shocked by the venom in his tone, and couldn't hold my tongue.

"The war is over," I said.

"It has only begun," he replied.

With that, he left me to set things up and ponder my *test*. I have a feeling a lot more is at stake than a few batches of bad aspirin.

✠

Diary of Adam Luce
Berlin, 19 February, 1924

I should have been prepared for Charlotte's letter. Her behavior has been erratic since the day we met, and, looking back on our more recent encounters, I can't deny that she dropped plenty of hints.

> My Dearest Adam,
>
> Could you but see yourself through my eyes for one brief moment you would understand why Love has become my only master, and how I am bound to you by fetters far stronger than any chains. Our Union has been preordained by powers few can understand, as is this separation, which works to your benefit at the cost of my pain.
>
> Apart, yet together in spirit, we have embarked on a new journey, and whether our paths will cross again is unknown to me, although it is my earnest wish.
>
> Please accept this forbidden letter as a token and reminder of my undying love. May you achieve your true destiny.
>
> Your Charlotte

I've read it two dozen times, and now I find myself simply staring at the fanciful loops and curls of her handwriting. I cannot find words to express my loss, nor the pain of the uncertainty her letter conveys. There's no doubt in my mind that behind the scenes she played a role in bringing me to the lab I now occupy. She said as much herself, although how she did it I'll never know. And beyond the walls of KDE she set me on a path that would have been invisible to my naive eyes. A descent into depravity, some would say, but one that afforded a glimpse of forces that the artists and philosophers at the Romanische don't even imagine. More than anything, she taught me how much I must learn if I am ever to make sense of the world. But at least now, after our time together, excess has nothing more to teach me.

What I must do above all is fix my mind on my goal and pursue it with unwavering intent. That's what Charlotte would want, what all who love and care about me would have me do, and what's in my own best interest. The transformation of Luce chemical is a damned worthy goal, and I have the lab of my dreams in which to pursue it I must not lose sight of that.

And should Charlotte reappear as she has so many times before, I'll ask for her hand before she can escape. That's fixed. I'll not let her slip through my fingers again. I now understand with certainty that she's the only woman I've ever truly loved, and I must act on that certainty. To commit to Margaret—to commit to any other woman—would be the lie of all lies.

And what if Charlotte fails to return to me? I must simply put that thought from my head, and indeed all thoughts that have no direct bearing on the synthesis of acetylsalicylic acid.

Diary of Adam Luce
Berlin, 20 February, 1924

The separation of the first batch has proceeded flawlessly, and I now realize that using methanol as the initial solvent to isolate the ASA was a stroke of good luck. Had I chosen ether, the hydroxyl radical would have interacted with the HCl that I used in the titration and forced me to start all over again.

The work is incredibly meticulous. Every variable must be measured and recorded. On top of that, I must be attentive to the possibility of experimental error. *My* error, to be precise. Against this eventuality, I have devised a system of random retesting that acts as a check against carelessness during the long hours I'm spending alone with my chemicals and my thoughts.

Tomorrow, armed with the new glassware Würtz requisitioned for me, I'll be able to prepare six more batches, enough to begin the real work. It could be as simple as

$$C_6H_{12}O_6 + 6O_2 \Rightarrow 6CO_2 + 6H_2O$$

But such a reaction would produce a measurable increase in a reactor's pressure, one that would certainly have been noticed. With a molecule like sucrose, however, there are multiple modes of oxidation, starting with the application of heat in the presence of oxygen.

Would it not be ironic if the whole problem stems from a small quantity of burnt sugar? Sugar is one of the essential components in the Luce company's Pills for Your Ills.

Diary of Adam Luce
Berlin, 21 February, 1924

I scarcely have time to spare, but I must record today's events, if for no other reason than to preserve the details in my memory should there be an inquiry.

I entered my lab at roughly ten minutes after eight this morning. The door was unlocked. I was surprised, because I've been careful never to leave it open, even when making visits to the john. But that surprise was nothing compared to what met my eyes on the lab bench. All my glassware assemblies had been dismantled, with the component parts washed and neatly set out on white towel to dry. A full day's work wasted!

I immediately sought out Würtz, who told me that when one leaves one's door unlocked it's a signal to the cleaning staff that whatever experiment was in progress has been completed. "We don't want our chemists wasting precious time washing the dishes," he said with a smirk. I was ready to plaster him, but I held back.

"I shall have to be more careful," I said, disguising my rage as best I could. The fact of the matter is, I locked that door when I left yesterday. And the only other person who has a key is Würtz.

During my lunch break I went home and prevailed upon Frau Schumann to lend me the cot stored in her son's empty room for occasional guests. It now leans against wall, soon to become my bed for as long as it takes me to finish this task. I'm behind schedule now, and I will need to double up on my work hours. I'll find a way.

Diary of Adam Luce
Berlin, 24 February, 1924

The use of cocaine is a supreme test of one's will power. Taken judiciously, the drug improves both concentration and endurance. My enthusiasm and productivity in the lab under its influence amply support this view, as well as my ability to skip a night's sleep without noticeable consequences. There is, I will grant, a temptation to take more of the stuff than necessary, a temptation to which I have succumbed on occasion, but to no ill effect that I can discover. Discontinuation of use can have a mild depressive effect, but that effect can be quickly mitigated by a small medicinal dose of, say, half a gram, or it can simply be allowed to pass of itself.

The Germans understand all this. The prudery that plays so great a role in the lives of Americans is in as short supply here as Virginia tobacco. Yes, there are half-hearted raids on the Friederichstraße cabarets from time to time, but everyone knows the true objective of these raids is to provide the Berlin police with intimate access to the dancers. It is through sexual favors that the girls avoid jail. There are no such efforts directed towards the reduction of drug use. Some thinkers on the right have gone so far as to suggest that the opium alkaloids are an effective means of cleansing what they refer to as the "Aryan Race" of its weaker members. Addiction leads the weak down the path of self-destruction so they die in some Neukölln alley instead of procreating in numbers comparable to their stronger, non-addicted peers.

I must admit, I myself give aid and comfort to these wretches by buying on the open streets. For some reason, I can't bring myself to make Johnny my supplier, although such an arrangement would certainly be more convenient. Presently, I feel compelled to dissolve the powder I purchase on the street in methanol and re-distill the crystals to ensure their purity, an easy task here at KDE, where I can obtain the requisite methanol, or any other chemical for that matter, with no questions asked.

For my efforts I am rewarded with potent crystals of pure cocaine that produce an almost immediate improvement in mental clarity. The only drawback is the numbness, which I find annoying, but it's a small price to pay.

Gefreiter Helmut Schreck

Field Notes, 25 February, 1924

If Rudy and his gang had a little patience they could save themselves a fee for this American. The way he uses cocaine, it's a wonder he hasn't died of heart failure already. What I don't understand is why he always buys in back alleys. You can get all the white you need in any of those clubs where he goes, and the quality's better. In Neuköln you get more filler than drug. Come to think of it, maybe that's why he buys so much.

Maybe I should step in. I don't want him overdosing on me. I could use the money for the hit. No, getting involved like that is a bad idea. You never know what could happen if you get to know the guy you're about to kill.

I wish he hadn't started sleeping inside the KDE building. I can't take him out if he never shows his face on the streets. But he will. It's just a matter of time, and for once Rudi isn't pushing me for quick results. Maybe it's time to take that trip to Dresden Marguerite keeps talking about. A few days away from Berlin wouldn't hurt. And that kid will be here when I get back.

✠

Diary of Adam Luce

Berlin, 25 February, 1924

Earlier this evening I left the lab to replenish my fast dwindling supply of cocaine. On my way to Neukölln I encountered Johnny, returning, I suspect, from the very locale that was my destination.

The first words out of his mouth were, "You look God-awful."

We adjourned to the nearest *stube* for what I presumed would be a friendly chat, but as soon as we were seated in one of the grimy booths he took me on.

"You're trying to move too damned fast."

"You're ignoring your sex life, and that's not healthy."

"You're pale."

"Your hands are shaking."

And so on.

When he was finished with his harangue, he reached across the small wooden table where we were seated and grabbed my forearm.

"I'm a Jew," he said. "I know all about hustle. We invented the concept! You are pushing yourself too hard, and what you are doing is not good. You cannot save the world if you die. And I would miss you, my friend."

The "what you are doing" was an obvious reference to my cocaine use, or so it seemed at the moment. And while I am hardly at risk of death, my consumption has increased substantially. One quickly acquires a natural tolerance, as with alcohol, and I need to level it off, or perhaps even cut back a bit. Having just looked at myself in the mirror Frau Schumann recently installed for me, I cannot deny Johnny's assertion that I look like Hell.

When this is all over I should probably join one of these sporting clubs that are so popular and run around naked in the woods on Sundays or whatever it is that they do. I should most definitely not work all night long more than once a week`.

The human body has its limits, and with the help of too many stimulants, I am fast approaching them. Johnny's got the right idea. I'll not work tonight. Instead, I'll write to Margaret, and then enjoy a decent meal for the first time in days.

Diary of Adam Luce
Berlin, 26 February, 1924

It's almost ten thirty in the morning and all I can think about is more black coffee and more aspirin.

I cannot remember where I spent last night, nor how I returned to my room. Good Lord! What sort of life am I living, that a night off for the purpose of relaxation should end with a black out? I am lucky I wasn't beaten and robbed blind. There was a match cover from the El Dorado, with a telephone number and the name "Adrienne" written on the inside flap. I hope to Hell I didn't make an ass of myself with some party of tourists. I'm damned well not going to ring up this Adrienne. Knowing the El Dorado she may not even be a woman.

There were a couple of white rose petals on the floor next to the bed. We must have indulged in some ether. That's what did me in. Not the alcohol by itself, although God knows I clearly drank my fill.

It's obvious my companion wasn't out to take advantage of me. My wallet is only a few hundred marks lighter than it was yesterday. That's about right for a night on the town. When I awoke my watch was still on my wrist. The two twenty dollar gold pieces that I'd left in plain sight on my dresser are still there. Yes, I'm damned lucky.

What is happening to me? Have I lost my wits? Anyone could have observed me – wherever I was – and that includes senior officials from KDE. They'll not entrust their secrets to a drunk.

I'm wondering if Johnny was with me for part of the night. I remember trying to reach him from a telephone at the Adlon after dinner. That was about half past eight. I was already half soused.

Then... I decided to go for a walk. I headed towards the Tiergarten. That's right. I passed by the very spot where I first met Charlotte. That called for another drink – and for the life of me, that's all I can remember.

For the second time this week, I've broken my rule against cocaine before noon, but at least I am still thinking clearly – and it's clear to me that I cannot go on like this. Word will surely get back to the powers that be at KDE. I need to take this lost night as a warning.

Diary of Adam Luce
Berlin, 26 February, 1924

I'm not sleeping so well on the cot, but it's the only way to ensure the safety of my work. I'm almost back on schedule. Today, with a little mental stimulation from certain alkaloids of the coca plant, I shall determine if sucrose is the villain in this drama.

Diary of Adam Luce
Berlin, 28 February, 1924

Tomorrow is Friday, and I'm running out of time. It's occurred to me that Würtz could again attempt to sabotage my efforts. Once the day is over, he'll not reappear until Monday morning. If I give him my results then, he could claim I'm late, only by a few hours, but late is late. I can't let that happen, even if it means a second all-nighter in a row. I'm as certain as any man can be that I've got the process right, but each iteration takes hours. And for all my conviction, what if I'm wrong? I must not hold that thought. If I'm wrong, I'm ruined.

Wolfgang Austerlitz
Überlegungen, 28 February, 1923

The maxim that best helps me keep in mind the dual nature of our work is one of the oldest: *Learn to separate the fine from the coarse.* It teaches us to purify the substances of the physical world so as to reveal their essential nature and exploit their true potential. It teaches us to purify our thoughts. And it teaches us how to choose those among us who can be trusted.

This young Luce would be a willing servant to our cause. So I believe. But I need to remind myself that his pluck and persistence often conjure up thoughts of my fallen Jürgen, and I must not let them affect my judgment.

Before all else, he must pass the test I've given him. I have confidence, but I need to bear in mind that success is by no means a certainty. If he fails, I'll simply have to make other plans and find someone else to carry them out. He can go back to America and cook up the next miracle cough syrup for his father's company. Better yet, I can use him as a bargaining chip. There are still those among the KDE directorship who would feel more comfortable if he were dead. I'll offer to remove the protections I've put in place and hand him over – for a price.

Diary of Adam Luce

Berlin, 29 February, 1924

The cause of the discoloration was a nitrate of cellulose, or bad cornstarch in layman's terms, and I can prove it should the need arise. Furthermore, that proof is now safely hidden here in my room where it would take a damned thorough search to find it. I shall pass my test, and I've done it with two days to spare.

As of today the final report is in Würtz' hands, on schedule, and he's to deliver it upon Austerlitz' return, the time of which is uncertain. I would hardly trust this Würtz with such an important document under other circumstances – I daresay no one can be trusted in this city – but in this case I have no choice. I did offer, a bit clumsily perhaps, to get the report to Austerlitz via my "close friend," Fraulein von Schwerin, an offer which he of course refused. At least he knows I have friends in high places. I never thought that phrase would apply to me, but it's apt. If I can find a way to control my impulses, I shall achieve my goal.

How long will it be before I can take leave of this dangerous city? A few months at best, I'd wager. The manufacture of aspirin is no scientific mystery. It's a series of simple procedures, ones, however, which must be carried out with discipline and attention to detail. There's the essence of a successful factory: discipline. Perhaps the employees at Rensselaer should be made wear uniforms to help instill that attitude towards their work. I'll wear a lab coat over my suit when I'm on the factory floor, and I'll let it accumulate some grease spots and stains to show the men that their boss knows his way around machinery.

I can't imagine we'll need new reactor vessels or piping, but the entire production line will need a thorough cleaning, and every gauge and valve will need to be inspected. With any luck, we'll be in production by early autumn. I need to write uncle Wyn and share these thoughts. Production is only half the battle. The other half is sales, and I've no idea what's involved in that end of the business. But no matter what it is that must be done to move my aspirin from the plant to the drugstore shelves of the nation, he'll be able to pull it off.

I have to add this. I never thought I'd be happy to return to this cold, dark room of mine, but it's beginning to feel like home.

Wolfgang Austerlitz
Überlegungen, 2 March, 1924

The so-called modern world we live in thinks the ancient texts that guide us are the work of fools, and thank God. If those who would oppose us understood the Law of Triads, they would already have an accurate model of the atom, and armed with that they would be only a few short steps away from harnessing its potential energy.

For now, at least, they know only of electrons and protons. Until they discover the third member of the atomic triad, the neutral particle, radiation will remain a laboratory curiosity whose only practical use is to make watches glow in the dark. But the fact is that Einstein and his circle of Jews at the University of Berlin are closer to the truth than they realize, and so is that Polish Jewess in Paris, Curie.

Thank God that the principles of separation and purification are not widely understood, much less refined through use. There we have a crucial advantage. Curie and her assistants are stirring vats of chemicals with wooden paddles, as though they were soup kettles, while we use electrical agitators that operate continuously day and night.

Diary of Adam Luce
Berlin, 3 March, 1924

Once again I'm in limbo. A communication from Austerlitz could arrive in a matter of minutes, or it might be days. More likely the latter, but nonetheless, I'm reluctant to leave the house for fear I'll miss a car he's sent for me.

From a small canister on the corner of my desk the White Lady beckons. Why not? She'll lift my spirits, and I'll be able to think more clearly about ways to profitably spend my time.

Diary of Adam Luce
Berlin, 5 March, 1924

Each day seems an eternity as I wait for a response from Austerlitz. I've as yet to begin the program of regular exercise I promised myself. I've learned that a little cocaine in the morning will give me the urge to go for a run, but somehow I haven't acted on it. I should join a running club – and cut back on the cognac and *Sekt*! But how many times have I lectured myself in this way over the past two weeks? It's always the same story. I wake up in the morning with a pounding headache, vowing never again to drink the stuff, and twelve hours later, there it is in my glass. I tell myself that I aspire to a life of purpose and accomplishment, and then piss away my time in cabarets. The finest chemistry library in the world are a ten minutes' tram ride from my front door, and I've not set foot in it once.

Is it simply our nature that, left to our own devices and with adequate funds, we'll choose self-indulgence over industry and sloth over effort? So it seems, at least in my case. Perhaps the sermons in the chapel about our fallen condition had more wisdom in them than I've been willing to admit.

Diary of Adam Luce
Berlin, 6 March, 1924

This morning I wrapped the apparatus I'd snuck back from KDE to re-distill my cocaine in a large towel and methodically smashed it to pieces with a poker. I then dumped it all in the garbage chute. It has been twenty-two hours since my last powdery dose.

Now what? That's the question. I'm not gullible enough to believe there's a God in Heaven who looks down on us and, if properly solicited, grants pardon for our sins. That's nothing but a child's fantasy. Yet I do wish there were some recourse for me, some penance by which I could redeem myself, unwind time and go back to undo the acts that brought me to this point.

Frau Schumann senses my distress, if not its cause. Before me on my desk lies a tray she brought more than an hour ago with two brötchen rolls, a small pot of butter, another of English marmalade, and a cup of herbal tea – but I am not hungry.

A new review debuts at the *Maus* tonight, one I'd anticipated viewing from my favorite table near the stage on opening night. But now I have no desire to leave my room. I feel no desire for anything... save for the one substance that I have forbidden myself. I know I must not waiver. It's best to stay inside and avoid temptation. As though anything could tempt me right now.

Darkness falls. In the alley below my window three war cripples have made a temporary home, complete with bedding and a make-shift cooking stove. That's what life is about. Finding a place for yourself. It may not be yours forever, but while you're there, you're there. And right now, I have no place anywhere.

I see with the most frightful clarity that without cocaine, the world can have no attraction for me. I know that as little as a gram would restore my appetite for life, but only at the price of strengthening my addiction. That is the conundrum of the White Lady: She will let you live in happiness, but only as her slave. And if you turn away, you are condemned to endless dreariness and unfulfilled longing as you march wearily through the years towards your grave.

Diary of Adam Luce
Berlin, 9 March, 1924

I can no longer pretend. I am suffering from an infection that's not going to cure itself, the evidence of which is a disgusting penile discharge that is worsening by the day. I think I have a fever as well, although in the absence of a thermometer, I cannot be certain. Indeed, at the moment nothing is certain.

This morning, I abandoned all reserve and approached Frau Schumann for the name of a doctor. It was both a touching and difficult exchange. She was obviously concerned, and couldn't keep from asking me what was wrong. When I replied that it was a "matter of some delicacy," a new sequence of emotions played across her face, emotions that verged on hostility – and I realized after a moment that she thought I was asking for the name of an abortionist! I resorted to technical language to describe my condition, upon which she seemed to be satisfied that I was not a villain, and furnished the name of a doctor who had treated her husband for stomach problems before he was taken away by the war. I'm to see him tomorrow afternoon, and until then I am reduced to sitting alone in my room, awaiting my diagnosis. Frau Schumann, kind soul, has brought me a fresh pot of herbal tea, which I am now sipping.

I should have gone to one of the government subsidized clinics instead of imposing on poor Frau Schumann for the name of a private physician. There are dozens of them in this city. But how have I fallen so low as to require the services of a clinic whose intended purpose is to contain infections spread by whores?

I am quite certain this affliction stems from my drunken night of what I chose to call "relaxation." One single indiscretion, or so I'll call it, although at the moment I feel as though my entire stay in Berlin is nothing but one extended indiscretion. What is my mission here if not thievery? That is my "new reality." I am a thief. I am a philanderer. And, smashed distilling apparatus or not, I am addicted to cocaine.

Diary of Adam Luce
Berlin, 10 March, 1924

The bells of the *Gedächtniskirche* just tolled three. The wounded soldiers' makeshift cooking fires having long been extinguished and it's pitch black in the alley outside my window, although the sky to the west still glows an electric pink from the neon lights of the clubs.

I can't sleep. I can't think. It's beyond belief that Uncle Wyn would betray me like this, but there's his crumpled letter, lying on the corner of the desk in semi-darkness to taunt me. The bastard!

There is no point to anything now.

For business reasons, he states, the Rensselaer facility is to be sold and converted into a plant for the manufacture of herbal purgatives. I am free to return to America "at my earliest convenience." I am offered the opportunity to participate in the conversion.

God damn him.

God damn him, and God damn him, and God damn him. May he rot in Hell.

Who does this man think I am, his butler? I have risked my very life to arrive at this point, and I will not have that effort negated for short-sighted "business reasons." The aspirin market is worth millions, and the secrets of that drug's manufacture are within my grasp.

I'm having none of this high-handedness. I shall make him understand his error.

But what nonsense have I written? The wheel of the Great Ship Luce is not in my hands, nor has it ever been. And if its compass bearing is set on the Seas of Deception and Quackery, who am I to pursue another course?

Where's the White Lady when I need her to stimulate my imagination? No. I can't go back to her, nor to Charlotte. She's gone. I'm alone here, and there's nothing for me back home save shame and ignominy. I've lost any opportunity to make my mark in the family business, and as this constant stinging confirms, I've lost Margaret as well. That's certain no matter what the diagnosis. How could I dare touch her after this? Indeed, I may well have lost all hope of sexual pleasure with any woman, and with it any possibility of fatherhood as well.

Perhaps there is hope, a German-made compound of arsenic or mercury that can defeat this disease. Or perhaps my condition is not so grave as I think. The fact is, I don't have a nickel's worth of knowledge about these things. I didn't grow up in a city where women spread their legs at the drop of a hat and venereal diseases are as common as winter colds.

Diary of Adam Luce

Berlin, 10 March, 1924

A uniformed *Freikorps* messenger from KDE arrived at the house at breakfast time this morning. He informed me that I was to meet with Herr Doktor Austerlitz at eleven o'clock at the Ruhrleben site, and that a car would be provided if I so wished. I declined the offer, saying I had my own transportation. In fact, I'll not be there. Given my dear uncle's betrayal, such a meeting would be pointless, as would the practical training that's likely be proffered.

What good would it do me? I'm kidding myself if I think I can reverse Uncle Wyn's chosen course of action, which has certainly been approved by my father, no doubt with profit in mind and nothing else. That determined, what am I to do?

My pretensions to the role of Chosen One – he who would lift Luce Chemical from the muck and mire of the patent medicine business to the shining heights of genuine therapy – are indeed pretensions, and nothing more. If I have learned anything during my stay in this city it's the uselessness of knowledge in the absence of power. I was chosen all right, chosen as a token in Uncle Wyn's game of hold-and-sell, giving the impression by placing me here that he had no intention of selling the Rensselaer facility even as its value went up and up with every passing month. He knew that would happen – understanding the mood of the market is his great skill – and his feigned reluctance to sell drove the price even higher until, at the optimal moment, he let it be known that he would entertain "an appropriate offer." The man is nothing more than a conniving back-alley *schieber* writ large. And what does that make me, who eagerly obeyed his every command like a well-trained hunting dog?

There is nothing left of my life now, nothing but this chemical automaton that wakes, eats, drinks and eliminates its waste. Even as I write these lines, with no reason to go on here, and no reason to go home, with no purpose whatsoever, I feel a craving for the warmth of a beer hall. That's what we are: beer cravers, meat cravers, and most importantly, sex cravers, so that the whole sham can be perpetuated for the span of yet another generation.

Were someone to ask me what wisdom I have gained in this city, my answer would be that there is no wisdom to be gained. Not here. Not anywhere. The beliefs that are the foundation of order in society are no more enduring than snow flakes, and the bonds we form in our personal lives can dissolve with frightening speed. This much I have verified through my own experience, and I don't care to learn more.

It occurs to me that when one owns a gun and bullets, suicide is not very complicated. It would be wrong to do it here in this room. Poor Frau Schumann has enough troubles already without having to deal with the blood and gore of some foreigner's corpse. I think the Oberbaum bridge would be an ideal spot. I would simply fall into the River Spree and the currents would carry me away to oblivion.

It's almost noon now, and my resolve is steady. I'm off to the river now, pistol in pocket. When I arrive, in the final irony of this Berlin adventure, I will turn the weapon I acquired for protection against others upon myself.

Frau Schumann will have no trouble dealing with my things. I've left her husband's amulet on the desk so her son can have it, as is fitting. I'll bring this diary along with me. My last act, then, will be to toss it into the river so that Margaret may never read its contents.

This is the best way for me to leave Berlin.

Diary of Adam Luce
Berlin, 10 March, 1924

I'm writing from a booth in a noisy beer hall, and perhaps I'm a bit tight. Nonetheless, I feel a strong need to record the details of my encounter now, while it's fresh in my mind.

In brief: In the dark sea of trouble that my life has become, I have found a beacon of light. I have set a new course, or, to be more precise, a new course has been offered to me: one that will place me in the most advanced chemical endeavor the world has ever known.

Only a few hours ago, when the heavy door of my apartment building closed behind me, I truly believed I would never return to Jägerstraße. I let my feet take me where they would, and eventually found myself walking north under gray skies along the vast expanse of Wilhelm Straße towards the river, alone with my sense of purpose among those *Hausfrauen* lucky enough to have extra spending money for the expensive shops in that part of the city. From time to time I reflexively patted the Mauser riding in my topcoat pocket.

The famous Brandenburg Gate loomed to my left as I passed Pariserplatz. Marschaller Brücke was now in full view. To one side, exactly at the point where the bridge began its arch over the river, stood a figure clad entirely in black. It was as though Death had come to meet me. I thought the city had produced one final hallucination for my dubious benefit, but no.

It was Austerlitz.

Arms folded across his chest, his stance – as I perceived it in any case – was that of a guardian whose purpose could only be to block my journey to the Next World.

"We should talk about this," he said, advancing towards me.

By "this" I was certain he was referencing my suicidal intent, and the chain of events that had brought me to ultimate hopelessness.

"You know," I said.

He nodded silently, then put his hand on my shoulder.

"Follow me."

He led me back to Pariser Platz where there is a large beer hall that caters to Berliners and travellers alike. It was half past noon and the place was crowded with well-fed types: *schiebers* and gangsters, to speak plainly. It crossed my mind that I was by no means the only man in the room who was armed, and with that thought the full significance of the act from which I had been deflected hit home. I felt a case of the shakes coming on. I desperately needed some alcohol to soothe my nerves.

Austerlitz gestured with a tilt of his head to a small corner booth, one of the few in the establishment that afforded any measure of privacy. I followed him through the throng in a cloud of confusion, brushing past customers and trying to avoid the harried barmaids with their heavy silver trays of food and beer. As we neared the booth, I experienced a moment of dizziness and instinctively reached for the Mauser in my pocket. It was still there and, I reminded myself, still loaded. At that moment I heard a male voice in my head, clearly audible in spite of the din. "You can still go back to the bridge," it said, and at these words the trembling in my limbs intensified. I eased myself into the booth.

Two steins of dark lager were brought to us almost immediately after we sat down to face one another. "To health," he said, raising his stein with an ironic smile. I drank, and set the mug down as steadily as I could, anticipating the alcohol's calming effect.

Under Austerlitz' gaze I felt both embarrassed and grateful. Embarrassed that I had not found the wherewithal to end the entire drama as I'd planned, and grateful that I was still among the living.

"The time of dissolution is over for you," he pronounced. "This much you already understand, or you wouldn't have been headed to the river with self murder in mind."

That Austerlitz could somehow read my thoughts didn't even surprise me. The man is omniscient, or so it seems. I have no option but to accept that fact, at least for the moment.

"How did you find me?"

He replied, "Your movements are quite predictable, Herr Luce."

I think that he must have arranged to have me followed, but I didn't voice this suspicion. Instead, I drank more of the fragrant lager. I felt a surge of energy.

Austerlitz was staring at me, and once again I felt weighed in a balance.

"I can give you a purpose," he said at last, and then paused a moment. "If that's what you're looking for."

I felt as though I had been stripped naked, so penetrating was his assessment of my situation. I could find no words to respond, a reaction which he had obviously anticipated.

"I assume you are aware of the threat to western civilization that was posed by its dependence on Chilean nitrates as a fertilizer for its wheat crops."

I nodded. That story was part of the indoctrination of every incoming class in the Yale College of Chemistry.

"Then you understand the importance of the Haber-Bosch process."

Again I nodded.

"The fixation of nitrogen. The synthesis of ammonia, and with it, the manufacture of cheap fertilizer. Without these, when the Chilean source ran out our race would have been condemned to a slow and humiliating death by starvation."

I assured him I understood.

"Perhaps you do," was his response. "But now, there is a new challenge, ultimately of greater importance."

At that moment, one of the amply endowed barmaids passed by and he commanded a plate of *wurst* for us. Then he continued.

"Today, Western civilization is as dependent on petroleum as it once was on the Chilean nitrate deposits, and the risks are equally grave."

I looked at him quizzically.

"Our transportation system depends on oil. So do our factories. Oil furnaces even heat our homes now, and without oil we could not fight a war to defend them. As things stand, the demand for petroleum based fuels will continue to increase, but the supply cannot. There is only so much oil in the ground, and it's only a matter of time before the wells run dry. When they do, society will collapse and disintegrate into savagery. We cannot allow this to happen, and we shall not."

Austerlitz drank from his stein, never taking his eyes off me. In that moment, the strangeness of my situation finally dawned on me. I was in a beer hall sitting across from the brains behind the entire pharmacopeia of KDE products. Surely such a man could find better ways to spend his time than discussing the fate of Western civilization with a chemical novice trained in a school he would surely view as second rate at best. Before intimidation got the better of me, I voiced my question: Why had he sought me out here? I, Adam Luce, who had not only spurned his offer of employment, but had done so by failing to appear at the appointed time and place, an affront in itself.

"You just skipped out on a meeting with the chief chemist of the most important chemical company in the world. I wouldn't have had the courage to do that at your age. I have to respect you then, in spite of your bad manners."

I immediately countered him, saying that my intent was by no means to insult him, but he waved my words away like so much cigarette smoke.

"You've had your moment," he continued, "and now you're at a fork in the path. Given the recent developments in your family's business, there's no future for you in aspirin. Nonetheless, I'm willing to offer you a quality control position at KDE. In six months you would learn more than many chemists learn in a lifetime, and that knowledge would serve you well in your homeland. He paused a moment, perhaps for dramatic effect. "But elsewhere there's a... more significant opportunity available to you, if you're willing to accept the danger."

To say that my interest was piqued would be an understatement. The suicidal thoughts that had held a tyrannical grip on my mind only moments ago suddenly seemed inconsequential. I asked him the nature of this opportunity. His answer was cryptic.

"Our society must harness the forces of nature in new ways if we are to end our dependence on petroleum. This is our new work." I felt emboldened enough by his offer, and perhaps by the lager, to press him for details, but all he would say is that the other "opportunity" involved a new source of energy, would require that I absent myself from Berlin for an indeterminate period of time, and swear a solemn oath of secrecy, the violation of which would have mortal consequences.

Charlotte's words come to mind as I turn all this over in my mind. *Don't let yourself be distracted. Just stay here in Berlin. Don't go elsewhere.* Why was she so insistent on this point? If I remain in Berlin and make experience with a German chemical company a part of my resumé, I might well win a position at DuPont on my own merits. The alternative is to join a clandestine group whose purported goal is to save Western civilization from ruin, a goal that seems a bit fantastical even when coming from a man of Austerlitz' stature. Saving Western civilization is the sort of thing Zsvilárd talks about. Am I up to that? And if I leave Berlin, will Charlotte somehow slip away from me?

Austerlitz closed our conversation by insisting that I not act on impulse, but respond only when I knew "in my bones" that I was making the right choice. He wouldn't allow me to argue. "I'm sure you have other appointments to keep this afternoon," he said, standing up and offering his hand. Then he left me here with my unfinished tankard of ale. I can't pretend to know what Austerlitz really wants with me. Yes, I'm smart, and my lab skills are strong, but surely there are dozens if not hundreds of chemists in KDE's employ who are my equal in brain power, and vastly more experienced.

In any case, Austerlitz was right about one thing. I do indeed have other appointments today, or at least one, and it has taken on renewed importance. I'm off to the doctor.

Diary of Adam Luce
Berlin, 10 March, 1924

Thank God, my affliction is not as bad as I feared. The symptoms will go away by themselves, my prick will not fall off, and, on a more serious note, my ability to produce healthy sperm has not been compromised. I am to abstain from intimate contact for one month from the onset of the symptoms, some two weeks ago, by my reckoning. Aspirin was prescribed for the pain, an irony that doesn't escape me.

The doctor was a Bavarian with penetrating brown eyes and none of the Prussian reserve one expects from the medical profession here. He was much more concerned for the fate of the girl. In females, the consequences of the disease are grave. As I am obviously rich by German standards, he suggested in the strongest terms that I seek her out and provide the means for her to spend the spring and summer in a *kurhaus* in the Swiss Alps, where a new treatment was available. As he put it, fifty of my American dollars could buy her fifty years of life.

✠

Diary of Adam Luce
Berlin, 11 March, 1924

I managed to retrieve the match cover upon which the mysterious Adrienne had written her telephone number, and we met today for tea at the Adlon. She's quite the looker, I must say, blonde and buxom like the girls on the beer posters one sees on occasion in the U-Bahn stations while waiting for a train. She's a shop girl originally from a small town in Bavaria which she fled to escape the oppression of Catholicism and the constraints of a domineering father.

I had forewarned her that we were to discuss a matter of some delicacy, and she showed no surprise when, in a low voice, I shared my diagnosis.

"What must I do?" she asked, as though her infection were a matter that could be cured by a quick visit to the nearest government health clinic.

I handed her an envelope, inside of which was a train ticket to Navos, a town high in the Swiss Alps that is known for its curative air and sunshine, along with enough money for a three-months' stay at one of its numerous spas.

She studied the contents a moment and then nodded. "I've always wondered what Switzerland was like."

Her easy acceptance of such a life-changing turn of events quite impressed me. I myself am poised to embark on a journey into the unknown, but not without endless inner debate, all of which in the end leads nowhere.

Brecon Hall
Bryn Mawr College
Bryn Mawr, Penn.
February 28, 1924

My Dearest Adam,

I shouldn't say this, but I will. There are other paths to a good life for us besides your family's company. Being the "Pills for Your Ills" scion has always been difficult for you, and I think you ought to consider a new direction. Please take this idea seriously. I'm sure you could arrange to do some post-grad work at Temple College. The science faculty there is renowned, and we wouldn't be separated by nearly so many miles. I might even get dad to buy me a Model T – I don't care who says we women should be banned from the roads. I would drive to you and attend to your every need, if you know what I mean.

You have a brilliant mind, dear Adam. Look at your grades! You could be a college professor if you wanted, or do very well in another company where you could be proud of your work.

The Polonia sails every five weeks. I looked it up. I hope you'll be a passenger soon.

All my love,

Margaret

Diary of Adam Luce
Berlin, 11 March, 1924

Margaret's letter is like a knife in my heart, and I'm at a loss as to how I am to respond. It would be cowardly to let her learn that we're finished by a letter in her mailbox. I must convey my decision to her in person, painful as that will be. And thus, for the present, I must find a way to correspond with her, although the love and caring she expresses are almost unbearable.

So much has changed. She writes of other paths to a good life. What a thought! I'm so far from the path that brought me here I doubt that I could ever retrace my steps. In point of fact, my old path no longer exists. Now I have no guide save Austerlitz, and God knows where he'll lead me.

Diary of Adam Luce
Berlin, 14 March, 1924

My telephone rang in mid-afternoon today, a rare occurrence. The caller was none other than Portia. Her purpose was to invite me to what she described as a farewell dinner at Hörcher's, a well-known establishment with a reputation for propriety and decorum reminiscent of the days before the war, when Germany was still a stable monarchy. I accepted, and assured her I would be appropriately dressed for the occasion.

When she arrived at my door in her chauffeured Mercedes she greeted me in the French style, as she afterward explained, with a kiss on each cheek. It was an awkward moment for me, and I could think of nothing to say during the short ride to the restaurant.

Portia is obviously well-known at Hörcher's. We were immediately shown to a well appointed table. In less than a minute, a cold bottle of *sekt* appeared in a bucket of ice. She regarded me across the white, starched tablecloth, and I couldn't help admire her beauty, dressed as she was in a black evening dress of a soft fabric that flattered her body. I found myself wondering how Charlotte would look in such a dress, but quickly set the thought aside. Portia had invited me, and I felt she deserved my full attention.

"Here's to a safe journey," she toasted.

"Journey?" I replied as we touched glasses. "What journey?"

She sipped her champagne and then set down the glass with a quizzical look. "You're not leaving Berlin? I planned this as our farewell dinner."

"I'm not certain."

"But you must," she said, and I suspect she spoke with more force than she had intended.

"And why is that?" I asked.

"There is great work to be done, and you've been chosen by fate to participate." Her eyes bored into me. "If a man does not follow his fate, he will be dragged by it." It was obviously a quote, but I couldn't identify the source.

"Where did that come from?

"It doesn't matter, Adam. What matters is your fate. And the fate of Western Civilization. I'm not exaggerating. Don't turn your back to greatness."

At that moment our waiter arrived. In Germany the man is expected to order for both himself and his companion. I was a bit uncertain about the choices, and was more than pleased when she suggested that I order the pressed pheasant for the two of us. Obviously, the new confidence I'm beginning to feel in the lab does not extend beyond its walls. Like the Charlotte of old, Portia had me off balance in less than five minutes.

I must say, the pheasant was spectacular, doused with a sauce that burst into flames at the touch of a match in the waiter's hand, and then just as quickly extinguished itself. I've never seen anything quite like that before, and Portia obviously enjoyed my surprise.

As we ate, she gently probed me about my plans. Under the influence of the several strong wines that accompanied the meal's many courses, I openly shared my dilemma.

"You're being offered the chance of a lifetime," she said. "I can't imagine why you'd choose to stay here in Berlin. Surely you're not awaiting my sister's return."

I couldn't deny that the thought had crossed my mind more than once.

"Is she well?" I asked.

"I don't know," said Portia.

I raised my eyebrows.

"It's true. I don't have any idea where she is right now."

At that moment, it was as though Charlotte somehow took possession of Portia's body. I was once again struck by her beauty, her dark eyes, the shiny black hair, the smooth skin of her slightly muscled arm extended towards me, all set off by her black dress, which made her quite the Sheba.

Trying to distract myself, I remarked that she and her sister always wore black.

Portia laughed. "That comes from our uncle. He used to call us his ravens when we were little girls."

I dared a delicate question. "Do you see your uncle often?"

"Not so much these days. He's so busy. It's important work, Adam."

Just then the waiter passed, and I signaled for two brandies to close out the evening.

As if that were a signal, she reached into her purse and produced a small leather-bound book and placed it in my hands with some ceremony. Its title, stamped with gold leaf into the worn cover, was *Der Ofen*.

The Furnace.

"What's this?" I asked.

"I don't really know. It's from Charlotte. I suspect it's nonsense, but she and I have different ideas. She said you're to open it only after you've left Berlin. You're to let no one know you have it in your possession. And you're to guard it as though your life depended on it. Knowing Charlotte, I suspect that being caught with this book could be very dangerous. To be honest, I didn't want you to have it. But she insisted, and she *is* my sister.

On this bizarre note our brandies arrived. We sipped them in silence, Charlotte's gift resting on the table. Portia seemed to be weighing something in her mind. As we took our last sips, she smiled at me, and there was a bit of a twinkle in her eyes, as though she were about to share a joke or a bit of gossip before we left. What she actually said staggered me.

"I brought a going away present for you myself."

"And what might that be?"

"It's warm and damp, Adam. And it's right between my legs."

I was speechless.

"It's yours tonight... if you make the right choice."

In my drunken state I attempted to calculate the number of days since my intimate encounter with Adrienne, but my mind wasn't working properly. I felt trapped, and not a little heated from the brandy and her brazen offer. I nodded towards the empty glasses and attempted a laugh.

"I think this isn't the moment for making any decisions," I spoke with as light a tone as I could muster, but she wouldn't abandon her intensity.

"Time is short," she replied, giving me a cold stare. "There's no place for indecision in our work." She paused for effect, then smiled. "I'll forgive you this once. But this opportunity will not remain open forever. I think you understand what I'm saying."

We left in separate cars, kissing cheeks in the French style before we parted.

There. I've recorded what happened, and now I intend to put it all out of my mind. I need to concoct a speech that will convince Austerlitz I'm committed. In the meantime, I've hidden *The Furnace* in a space behind the wall that's accessible from my closet. I won't open it until I've left the city. So far as I'm concerned, that's Charlotte's last wish.

✠

Diary of Adam Luce
Berlin, 15 March, 1924

As I set pen to paper here I feel quite safe, but is my sense of safety merely an illusion? I'm far from the city center, far from the swarms of partisans that are no doubt being goaded into marching somewhere or other at this very moment. I've chosen a booth in this crowded beer hall where no one will disturb me, where no one can *see* me, for that matter. I need to settle my nerves and think things through. A man leveled a pistol at me this morning at point blank range. This incident was no mere consequence of life in a violent city. Someone sent that man to kill me, and I want to know who. No, that's a lie. I don't want to know. The answers I can conjure up are all too frightening to contemplate. But forward I must.

I live within walking distance of both the old Imperial Palace and the Reichstag where the much-maligned National Assembly meets, and I often find myself at the periphery of some mass demonstration or another. That's Berlin for you, and I've learned to live with it. Most days I can simply ignore the noise, even the popping of rifles in the distance, as do the merchants at the open air market where I pick up an occasional loaf of bread or wedge of cheese to tide me over when I'm not in the mood for the noise and distraction of a restaurant.

Today, however, was quite unusual: a demonstration against the occupation of the Rhineland. It's the one issue where the Reds and the Whites can find common ground and march, as the song goes, *mit Reihe fest geschloßen* – "arm in arm," I suppose you could translate it. To be accurate, marching was quite out of the question this Saturday. The square in front of the Imperial Palace was jam packed, as were the streets and boulevards that radiate from it in all directions. Communists with their red armbands stood side-by-side with Freikorps militiamen in old Prussian uniforms as one speaker after another condemned the Treaty of Versailles, the "November criminals" who validated it with their signatures, and *The System* – a pejorative term favored by the Whites to describe Germany's new democracy, which the Reds despise as well, although for different reasons.

I should probably not have gone out, but the furnace in my building has failed once again, and after the previous night's heavy dose of *sekt* with Portia I was in need of some strong German coffee and a warm place to drink it, not to mention three or four of the miracle tablets our people in Rensselaer can't seem to manufacture. So I pulled on my coat and scarf – both purchased here in Berlin at the KaDeWe so as to give no hint of my nationality – and descended the cold stone stairs. I opened the exterior door that leads from the small foyer into the street with downcast eyes, wary that last night's half-melted snow might have iced over. When I looked up, my assassin was there, not six feet away, facing me against the background of the moving crowd of Berliners on their way to the demonstration.

He had the look of a Bavarian: husky, with a broad (and rather flushed) face, an unkempt brown beard and incongruous blue eyes which regarded me with pure hatred. I cling to the memory of his wild demeanor as evidence that what happened could be attributed to chance. Caught up in the patriotic fervor of the moment, a drunk who's come up from some village near Munich sees an American exiting an expensive building and, filled with rage, draws his pistol and fires without thinking The problem with this analysis is that

I don't look like an American. The son of a wealthy *junker* from Schleswig-Holstein, perhaps, if I were to affect a monocle. But not an American. Why, then, should he single me out?

And who killed him?

I only know that the shot came from a distance, that the force of the bullet was powerful enough to knock my would-be assassin to the ground and, judging from the blood that poured out onto the snow, to destroy his heart. As I stared, not fully comprehending what had just taken place, two uniformed men appeared and dragged the man's body away, leaving a bright red trail in the snow. They threw him in the back of some sort of military vehicle, in which they sped off at high speed in spite of the snow, scattering the arriving demonstrators in their path. After their departure I noticed a small black notebook in the snow, a diary as it turns out. I have it in my possession, but truth be told, I'm not eager to read its contents.

Whatever the story behind this event, there's no doubt of its message. I must get out of Berlin, and soon.

Diary of Adam Luce

Berlin, 15 March, 1924

This, from my would be assassin's diary. "Rudi said there was foreign money behind this hit." Were Johnny to see those words, he would insist that they point the finger directly at Uncle Wyn. In fact they're ambiguous—like everything in this bedeviled city. Elsewhere, the man writes that he's paid in dollars or gold, which I must admit is hardly suspicious. Who would want to be paid in marks, given that currency's unstable history? But the fact is, the rentenmark *is* stable. So why dollars? And more to the point, what was the source of those dollars?

I don't want to believe Uncle Wyn was behind this, but given what he's already done, I wouldn't put it past him. I'm sure he has Berlin connections I don't know about, and they might well extend into the underworld. What I do know is this. If he paid somebody to have me clipped, the money probably came through Houghton, the legate, the man who set up my bank account when I first arrived in Berlin.

Diary of Adam Luce
Berlin, 16 March, 1924

I took a taxi over to Houghton's residence this morning immediately after breakfast. The American diplomatic presence in Berlin has never been housed in a specific edifice, but rather a succession of mansions occupied by the current legate. Houghton's home is in the northern part of the city. A long, curved driveway leads one to a columned portico that reflects, I suppose, the level of ostentation he thought appropriate to his station.

As luck would have it, he was available, and I was ushered into his office in less than five minutes. Seated behind his polished desk, Houghton gives a scholarly impression, with round, steel-framed glasses and the slightly hunched posture of a man who had spent years of long hours reading books. He rose, offered his hand and then invited me to take a seat.

"What brings you here at this early hour?" he asked. "Nothing grave, I should hope."

"Not at all," I replied. I had rehearsed my speech carefully. "My Uncle Wyn cabled me to look into a transfer of money that he suspects didn't go through. I don't know why he didn't contact you directly. Perhaps he didn't want the cable to go through official channels. He can be secretive when it comes to business."

Houghton said nothing for quite some time. Was he questioning the legitimacy of my enquiry? If so, I passed the test.

"I can recall only one transfer of funds. It was in the sum of five hundred dollars, I believe. Here, let me look it up."

He retrieved a rather battered ledger from one of the desk drawers and proceeded to meticulously thumb through its pages. I fought to appear relaxed, although my heart was pounding.

"Ah, yes. Here it is. The money arrived on the twenty-second of February and was disbursed the next day in person to one Rudiger Kopf. I think he said he was in the insurance business, but he didn't leave a card."

I couldn't totally conceal my reaction, but to tell the truth, I didn't really care what Houghton might be thinking. I nodded and stood up somewhat unsteadily. "I'll let my uncle know. Thanks so much for seeing me."

We shook hands again. "Give him my best."

I felt like a target was painted on my back as I waited for my taxi outside the Houghton mansion, even though reason told me it was unlikely that a new assassin was stalking me this soon after the previous failure. Better safe than sorry, as they say. In my case, make that better safe than dead.

My God, how did I end up in this mess? My own uncle tried to have me murdered, and may well try again.

I need help, and there's only one man to whom I can turn.

Wolfgang Austerlitz

Überlegungen, 16 March, 1923

If I don't do what this American demands and remove him from Berlin in the very near future, he's going to end up leaving in a coffin. It was sheer luck that the man I had tailing him was armed and took matters into his own hands. I can't protect Luce forever, not in this city. And if he's dead he'll be of no use to me.

I have to admire his drive, and I need more people in the project who aren't afraid of me. Perhaps he could even be taken into the inner circle. No, that's fantasy. Nonetheless, he has what it takes.

The safest place I can put him is Joachimsthal. I've already laid the groundwork. But if I do that, is there a risk he'll learn too much to soon? Of course there is. But no great enterprise is without risk. And I can't keep him entirely in the dark anyway. He needs a sense of belonging and purpose. He needs to believe he's helping fuel the industrial might of the Western world.

Let him learn the truth about the fuel we're using. Let him go so far as to broadcast that fact. He would be ridiculed. But I will keep him away from the device itself, at least until it's time for deployment. And when he sees it, he'll have no idea what he's seeing.

RADIOGRAM

Radio Corporation of America

233 Broadway, New York

RKBEX 4311 2MAR24

JägerstraSSe 45

Berlin C23

Deutschland

MY MAILBOX HAS BEEN EMPTY FOR TWO WEEKS. FEAR FOR YOUR HEALTH AND SAFETY. MARGARET

RADIOGRAM
Kopie
Betriebsgesellschaft für drahtlose Telegraphie m.b.H, System Telefunken

RKBEX 4311 2MAR24

MISS MARGARET SHIRER
BRECON HALL
BRYN MAWR PENN
FEAR NOT. A LETTER IS POSTED. ADAM

Diary of Adam Luce

Berlin, 16 March, 1924

If I so wished, I could simply go home as Margaret entreats me to do, and leave all this behind. Indeed, passage has already been booked for me on the Lituania, one of the Polonia's sister ships, which is due to sail in less than a week. I won't be aboard that ship. I would rather die than have Uncle Wyn once again plotting out the course of my life. Indeed, there's little doubt that with Uncle Wyn in charge I *will* die, and long before my time. No, I'll pay for my own passage home when the time comes, thank you, and with any luck I'll not be alone. But for now I'm casting my lot with Austerlitz.

A painful but necessary encounter with Johnny is in store for me tonight. I cannot leave Berlin without giving some explanation for my departure. It's no exaggeration to state that he risked his life to further my initial mission here, with only the slightest hope of recompense. Shall I simply lie and tell him I'm off to America to marry a blonde wife and father blonde children? That I'll write as soon as I can find him an opportunity? He'd see through me in an instant. But I am solemnly bound to reveal nothing of the work to which I've committed, and most certainly not the name of the town where its activities are centered.

I think the best course of action is honesty. "Johnny, I'm going away, I shan't be back any time soon, and that's all I can tell you." That's what I'll say.

Diary of Adam Luce
Berlin, 17 March, 1924

That damned Jonny never ceases to amaze me!

We met at the Jospy on Alexanderplatz. The huge traffic light there is a symbol of Berlin today: the technical ingenuity, the ability to impose order on chaos, the obsession with electricity and artificial light, the need to show off to the rest of the world... in sum, the symbol of all I'm leaving behind.

It was after five o'clock and the amateur prostitutes, "half-silks" as they're called here, were out in full force now that the workday had come to an end. Some of these women look as innocent as kittens with their elegant hats and spring dresses.

Johnny had already arrived, dressed in a sharp brown suit and a jaunty fedora. The minute we shook hands he knew something was up. But when I told him of my impending departure he didn't react with shock. Rather, he displayed a knowing smile. "Off to work on Project X, eh?"

"Project X?"

"That's what I call it. There's something going on down south that no one will talk about. Sometimes the higher-ups disappear for days on end with no explanation. That's not the way KDE normally works." He offered me a wry smile. "I suppose you're sworn to secrecy."

I nodded, feeling no small measure of guilt for not sharing all with a friend who had done so much for me.

Johnny's face darkened. Then he began to lecture me.

"Listen, my friend," he began in his typical fashion, "You don't know what you're getting yourself into. And for once, neither do I. But I do know that the first thing a man should do when he walks into a strange room is to make sure he knows where the exits are."

He then asked me if I had money. The fact is, I'm running low, and I told him so. He nodded, as though he expected that response, and then reached into his coat and grabbed a handful of fifty rentenmark notes. He pressed them into my hand. "Just remember, if you get into trouble, I'm your exit door."

Thus Johnny showed himself once again to be the true friend that he is. I expressed my embarrassed gratitude as best I could.

His response was a hearty pat on the shoulder. "You'll find a way to pay me back."

Herr Adam Luce
Jägerstraße 45
Berlin C23, Deutschland
17 March 1923

Dear Margaret,

As always, you're right. It's high time for me to make my own way in the world, and there's no better preparation than the training I can obtain right here in Germany (and, to speak frankly, in no other place in the world).

I have accepted an assignment of indeterminate length that involves travel to a region beyond the reach of the postal service. I pray you'll endure my silence for a time. I do believe my future is at stake, and that I am making a wise decision.

I assure you I am in excellent health and more than up to the challenges that await me. As you may gather, there is an element of secrecy in all this, and I dare not relate detailed information in a letter that, through no fault of your own, might fall into the wrong hands.

With deepest affection,

Adam

Diary of Adam Luce
Berlin, 18 March, 1924

If the truth be told, I've no idea what lies ahead nor what to make of the hints Austerlitz has dropped of mysterious energy sources, and I am not disposed to speculate. It is enough to know that I shall soon be on a train headed south. My destination is to be a mining town called Joachimsthal in the Erzgebirge, a heavily forested region whose mountainous spine forms a natural border between Germany and Czechoslovakia. Save for the miners and the aristocratic guests of its famous radium spa, the *Kurhaus*, its only inhabitants are wolves and bears – and trolls, if legend is to be believed. To my knowledge there is no telephone service in Joachimsthal, and the nearest post office is some thirty kilometers away in a town called Zwickau. In other words, I am to live in virtual isolation.

It's a brilliant choice on the part of Austerlitz. The guests of the spa are European aristocrats, business tycoons and celebrities who are unlikely to venture outside the doors of an edifice wherein they are waited upon hand and foot. Secrecy is thus ensured.

I must say, I have never felt such enthusiasm for a venture since my conversation with Uncle Wyn at the Waldorf. Perfidious as he has shown himself to be, I should probably thank him, for without him, I wouldn't be in the position I'm in.

But enough. I'll now post letters the letters I've written, inadequate as they will seem to their recipients. Then, it's time to pack.

Pitchblend

> *The alchemist's laboratory is an exteriorization of the human body, where the heat of the furnace represents the heat of the struggle between duty and desire, the retort the corporeal body of the Adept, and its contents the soul in the process of transformation. The tedious and repetitious nature of The Great Work, which demands unflagging attention, creates the conditions under which the internal transmutation which is its ultimate goal can take place. And what is the result of this transmutation of inner lead into inner gold? As the Sun rules the motions of the Earth and the Earth those of the Moon, so the fully developed man is the master of his own life: "He Who Rules," and bends not to the force of lesser influences.*
>
> *– Mercurius, The Furnace*

Diary of Adam Luce

Joachimsthal, 19 March, 1924

Sitting alone in this Pullman coach as the train steadily carries me towards an unknown future, I feel as if I am holding in my hands the book I have sought my entire life, but did not know it. And this book is without any question the work of an alchemist. How can a book of such questionable lineage so captivate my mind? Has my intellect been confounded by the influences of Berlin to the extent that any treatise promising an end to confusion and doubt can win me over? Is there indeed truth to be found in the trappings of superstition and myth?

Every general chemistry text tips its hat to alchemy as the precursor to today's scientific chemistry and acknowledges the alchemists' early achievements in distillation and metallurgy. But, says science, its practitioners stubbornly clung to theories that lacked experimental validation. Those theories were thus abandoned, and rightly so. Have I then lost my wits to study them seriously? The note Charlotte tucked behind the first page is of little help.

Dearest Adam,

This journey to the Erzgebirge is your destiny. I see it so clearly now. In those mountains, many things will be hidden from you, and men you have come to trust may seek to deceive you. It is my deepest wish that this volume will be a touchstone against which you can measure the authenticity of anything you may encounter.

Know this, my Darling. All that I am is yours.

Charlotte

That some may seek to deceive me is no revelation. Deceit has been the primary motive of half the people involved in this German excursion of mine, Charlotte included, at least in the beginning. Even now, I know I cannot fully trust Austerlitz, much as I wish to, but in his case I have no other option for the present.

The reference to hidden things is more troubling. I believe Austerlitz will teach me everything I need to know about the operation and use of the electrical generators that are now in their final stages of development. Will he also share the secrets of this hidden chemistry to which Charlotte introduced me, and to which The *Furnace* alludes? And how can the material in *The Furnace* help me evaluate the "authenticity" of anything he might tell me? *The Furnace* speaks clearly about the failings of humanity, failings that I see all too clearly in myself. It speaks only indirectly of that chemistry by virtue of which a man can evolve beyond his natural state and, in the words of the book, "arise from the ashes of confusion."

How one achieves this transformation is not at all clear. It's all told in the guise of symbolic chemical reactions which I can hardly begin to fathom, but which nonetheless compel my attention. Beyond that, there are references to Christian doctrine on almost every page, references that I would have dismissed out of hand a few scarce months ago. The illustrations are not in the diagrammatic style one would expect in a chemistry book, but rather woodcuts that would seem more appropriate in a book of fairy tales, excepting of course, those that depict copulation.

What strikes me with the most force is the fundamental idea that the study of the external world and the study of man are one and the same, and that the laws governing elementary particles not only extend to the metals but to all forms of life as well, and indeed comprehend the behavior of men and societies, extending even to the planets and stars. This idea would most certainly be met with ridicule in the hallowed halls of Yale, but on the labyrinthine journey my life has become, it rings true.

Be that as it may, I must still ask myself, why did Charlotte arrange that I should have this book, and why is keeping it hidden of such great importance?

The canonical metals of antiquity are said to respond to the influence of celestial bodies like tuning forks: silver to the moon, gold to the sun, iron to Mars, copper to Venus and so on. This must be understood in a figurative sense. The metals represent certain faculties of the mind and heart that can only be awakened by stimulation from the central ideas that animate the Great Work. This phenomena, analogous to sympathetic vibration in the physical world, will occur whether the encounter with hidden ideas is the result of a conscious search, or mere chance. The biblical reference to "those who have ears to hear" is a reference to sympathetic vibration in the psychological sense.

– Mercurius, The Furnace

Diary of Adam Luce
Joachimsthal, 19 March, 1924

I feel a vague sense of unease as I sit down in this rustic cabin to record by the light of one dim candle the next step of the journey upon which I have embarked. There is no rail service to Joachimsthal. I was met at the nearest train station – in the industrial city of Chemnitz – by a driver in a faded gray uniform which I later learned was that of the local spa, the *Radium Kurhaus*, which apparently has an international reputation now. My transportation was a horse and buggy that seemed not at all out of place even in the city, and ideally suited to the dirt roads we encountered once we reached the mountains.

We arrived at the edge of the town just as the sun was setting. In the fading light I followed my driver down the main street, toting my single piece of luggage filled with books, clothing and little else. We passed the old silver mint, the graceful stone church, several taverns, and then the imposing *Kurhaus*, which stands directly across the street from a manufacturing facility devoted to the production of yellow dyes derived from uranium. My guide proudly recounted the history of these buildings in a thick rural accent.

We soon left the town behind. He led me up a heavily wooded trail to this cabin, one of more than a dozen maintained by the *Kurhaus* for those who prefer to live in privacy while taking the radium waters. In addition to this wooden table with its two straight-backed chairs, it offers a decent bed with a thick, quilted coverlet, a fireplace, a little bathroom and an indoor toilet. The door is sturdy enough to withstand a heavy storm, but it has no lock, although it can be barred from the inside.

I noticed a loose floorboard near the foot of the bed where *The Furnace* could be easily hidden, along with this diary. I think it is a trap. Anyone could enter this cabin at any time and search it from top to bottom. That floorboard is an invitation to indiscretion, like a garter left on your pillow in a Berlin hotel. I shall stash what I need to hide in the stonework of the cabin's foundation and hope the dry weather holds until I can find a more suitable place in the woods.

Before leaving me, with a smart salute no less, my driver explained that there is a small dining hall adjacent to the kitchen on the ground floor of the *Kurhaus* where I am to take my meals with the other chemists of rank, as he put it. A maid will visit the cabin daily to clean and pick up any items of clothing that may need to be washed.

I am slowly coming to accept that this cabin in the woods is to be my home, perhaps for quite some time. Joachimsthal has been a mining town for centuries. From a brochure I was able to find in Berlin before my departure I have learned that the silver coins known as '*thalers* minted here in the sixteenth and seventeenth centuries were one of the most respected currencies in Europe in their day, and gave the American dollar its name. When the silver ran out, bismuth and cobalt maintained the mines' economic viability. Now, in the twentieth century, it's uranium, which is prized as a tint for glassware and now, if my speculations are correct, for something much more important.

Why locate a research project devoted to the generation of cheap power near a cluster of uranium mines unless uranium plays a key role in their operation? If remoteness and secrecy were the only criteria for such research, there are endless other locations – the whole of the Black Forest, for God's sake. And why should Austerlitz have the astronomical symbol for the planet Uranus tattooed on his wrist? It's hard to chalk that up to coincidence.

Ordinary men and women are trapped in a prison of causality from which there is no possible escape, because they do not realize that they are prisoners. They wake up, drink

their coffee, march off to work, court the favor of their superiors, search for sexual release, all drawn, as if magnetized, from one object of desire to the next... until they eventually die. The Adept, in contrast, responds to the higher causality of intentional evolution. His work is self-chosen, and it consists in freeing himself from the frivolous attractions that govern the aimless lives of others. This freedom is the true goal of the Great Work.

– Mercurius, The Furnace

Diary of Adam Luce
Joachimsthal, 20 March, 1924

The second in command here is one Alex Weiß, an intense, thin fellow not much older than I am, with close cropped hair and piercing blue eyes. He approached me at the breakfast table this morning, and I somehow felt I should stand up to introduce myself, much as an *unteroffizier* would when a captain entered the room. As we shook hands I noticed that his inner wrist bore the same tattoo I had seen on Austerlitz.

He asked if my quarters were adequate, although it was obvious he couldn't have cared less. Then he proposed, if I had the time, mind you, that we walk over to the mine so he could introduce me to my duties. He spoke of "the mine" as if there were only one, and seemed to assume I knew all about it. His style is one of command with a careful veneer of politeness, which deference I can only attribute to my relationship with Austerlitz. I of course assented to his suggestion.

We walked at a brisk pace. The road to the mine, which is indeed a uranium mine, winds for about half a mile around two steep, grassy hills that hide the buildings of the nearby uranium processing plant from the town, and in particular from the elegant *Kurhaus*. The buildings are interconnected by a maze of piping. It will be my responsibility to monitor pressure, verify valve operation and in general assure that all is in order in these external connections. I will also supervise the transfer of the uranium ingots that are the end product of the refinement process to a guarded storage facility with a vault-like door whose combination changes daily based on, of all things, the sidereal tables used by astrologers. The ingots are to be handled with great care, and for some reason I don't understand must never come within one meter of one another. I didn't ask Weiß, as he is obviously a man who doesn't welcome questions.

Weiß concluded his review of my duties by introducing me to the men in my crew, or rather, by lining them up so they could introduce themselves. They are Abraham, Sebestian, Jakub and Bruno, four Czechs who speak only the most rudimentary German. They touched their caps as they spoke their names and avoided looking me in the eye. My job, said Weiß after dismissing them, will be to supervise their work and in particular enforce the prohibition against smoking and drinking while on the job. They were not to be trusted, and I must never allow them to watch me when I unlocked the storage vault lest they steal the combination.

After Weiß left I spent nearly an hour tracing the path of the various pipes that connect the buildings as best I could. It strikes me that my situation here is hardly different from what it was in Berlin, that of an outsider with very limited knowledge of the chemical processes I want to understand. I do know, however, that uranium is at the core of them all.

Diary of Adam Luce
Joachimsthal, 21 March, 1924

I have quickly fallen into a routine. Each morning on my way to the mine I pass by the *Kurhaus*, whose guests often take their coffee on the terrace now that the spring weather has arrived. I wear a modest wool suit of local cut that I bought down in Chemnitz, heavy shoes and a worker's cap. The cap shades my eyes from the sun, and in doing so also blocks the view of my face from any guest who might hail from that city whose decadence I have left behind. Austerlitz doesn't want my presence here to be known, nor do I. It's a matter of safety.

The walk to the mine takes but ten minutes, and it's pleasant enough. When I reach the gates that enclose the processing buildings I display my badge to one of the black uniformed guards who stand watch at the entrance. They're taciturn Teutonic types, obviously recruited from the north, and they know damned well who I am by now. Nonetheless, they're not satisfied until they inspect my badge and verify that its number is on their list. It's the same list, I might add, that was in their possession the day before. I suppose orders are orders, and like good Prussians, they no doubt hold that discipline is a virtue in itself.

I exchange idle pleasantries with the night supervisor, a middle aged Bavarian whose name I've as yet to learn, collect my clipboard off the metal desk in the small outbuilding that functions as our office, and then head off with my crew to conduct my first round of inspections. Together we check the external piping that conveys liquefied uranium compounds from one building to the next, monitor the various gauges, and make sure that all the valves are operating properly. I've no idea exactly what chemicals these pipes carry, only that they are highly poisonous and highly corrosive as well.

I have vowed there will be no accidents on my watch, and I personally verify that every connection has been inspected with care. In this regard, my summer shifts at the family factory have served me well. The Czechs can see I'm handy with a wrench, and they're coming to respect me. One, whose German is not nearly as bad as he lets on, shared with me that there have been accidents in the past, and that his crew mates have learned the hard way to respect the need for caution. Unfortunately, he was unable to explain the exact nature of these accidents. I don't think it's a good idea to ask Weiß.

When the day is over I take an early dinner with the other supervisors and chemists, entering the *Kurhaus* through a back door reserved for the help, a role which I accept with difficulty. By unwritten rule, we don't speak to one another beyond the briefest of comments. After dinner, if I don't succumb to the temptation of a tavern, I take a walk in the hills, being careful to return before nightfall. Wolves own the night here.

I am not denied access to the rural society of Joachimsthal, such as it is. There are two taverns where German is spoken, the Blue Boar and the *Wolpertinger*, the latter named after one of the region's numerous mythical animals, in this case a jack rabbit with sharp antlers. Both taverns are convivial, with large round wooden tables where the locals gather, many of them miners who usually bring their wives. The Blue Boar and the *Wolpertinger* both have a long bar in the back for the single males, the majority of whom are outsiders, a fact made obvious by their northern accents. I believe most of these men are attached, as am I, to the uranium processing facility, although none will admit it. "We don't talk about work here," is their common refrain.

The bar maids are friendly, buxom and the picture of German health. It's rumored that they are available for other services beyond filling empty steins, but that's a not a theory I'm disposed to test at present. The fact that a couple of them have learned my name is discomforting enough, although in that regard I'm most likely being a bit over-suspicious. The somewhat paranoid habits of mind I acquired in Berlin are hard to set aside.

One of the few fellow northerners who would speak to me volunteered that sex is cheaply available from the Czech girls, although those Germans who avail themselves of this opportunity on occasion end up with a knife in their back. There is no love lost between the Germans and the Czechs, who are unquestionably oppressed when it comes to working conditions, and thought to be racially inferior, an opinion that my personal experience does not confirm.

When it comes to girls, I can't deny that I'm lonely. I feel it most on the walk along the narrow, winding path back to my cabin, where I'll sleep alone.

Indeed I must stop writing and get some sleep now, alone as I am, or I won't be sharp tomorrow when I'm on duty.

Diary of Adam Luce
Joachimsthal, 22 March, 1924

I continue to study *The Furnace* every night, re-reading passages again and again in the hopes that sheer repetition will somehow bring understanding. Charlotte revealed its central premise back in Berlin, that human body is a chemical factory. The text goes on to assert that knowledge of the laws governing its operation can bring freedom from unnecessary "reactions" that drain one's energy while producing no useful results, processes like worry or longing, which I know all too well. I strongly suspect that the superiority of German chemical industry has its roots in this alchemical manipulation of the mind.

Foremost among these laws is the Law of Triads, which states that all manifestations at every scale have three components: one that is positive, or active; one that is negative, or passive; and one that is neutral. This concept is simple enough in theory, but I find myself unable to apply it either to the chemistry of the physical world as I know it, nor to myself. If I could, my capacity for analysis and invention would soar beyond the bounds of what I presently know as thought as surely as my perceptions extended themselves beyond all ordinary limits when I was in the woods with Charlotte. But I cannot confirm this, nor progress beyond speculation without a guide to the practices of which The Furnace offers but hints.

So I must ask myself, what good does all this do me? I do believe that Mercurius' system has a breadth and depth modern science lacks, and that if I could pursue it I would find a way to live my life more intelligently. I've had fantasies about seeking an adept, to use the language of *The Furnace*, who could instruct me further in this system after my work here in Joachimsthal is done, I don't doubt that Austerlitz is such a man, but fate has made him my employer instead of my teacher.

Wolfgang Austerlitz
Überlegungen, 23 March, 1924

I tell myself that the writings of *Mercurius* belong to a time when our predecessors lived like hermits in the forest, working with crude furnaces and hand blown glassware that couldn't even be sealed against contamination. So much for purity. But of course, Mercurius would say that the purity in the old texts has nothing to do with glassware. For him, what we're striving to achieve in Joachimsthal would be of no consequence. Well, he would have that opinion if he had lived through the war. Or so I tell myself. From my perspective, this philosophical gold he writes about is an illusion and a distraction to boot. We are what we are, and we just have to make the best of it. I don't believe I was put on this Earth to find hidden meanings in old books. I am here to serve the Fatherland.

Diary of Adam Luce
Joachimsthal, 23 March, 1924

Saturday afternoons and all of Sunday I have no official responsibilities, and I take pleasure in hiking the numerous trails here. One cannot roam far in the woods and fields behind Joachimsthal without coming across abandoned mines with rusted rails leading to a long-shuttered shaft where miners of another century toiled to win silver from these mountains. The mines remind me of gagged mouths that would tell lurid tales if they were but to open. I'm aware that this is a strange thought, and it's only one of many that have begun to possess me since my arrival. If I've time and can obtain the right gear, I'm tempted to do some exploring. Years of neglect have had their way with these mines. I'm confident the entrances could be easily breeched.

Yesterday I passed the *Svomost* mine. It's no longer active, but there is a natural spring deep within it that supplies the waters for the medicinal radium baths located in the basement of the *Kurhaus*. The spring may explain the presence of the two guards at its entrance gates. In my opinion, they lend it a sense of importance. It's hard to imagine there's anything in this mine that would be worthy of plunder.

Diary of Adam Luce
Joachimsthal, 29 March, 1924

A well-appointed horse drawn carriage departs for Chemnitz from the *Kurhaus* daily at nine a.m. for the convenience of guests who are in need of items that can't be purchased here in Joachimsthal, which is to say virtually anything other than food and drink. Although it's intended for the guests, chemists of rank are tolerated, and today I took a seat, being in need of a sturdy coat for warmth at night. Unless I receive an invitation for dinner in the formal dining room of the *Kurhaus*, a highly unlikely prospect, all my Berlin clothes will likely remain hanging on the rack in my cabin for the duration of my stay.

Chemnitz is a true city, with the same sort of fine buildings one sees in Berlin, motorized trolleys and outdoor cafés that face onto busy boulevards. Tall, tapering smoke stacks arise from the factories near the river, confirming the city's reputation as a manufacturing powerhouse.

I easily obtained the coat I needed, and used the remaining hours to hunt for one of those shops that sells gear left over from the Great War. I found what I was looking for: a portable dynamo flashlight that hangs around one's neck on a leather strap. It's a true marvel of German ingenuity. A pull cord that dangles from the lamp is attached to a miniature electrical generator inside the lamp's housing. Each pull on the cord provides about fifteen seconds of strong light – more than enough to guide me through an abandoned mine shaft.

The ride back to Joachimsthal was like a trip into the previous century. With the exception of the *Kurhaus* and the factories, there is no electricity to be had. The majority of the inhabitants have never even seen a telephone, much less put one to use. These people are close to the Earth, and for them the bright lights of a city have no attraction.

Wolfgang Austerlitz
Überlegungen, 30 March, 1924

I don't like it, but deception is an important part of leadership. There are times when force by itself won't do the job, and so it is with Luce. I wish he were one of us... but he's not. And the longer he remains in Joachimsthal, the more likely he is to piece together what's really going on. I must find a way to throw him off the track, and for that I need some credible sounding science. I think I'll make the electrons the heroes of my false story. They're known to conventional chemistry, and a breakthrough involving them wouldn't seem unbelievable. He'll want to see the prototype "generator" he's supposed to demonstrate when he gets back to America, but I can put that off for now.

How willing he'll be to use the Luce Company's warehouses for temporary storage is another question. He probably hates his uncle now, and maybe I can use that to my advantage. I could give him a chance to approach his elders as an equal, with a product that will make their Pills for Your Ills business look like a child's lemonade stand. That may appeal to him. But if it doesn't, he can surely find a suitable storage alternative. He's an America citizen, and that's a huge advantage for us. He won't have to deal with the government scrutiny a German would encounter, and the last thing we need is scrutiny.

I'll talk to him the next time I can get to Joachimsthal and see where things stand. That had better be soon. I wish my role at KDE here in Berlin didn't take up so much of my time.

Diary of Adam Luce

Joachimsthal, 30 March, 1924

Much as I try, I cannot make sense of what's really going on in the buildings adjacent to the mine.

Here's what I know.

Austerlitz claims he's invented a chemical generator about the size of a steamer trunk that can produce enough electricity to light up an entire town.

His new source of power will cost less than those based on oil or coal.

The fuel for this generator is specially processed metallic uranium.

The processing of the ore – its purification, as he expresses it – is carried out under conditions of extreme secrecy.

All the chemicals involved in the processing are highly explosive, including the uranium itself.

The one item that makes sense in all of this is the explosive properties of the fuel. An explosion, after all, is nothing more than the sudden release of energy. If Austerlitz and his team have figured out a way to make an explosion happen at a slow, controlled rate instead of all at once, perhaps he's got something. What's certain is that the Germans working on this project will barely engage in conversation with me, much less share the nature of their work.

I am convinced that there is a secret laboratory dedicated to the chemistry of the generators, and I think I know where it is. If I'm right, it's in the basement of the *Kurhaus*, with access through a door—most likely a secret one—in the kitchen or the adjacent pantry. Half an hour inside that lab would likely yield up information that would take months to acquire in my current position as an outsider. I could never get in through an entrance that's securely locked and perhaps guarded, if I could even manage to find it. But there may be another route, albeit a dangerous one.

So what if it's dangerous? I've already devoted half a year to penetrating the secrets of German chemistry, all to no avail. My patience is wearing thin.

The concept of purity will always be misunderstood by the coarse sensibility that reigns in these terrible times. Men imagine they must abstain from sex, or beer, or whatever vice they may nurture. This is not what was meant by the masters of the Great Work. True purity is purity of intention. An ordinary man, if he examines himself with honesty, will see that he has no consistency of intention. One moment he wants to climb to spiritual heights, the next he is worried about his bank account, and the next he craves

a Sachertorte. Such a man can achieve nothing. Thus the first task for he who would undertake the Great Work is to embark on an inner search for the core from which one single intention can arise. We call this core the Lapis. It is the true Philosopher's Stone.

– Mercurius, The Furnace

Diary of Adam Luce
Joachimsthal, 31 March, 1924

At last I've been granted some information about the research Austerlitz is conducting here in Joachimsthal.

This afternoon I was interrupted while adjusting a pressure valve by a uniformed messenger. Herr Doktor Austerlitz was in town and requested my presence *sofort*—straight away. I handed the wrench I was using to Abraham, who was observing me as I worked, and explained the last two steps to be taken. (His German is much better than he lets on, and he seems quite intelligent.)

Austerlitz was standing in front of the old stone church when I arrived, for once without a lab coat. After we shook hands he suggested a walk in the forest. The path he chose was lined with tall conifers and led northward away from the mine. We walked for some time in silence. Then, without preamble, he began to explain the scientific principles behind his generators.

The chemistry that will drive them lies beyond anything I could have imagined. Indeed it transcends chemistry as it is known to the world. I'm not yet privy to the details of how these generators will be constructed, but the theory of operation revolves around purity, a concept with which he seems to be obsessed, as was Charlotte, come to think of it.

The key to it all is the behavior of electrons. He explained that when uranium is purified, its electrons become so highly energized that they spontaneously fly from one uranium atom to another. The flow of electrons becomes increasingly powerful as the quantity of uranium increases. And what is electricity but the flow of electrons?

The generators will be designed to hold two ingots of purified uranium fuel, separated by a distance such that the flow of electrons he described cannot take place. A crank will allow me to diminish that distance and unite the two ingots, resulting in a quantity of electricity equal to that of a small hydroelectric dam.

The lead Germans hold on the rest of the world in science is astonishing, and as I write these words, I can't help but think they owe this lead to the techniques referenced, but never explained in detail, in the pages of *The Furnace*. Their thinking is on a different plane. I must say, my walk with Austerlitz has whetted my appetite for more knowledge about the design of the generators themselves, and the thought of sneaking into the secret lab—assuming it exists—is more attractive than ever. Were I to be caught, the price could be death. But somehow I doubt it. I think Austerlitz respects risk-takers.

✠

The faith of the Adept is not the faith of a pious peasant who prays for rain, but rather that of a scientist, whose only belief is in the existence of natural laws, whether they be known to him, or as yet hidden. His work, then, is a work of discovery and verification, not slavish devotion. And through this work, the power of The Almighty is not merely acknowledged, but directly observed and felt.

– Mercurius, The Furnace

✠

Diary of Adam Luce
Joachimsthal, 1 April, 1924

Today I walked out to the *Svomost* mine immediately after my shift ended. As usual, two guards were posted at the gates, obvious northerners like all the others. I was still wearing my supervisor's badge from work and, per my plan, I simply walked by them into the mine as though I were there to make a routine inspection of the flow control valves at the head end of the pipeline. Carbide lamps cast uncertain light on the timbered passageway, creating bizarre shadows on its rocky walls as I passed. I found my way to the natural spring quickly enough. It was surrounded by a safety rail, such that no one could accidentally fall in, even in pitch blackness. The path that led around the spring to the pipeline itself seemed safe as well. I briefly inspected the pipe fittings and cut-off valve and then turned back. As I approached the entrance, I spotted what I had hoped to find: three thick keys hanging from nails that had been pounded into one of the support timbers near the entrance. They looked to be identical. I stuffed one of them into the inner pocket of my coat and walked out without giving the stone faced guards a glance.

I arrived back in town in time to take my dinner, but afterward, instead of stopping by one of the local bars, I went straight to my cabin. Then, with my new portable light hanging around my neck and the stolen key in my pocket, I set out for the mine.

The guards were no longer on duty, the assumption being, I suppose, that no one in his right mind would venture out at night to visit an old mine. My key worked, and I easily made my way to the spring using bursts of light from my newly acquired dynamo flashlight. From there on, the going was tough. The builders of the radium water pipeline had realized that a maintenance shaft would be required, which meant I was able to walk, rather than crawl, but the footing was unsure and more than once I banged my head. After about half an hour I reached the *Kurhaus*, and here luck was with me.

Above the point where the pipeline passes into the *Kurhaus* the builders had installed a long air vent. For a moment this perplexed me, given that a narrow maintenance shaft some fifteen feet under the ground is hardly an ideal source of fresh air. Then I realized that the louvered panels provided an excellent peeping Tom's view of the tubs where movie stars and other celebrities bathed, and obtaining that view was no doubt what the workers had in mind. Fortunately the "vent" extended beyond the baths to another room that could only be the secret lab.

Both the baths and the lab were in total darkness, and from my position I couldn't manage to angle my portable light satisfactorily to gain a full view of the lab. I was able to make out complex assemblies of glassware against the far wall, but that was all I could see.

I will return soon, and continue to return, until I'm there when the lights come on. I'm sick of waiting for an invitation to see first hand what these generators look like.

Diary of Adam Luce
Joachimsthal, 2 April, 1924

With Austerlitz, my advancement towards any knowledge of value seems destined to take place in small, measured steps, each one of which, I must note, takes me farther away from the realm of chemical practice. Given the Rensselaer fiasco, I suppose I should be grateful that he not only kept me on, but chose me to be his American emissary for the chemistry closest to the heart of scientific and industrial progress.

From that perspective, today's developments are promising to say the least. We again met in the shadow of the old church and followed the path that leads away from the mine. The air was hot, and one could hear the rustle of insects in the grass.

During our walk Austerlitz surprised me by laying out a detailed business proposal. Once the time arrived for shipping the generators, I would no longer retain my employee's status at KDE. Rather, I would become the company's agent, operating independently to secure storage space and arrange transportation for the generators as necessary for on-site demonstrations. He suggested that I might even approach my father and uncle to see if appropriate storage space might be available in the company's numerous warehouses scattered across the country.

I would be paid a flat fee for each demonstration in which I participated, and a commission on top of that for every sale. My role, he assured me, would be entirely technical, with the responsibility for drumming up business, arranging sales calls and the like to be handled by one of the several American sales organizations with whom he'll be meeting when he returns to Berlin.

The proposal seemed more than fair, the financial terms generous. Nonetheless, I continue to harbor misgivings, born of his insistent secrecy. What must I do to win his trust? As soon as I pen those words, the converse thought arises: What must he do to win mine? I am the one secretly peering into his darkened laboratory, awaiting the moment when the lights come on.

The quest for inner psychological development has always been at the heart of The Great Work. The accumulation of formulae and data about the outcomes of experiments is of little importance when compared to the spirit of enquiry that produced them. In these modern times, as always, no

assertion of truth is to be taken on faith. The anticipated results of any process must be personally verified. To repeat the arcane chemical procedures found in musty tomes is to confound the material with the psychological, or, more precisely, historical formulae designed for external manipulation with the timeless pursuit of inner growth.

– Mercurius, The Furnace

Diary of Adam Luce
Joachimsthal, 3 April, 1924

It's again well past midnight, and the town of Joachimsthal is as silent as a tomb. I've numerous scrapes and scratches on my hands as well as a gash on my forehead resulting from my ongoing difficulty negotiating the rocky maintenance shaft that leads from the *Svomost* mine to the *Kurhaus*. I'll find a way to explain the gash should anyone ask about it, but I'm not sure how I'll ever explain to myself what I witnessed once I reached the cramped space from which it's possible to spy on the lab. Austerlitz is an alchemist. And he's been lying to me all along.

The sun hadn't quite set when I entered the mine using my stolen key. I struggled along the maintenance shaft as quickly as I could manage, the water from the large pipe that led to the *Kurhaus* gurgling beside me. When I reached the air vent I could see three young chemists whom I recognized as newcomers to Joachimsthal. They were seated on metal chairs facing a black board covered with chemical equations related to various uranium compounds. With no means to take notes, I can't reproduce them all. I do recall that three of those compounds were circled: U_2O_3, $U_2(NO_3)_2$ and UFl_6.

I was puzzling over the equations when I heard a door open out of my range of vision. A moment later, Austerlitz strode into view. Without a word, he erased the black board, replacing the complex formulae with a simple triangle. Then he began the lecture that has thrown my mind into utter confusion.

"Our work is based on two tenants of faith," he began. The first is that the operations of nature are governed by laws. The second is that, with the proper effort, we can understand these laws. You are all familiar with the Holy Trinity of Christian doctrine. No doubt you were all baptized in the name of the Father and the Son and the Holy Ghost." Here I detected a note of irony, but only for a moment.

"What you do not understand is that this doctrine, as it is proclaimed in contemporary Christianity, is only a faint echo of a fundamental *law* that governs every aspect of the physical world: the Law of Triads. This law states that every manifestation involves the interaction of three forces: the active, the passive and the neutralizing. In electrolysis, for example, when an electric current is passed through water to produce elemental hydrogen and oxygen, the anode represents the active or positive force, the cathode the passive or negative force, and the water itself the neutralizing force without which the current could not flow."

He continued, amplifying passages from *The Furnace* I had read a dozen times, but with a somewhat different slant.

"In human society, the male represents the active force and the female represents the passive force. The neutralizing force in this case is what we call love. In alchemical texts, the Law of Triads is symbolized by salt, sulfur and mercury, which are represented by the colors black, white and red.

"What's important here is that no phenomenon in the universe can exist without the participation of all three forces. In the currently accepted models of the atom only two forces are represented. The positive by the proton and the negative electron. As such, in light of the Law of Triads, these models are obviously incomplete."

He went on to describe a model of the atom in which electrons orbit like planets around a nucleus composed of not one, but two types of particles: protons and *neutrons*, the result being a triadic entity.

"The neutron is the most important particle for our purposes. The neutrons of one atom can be made to interact with those of another, and that possibility is what make the production of energy possible."

At that point, I stopped listening carefully. When he explained the generator to me, the key particle had been the electron. I know that's what he said. I wrote it down. But in this discourse, the key particle was the neutron.

It's hard to say what emotions ruled me at that moment. The thrill of being privy to knowledge that's as yet undiscovered territory in the labs and universities of the world? Wonder, that the chief chemist at KDE was designing his miracle generator based on the theories of alchemy, theories which I myself have begun to embrace? Anger at having been misled about science by a man to whom I have entrusted my future? Confusion as to what it all means? What's certain is that the principles of alchemy – at least some of them – are valid. It would seem that the German chemical industry is in fact built on them!

In the light of tonight's discoveries, need I re-evaluate my understanding of *The Furnace*? Can it be that alchemy is not, as *Mercurius* avers, a unique guide to self-improvement, but rather the ultimate empowerment of villainy? *Mercurius* never misses a chance to disavow the importance of the practical techniques alchemy has contributed to modern chemistry. He exclusively recognizes psychological interpretations of the texts, while Austerlitz presents quite a different orientation, one that embraces and secretly stimulates the advancement of modern science through a single-minded focus on the physical world.

I can't think this through clearly right now. To tell the truth, I can't think at all.

Diary of Adam Luce
Joachimsthal, 4 April, 1924

Tonight, as I crouched in my hidden observation post behind the air vent, Austerlitz again eschewed complex formulae and instead wrote but three words on the blackboard:

Separatio
Purificatio
Conjunctio

Separation. Purification. Conjunction. These processes, he said, comprise the fundamental triad that governs all alchemical transformations.

"The elements we encounter in the physical world have without exception been adulterated with impurities, and this includes even the most noble metals. For those of us who pursue the alchemy of metals, then, the first task is to free them from the chemical bonds by which they are imprisoned. Over the centuries, in this very region, numerous methods have been developed to extract valuable metals from the earth. I'm sure you are familiar with these methods, and I won't go into detail.

"The second task is purification. In the case of uranium, the final extracted metal is not truly pure, and requires methods that are known only to us. In this regard, we are guided by the words of Hermes Trismagistus."

Here, he wrote on the blackboard:

Learn to separate the fine from the coarse.

With that, he moved on to a discussion of the chemistry of explosives, specifically, the properties and merits of gels as opposed to powders.

I am more baffled than ever, and growing more suspicious as well. What role could gun powders or more modern explosives like trinitrotoluene have in the generation of electricity?

Diary of Adam Luce
Joachimsthal, 5 April, 1924

It's well past midnight and very cold now that the logs in the fireplace have been reduced to embers, but I don't want to take time to build a new fire. I need to capture the insight that came to me like a bolt of lightening as I slept. The triad of alchemical transformation Austerlitz described has been right in front of my eyes every day! *Separatio* refers to the processes that extract elemental uranium from the pitchblend the miners bring up from the mines. *Purificato* is the mysterious process the uranium undergoes inside the locked buildings to which I have no access. *Conjunctio* refers to the moment when the cranking mechanism brings the purified uranium ingots back into close proximity to unleash the flow of energy in the generators.

In America, alchemy has been abandoned. Here, it has merely gone underground, where it apparently serves as a source of inspiration to Austerlitz and his followers, and the whole German chemical industry for all I know. If they've learned how to electrify an entire city with a generator no bigger than a steamer trunk, what's next?

Diary of Adam Luce
Joachimsthal, 5 April, 1924

I thought it impossible that my life should become more complicated, but now it has. Portia is staying at the *Kurhaus*. I saw her this morning on my way to work. There's no mistaking the way she enters a room, or, in this case, a sunlit veranda. Charlotte attracts attention. Portia commands it. She wore a white summer dress and, surprisingly, sported a pair of sunglasses whose movie star flash would have been more appropriate to Charlotte's wardrobe.

She took a table near the thick wooden rail surrounding the veranda and a formally clad waiter approached immediately to take her order. I wanted to stop and observe her, but I dared not. Instead, I walked on, stealing one backward glance. Her attention was focused on a newspaper. I'm sure she didn't see me, but I wouldn't be surprised if she knows I'm here. I can't seek her out. That's out of bounds. But she may come to me. With that in mind, I'll forego my visit to the mine tonight.

Diary of Adam Luce

Joachimsthal, 6 April, 1924

It's almost dawn. There's no point trying to sleep now. Not after what took place earlier.

I heard a gentle tap on my door just as the church bells of St. Joachim completed their announcement of the midnight hour. To arrive at the stroke of midnight was the sort of theatrical touch I would expect from Charlotte, never from Portia. But, I reasoned, who else could be there? I opened the door, and there, candle in hand, stood Charlotte. The woman I would have as my wife. She was dressed in a red, foot length garment with black piping, fastened at the neck by an iridescent clasp inlaid with images of the sun and moon. Her face was pale and tense. Her first act was to blow out the candle.

"The moonlight will be enough for us," she said, and she was right. The moon was only one night short of full. As we stood in the doorway our bodies cast shadows onto the cabin's wooden floor planks.

"Are you going to let me in?" she asked, and for a brief moment I caught a glimpse of the endlessly flirtatious Charlotte I had come to know so well in Berlin.

I stood aside and she entered. In a moment we were sitting cross-legged on the bed, facing one another once again. Memories of our time together in Berlin flooded into my mind.

She took my hands in hers. "We've waited so long, Adam, and at last the stars have aligned for us. I know you've wanted me, and now I can be yours, every night if you like, until the moon is dark again."

She squeezed my hand. "Don't worry, I've quite successfully corrupted my guard. These Bavarians are no match for a Berliner."

That Charlotte should have a guard struck me as more than strange, but I said nothing. Frankly, I had no wish to know how she had managed to corrupt him.

When she spoke again, it was as though in answer to this thought.

"I'm pure as snow, now, Adam. I'm here of my own free will."

I stared at her. Was she implying that in the past she was sent? And if so, by whom?

"I know what you're thinking," she said. The past is the past. The stars are out only guides now."

A silence fell between us. Somewhere in the forest a wolf howled at the moon. As if that were a signal, Charlotte reached up and unsnapped the clasp at her throat. She shook herself and her garment slid down over her shoulders.

Wolfgang Austerlitz
Überlegungen, 6 April, 1924

The I.G. Farben *kartel* has existed in spirit for decades, and now it is to emerge from the shadows. Its power will be mythical. Such power is our destiny, the work of generations. The base of our pyramid of dominance will be the array of artificial fertilizers that provide sustenance to the civilized world. At its peak, in the place of honor, will be the Dark Queen, released from her prison deep in the mines of Joachimsthal. Atomic chemistry, which will give the civilized world an inexhaustible source of power so that industry can advance without limits. New drugs will ensure long, healthy and productive lives, and new genetics will teach us how to ensure the purity of our race. Architecture, music and drama that embody the spirit of our Work will guide the moral lives of the people, because where chemistry leads, civilization will follow.

Diary of Adam Luce

Joachimsthal, 7 April, 1924

Late as it is, I must capture all of this before I sleep.

I was so shocked by Charlotte's appearance last night I didn't ask when she had arrived in the village or where she's staying, but I can safely assume the *Kurhaus* with Portia. In any case, her accommodations are of little importance. She's here in Joachimsthal, and last night when I finally lay down on my bed long after she had left her scent lingered on the hard straw pillow she found so charming and rustic.

Tonight, as before, she arrived at my door shortly before midnight, bearing a flask of strong red wine, which we drank from crystal goblets that would have been more at home in the formal dining room of the *Kurhaus* than on my rude table. In fact, that was most likely their source.

"It's nothing special," she said as she poured the wine.

"Anything we share is special," I replied.

"Such eloquence!" she said. "Not at all what I'd expect from someone trained by Berliners."

In contrast to her behavior of the previous evening, which bordered on the ritualistic at moments, she seemed relaxed, and we spoke as old friends might. Nonetheless, it was obvious that there was something of importance on her mind. She waited until we had finished off most of the wine from her flask to reveal her purpose.

"There's a lot you don't know," she began at last.

"That's the understatement of the year," I replied with a smile.

"I am deadly serious," she said.

"I can see Berlin as you saw it, Adam," she began. The chaos and debauchery and death in the streets, and in the midst of it all, the KDE building with its iron gates and thick stone walls and *Freikorps* guards. Those walls lay between you and everything you want. A monocle, a mansion, parties where string quartets play Beethoven."

I attempted to take issue with this materialistic vision of my wants, but she shushed me with her finger.

"Listen. I need to tell you something important. You must share this with no one. Promise me that, please."

I had never heard Charlotte speak in such grave tones. I made the promise.

"There was a time when that stone building that holds so many secrets wasn't there, nor were the busy streets with their modern automobiles and traffic lights and all the rest. Instead, there were hills and trees and a few wooden houses with pointed roofs... and a hunting lodge. An important group of men gathered in that lodge more than a hundred years ago, men who had only known each other through obscure books and secret letters. They were alchemists."

Until the revelations of three nights past, I might well have scoffed at her. But I've come to realize that there's more to alchemy, or whatever it is that Austerlitz and his team are practicing, than a quixotic attempt to convert base metals into gold. I listened intently.

The men who met in that lodge knew that alchemy as practiced in their day was a sham," she continued, "and for the first time in their lives they admitted to one another that their quest was hopeless. I can't even imagine what that felt like, to abandon a life's work." She looked down at the table, and then into my eyes.

"But all was not lost. They also realized that if they worked together using what they had learned, they could formulate dyes and chemicals of enormous commercial value. There hasn't been a collection of minds like that since ancient Alexandria. They were inspired, and over time they had developed drugs to help discipline their minds.

"They determined they would introduce the fruits of their labors to the world indirectly, through existing dye and glass makers, which of course grew large under their influence. Then they branched out. All the ideas for all the important chemicals manufactured by KDE and Agfa and Bayer and all the others came originally from this small group. The explosives, the fertilizer, heroin, all of it.

"The chemists in Germany's commercial laboratories are being guided by them to this day. Those chemists will see a formula in the corner of a black board, or find a journal article tucked in their lab notebook, or there'll be an encounter in a beer garden with a stranger who passes himself off as a chemistry professor from a foreign university. The successful chemists aren't fools. They learn to look for these things and follow the hints they're given. In return for this stream of guidance, the alchemists receive a small part of the profits in ways that can't be traced."

She stopped to take a last sip of wine and studied me, gauging my reaction. I had to admit that what she proposed had some measure of credibility.

"There were some among the gathering who saw things differently. They didn't disdain money, but they believed there was more to alchemy than a bunch of old recipes for gold that didn't work and lab techniques that did. The way they saw things, the lead and the gold in the early texts weren't metals at all. They were faculties, like perception and reason, that they could elevate through purification. Some thought there was a whole model of the universe hidden in those texts.

"Their leader was a man named Walter Hauptman, but he took the name *Mercurius. The Messenger*. He was a powerful speaker, and he argued that to lose touch with the tradition that had brought them all so far was a grave mistake. In the end, he carried the day. The practical chemists agreed to share their wealth and support the studies and travels of the others, the philosophical chemists. I suspect they hoped that knowledge of material value would be uncovered by these efforts, but of course I can't be sure.

"The group disbanded soon after that, and a few years later the hunting lodge where they had met was struck by lightening and burned to the ground. They continued to meet elsewhere in Berlin, but they always referred to what they did as the work of The Lodge."

Charlotte's revelations rendered me speechless. Hidden behind KDE and the other chemical giants of Germany was a secret fraternity of alchemists led, so it would appear, by Austerlitz himself. No wonder he concealed so much of the truth from me. It was not his to reveal to an outsider.

Once my mind quieted down, I immediately began to ask myself what I might do to gain membership in The Lodge. Charlotte rested her hand on mine. "There's more to tell," she said. "I'm worried."

I wanted to protest that there could hardly be more to this incredible tale, but the concern in her dark eyes kept me silent.

"Uncle Wolfie changed after his son was killed in the Great War. He became obsessed with pitchblend. It's the black ore they mine down here."

"I know," I said. "The ultimate source of uranium."

"Yes, and black is the color of new beginnings. He says that uranium should displace gold as... the emblem of our work."

Her reference to *our* work was not lost on me. She had clearly chosen that pronoun deliberately.

"Adam, you cannot know how difficult it is for me to say this, but I think he's lost his way. Gold – I mean the gold of *The Furnace* – isn't just some valuable metal one can mine. Gold is sunlight. It's *our* light, yours and mine. But now he says we're to revere blackness."

She looked into my eyes with love – there's no other word for it. "Do you know what he's doing here in the mountains?"

"No," I said, although that was not strictly true. But what I knew, I doubted.

"Neither do I," she said to my surprise. "He won't talk about it. I only know he's on a different path. "

"I didn't realize you were in the dark."

"We're all in the dark, Adam. That's what I fear."

"I meant, I assumed you knew much more than I. Your uncle *has* spoken about his research here, but I'm not sure he's comfortable sharing information with me. I think he leaves out quite a bit."

"Tell me what he said."

In non-scientific terms I sketched out his plan for the cheap generation of electricity, and its importance for Western civilization. I wasn't ready to trust her with any knowledge of my spying, although as I think it over, I should have been totally candid. Thankfully, it's a mistake I can easily correct.

She reacted to my description with visible relief, although I can't imagine what she had thought I'd say.

"What makes you think he's not telling you the whole truth?" she asked after a moment's reflection.

The answer was easy. "When all is said and done, I'm still an American."

She rubbed my thigh affectionately "that hasn't made *me* want you any less." At that point it became clear that our time for serious talk had come to an end.

I have been so overwhelmed by Charlotte's sheer intensity and the nature of the secrets she revealed that I've been unable to turn the conversation to our future, but I must and I will. Tonight I'll pop the question.

Diary of Adam Luce
Joachimsthal, 7 April, 1924

My fluttering candle casts grotesque shadows on the rough hewn walls of this cottage, evoking the shadow play my life has become, where the true identities of the actors are but partly revealed, their motives forever hidden.

I've just returned from dinner with Portia in the grand dining room of the *Kurhaus*. Portia! Her invitation, contingent upon my ability to arrive appropriately dressed, was conveyed to me at the end of my shift by the uniformed messenger who is apparently at the service of the entire Austerlitz entourage. I felt I couldn't decline, so I put on my best suit, walked the half mile or so to the town and for the first time entered the famous spa through its massive front doors.

The dining room sparkled with polished glass and silver set out on starched white linen, the napkins folded into stiff fans. Portia had chosen a table by the window in the far corner. As I searched for her, I'm sure I saw Gloria Swanson sitting alone at a table nearby. I wondered what other celebrities might be among the guests, seated at tables not within my view.

I made my way to Portia's table and she rose to kiss me on both cheeks. We sat, and without being summoned a waiter approached with a bottle of champagne and two fluted glasses. When he had filled them, Portia raised hers in a toast that set me on edge.

"To your health... and continued safety."

"Is my safety in doubt? I asked.

"In these times, who knows? Anything can happen. Five years ago, our countries were at war. And here we are."

I raised my own glass. Here's to peace."

She glowered at me. "You know I can't drink to this shameful peace."

"To what then?"

"To the return of order."

I let my eyes play over her face as she drank. Charlotte's face, yet inhabited by another.

"There is a natural order that exists everywhere," she said. "In the forest, in all nature, some animals are prey and others are predators. You and I are part of nature, Adam, just like every man and women in this room, every man and women in this world. The question is, are you the prey, or are you the predator?"

Our first course arrived, cold tomato soup crisscrossed with a geometrical pattern of white cream. I hoped the start of the meal would distract her from this disturbing theme, and it did.

"I don't think you realize what an honor it is to be here," she said.

I glanced around the room at the elegantly dressed guests. I must confess, I fit right in, in appearance if not in wealth.

"Not this spa," she said sharply. "I'm talking about the mine, and the chemistry of pitchblend that's being developed here in this little village. It will change the world, Adam. And you're part of that. You'll have the honor of carrying the torch of progress to America. The chemistry of the future."

I protested. "I'm the foreman of a small work crew. I know nothing of the chemistry of the future." I couldn't completely remove the sarcasm from my voice.

"That will come in time. I can assure you of that."

My heart leapt. I was painfully aware that she might have a clearer picture of what's in store for me than I myself do. But it was also possible that she was bluffing. She was about to continue when a second course of delicate fish arrived.

While Charlotte either wolfs down the food that's put in front of her or savors and analyzes every bite as though she were a chef, Portia takes a practical approach to eating, sipping her soup at a measured pace and wielding her knife and fork with no wasted motion. I caught myself wondering if she brought that same style to the bedroom.

We ate in silence, and I could hear snatches of French and English from the conversations that floated over from the nearby tables. Our waiter was quick to replenish our wine glasses and I soon felt the effects of the alcohol. I think that was her intention.

"Sometimes I feel like your older sister," she said, taking a generous sip of the red that had replaced our Mosel when the main course arrived.

I considered this remark. She grew up here in Germany, part of a powerful family and an insider to everything that's transpired since the Great War. In comparison, I'm little better than a tourist. No wonder she's always a step ahead.

"If I were your sister, that would make kissing even more forbidden."

This remark, delivered in a casual tone, actually made me blush. Her lips curved into a flirtatious smile worthy of Charlotte. Then, she abruptly turned the conversation away from this uncertain territory.

"How do you like your new work?"

It crossed my mind that with any other dinner companion, this question would have been an innocuous one. With Portia, I had to assume that it might be a test, and that my answer might well reach Austerlitz' ears.

"It demands unflagging attention," I said, hoping a neutral answer would satisfy her.

"Are the chemicals dangerous?"

"Yes. They're corrosive and poisonous as well."

"All of them?"

I thought, another test. "I'm not aware of every step in the process. It's kept secret, and I don't have 'need to know' status."

"Does that bother you?"

"That I'm dealing with dangerous chemicals? Of course not. I've always thought that strolling down Unter den Linden in Berlin was far more dangerous."

"I meant, does it bother you that no one has explained the chemistry of these processes?"

"You're over-stating my importance, Portia. I'm nothing but a glorified plumber. My main job is to check the valves and prevent leaks."

"Leaks of chemicals that can eat through steel pipes and kill on contact? I'd say that's quite an important job. And you're part of something much bigger. You should remember that."

Now she returned to the didactic style with which I've become accustomed.

"This food would not be on our plates without German chemistry. You realize that, don't you?"

I nodded at her reference to the Haber-Bosche process.

I've been to Oppau, Adam," she said. "The vessels where they synthesize the ammonia are the size of trolley cars, and they produce almost ten thousand tons of it each month. Without our scientific achievements, civilization would be on the verge of collapse. Instead, the genius of the past is reawakening. And, I'll say it again, you're part of it. You must understand that this research here in Joachimsthal isn't only about Germany. It's about the Western world. Where chemistry leads, civilization will follow.

"I shouldn't tell you this." She paused, frowning. "You'll find out soon enough anyway. The giants of the German chemical industry will soon be united. Farben, Bayer, Hoechst, BASF, Agfa and KDE will be one. They will dominate the world, Adam."

She put her hand to her mouth, and her gaze, which had become intent, quickly softened.

"I'm lecturing you again. I'm sorry. We should be chatting about the weather or something like that and enjoying this lovely food and wine." She surveyed the dining room with its high ceilings and large windows. "I love it here. Who would imagine finding this sort of elegance in an old mining town?"

I thought, and who would imagine finding a research project that could change the world in that same town? I said nothing. A new vision was forming itself in my mind: a hidden Germany that had survived the Great War whole and intact, a Germany that was growing stronger by the day despite the economic struggle and political chaos the world could see, a Germany secretly led by men holding a set of heretical beliefs that would evoke ridicule within the scientific community, but had yet produced a discovery that literally saved the world from starvation.

I wanted to ask Portia why should I of all people be an object of interest to this secret fraternity. I won't sell myself short. I have the makings of a damned good chemist, but I'm no Fritz Haber. What was my place in this program of "domination?" I hesitated, however, because it was by no means clear that Portia was even aware of its roots in alchemy, and I had promised Charlotte to share this knowledge with no one.

Upon reflection, my place is obvious. I am to bring to America a means of generating power that, by virtue of its superiority and low cost, will supplant all existing means, and upon which the entire American economy could quickly become dependent. Germany would control the mines providing all the fuel, and hence would be in a position to easily cut off our supply. Under those circumstances, Germany would indeed dominate us, and be well-positioned to undercut the industries of its European neighbors as well using the same tactic. In a word, Germany could indeed achieve the domination of which Portia spoke, at least in the economic sphere.

Of course, the situation isn't quite that simple. Nonetheless, Austerlitz' argument that the Western world needs power to grow is hard to refute.

Our meal ended with strawberries and whipped cream, followed by coffee but no liqueur. Spirits, Portia explained, were believed to weaken the action of the radium cure.

"Luckily, I have a bottle of cognac in my room," she said. "Come up with me so we can finish this wonderful meal properly."

We were already more than tipsy, and I knew full well how the evening would end if I accepted her suggestion. I was tempted, I can't deny it. Seeing my hesitancy, she added, "My sister wouldn't mind at all. She wants you to be happy and have what you need."

"Not tonight," I said, and I must add that I expected the invitation to be repeated in the near future. To my shame, I couldn't bring myself to fully close the door on that possibility.

"I understand," she said. "Not tonight." We parted with a brief touch of the lips.

Zozzled as I was, the import of her statement about Charlotte wanting me to "have what I need" didn't hit home at the moment, and I'm in no state to think it through now. Even though it's dark, I need a walk in the fresh air to clear my head before Charlotte arrives.

Diary of Adam Luce
Joachimsthal, 16 April, 1924

When Charlotte did appear at my cabin door, dressed in white as before, I could smell alcohol on her breath, and I experienced a wild flash of jealousy. Where had she been drinking, and with whom? I couldn't imagine her in either of the two taverns frequented by the locals, nor could I picture her sitting alone in her room with a bottle.

"How gallant of you to refuse my sister's invitation," she said, putting her hands on my face and kissing my lips.

"You were there in the dining room?"

"Of course I was. We share the same body. Where else could I be?"

"What? The same body? What do you mean?" I stepped back and sank onto the bed, my head spinning as much from her bizarre declaration as from the alcohol that continued to circulate in my veins. She sat down beside me and put an arm around my shoulder.

"It's okay," she whispered in English.

The bed seemed to be dissolving into a cloud-like substance into which I was sinking against my will, as though we were back in Berlin and I had inhaled ether. I fought for control and the sensation finally subsided, but the avalanche of disastrous thoughts continued. What this would mean for our future? Were all my plans to be dashed? How could something like this be *okay* in any way?

She continued speaking. I had the sense she had rehearsed every word of this speech. "It's not an unknown condition, Adam. It's called 'exchanged personality.' There was a woman in Stuttgart at the end of the last century who was just like me, except she spoke German and her sister spoke perfect French. Well, I say 'her sister' but the monograph I read used the term 'alternate identity.' Her name was Caroline Halsbeck. And there was an American woman too, I forget her name. I looked them up in the medical section of the Universitätsbibliothek. I'm sure there are others."

"Have you always been... sisters like this?" I asked, although the real question in my mind was whether or not this condition was permanent. If that were the case, what was I to do? Propose to two different women?

"I emerged when we were nine. It was after my mother died in the influenza epidemic. We have no real memories of the time before that, only what we've been told by others, mostly Uncle Wolfie. No one in my family talks about the past very much, and when they do it's always about politics or history."

"Why didn't you tell me? Don't you realize what this means?" I was almost shouting.

Tears trickled down Charlotte's cheeks. "I was scared." She stared into my eyes. "We've always kept it a secret, Adam. There was just this girl named Portia who had a little wild streak. I got us into trouble sometimes, but I'm careful now." She squeezed my hand, smiling through her tears. "Except when it comes to Adam Luce. I lose all control with him."

"Charlotte, this is serious."

"I am serious. What I just said is true. Don't you see? The stupidest thing in the world a woman in my situation could do is fall in love. And here I am."

"And is Portia with us?"

"What does it matter?"

"I want to know."

"When I take over, it's like she falls asleep. I can do anything I want, so long as I protect her from harm. Sometimes I tell her the things that happened while she slept, and sometimes I don't. She knows a lot about you, Adam."

She pushed me back against the wall and leaned forward so that her face was very close.

"About Portia. I'm sorry I didn't tell you sooner. I should have. I know it puts limits on some things."

"I would say so," I shot back, my confusion now mixed with anger and frustration.

"Just treat us like you would any twins, my darling. Make it simple. We'll manage."

I couldn't speak. She could see that I was taking it hard, and she brushed my forehead as she might a child with a fever. "You'll get used to this."

Gradually I regained my composure. There would be no proposal that night, no marriage, no bohemian apartment in Manhattan where my scientist colleagues and her artist friends drank brandy and debated the future of the world. What we have is what we have right now. As I write these words, I can't help but remember her admonition in the park at a time that now seems in the distant past. "Every minutes is important to us."

Diary of Adam Luce

Joachimsthal, 9 April, 1924

First Charlotte's revelation and now this. I felt like my heart might burst from my chest after what I heard in the cramped space behind the air vent tonight. The rough calculations I've just completed only heighten my distress.

Austerlitz' discourse began innocently enough with references to the transmutation of metals, references which, taken symbolically, I could easily link back to *The Furnace*. He dismissed the notion that lead could miraculously be transmuted into gold, but then asserted that in some cases literal transmutation could take place, notably in the case of uranium.

Because of their surfeit of energy, as he put it, the atoms of purified uranium throw off excess neutrons which, striking the nuclei of other nearby atoms, cause them to split in two, the result being an atom of barium and one of the noble gas, krypton. Three neutrons are also thrown off in the process, and these strike and split other uranium atoms, generating even more neutrons to do their destructive work and causing a chain reaction on the level of atoms.

What's most important, though, is the energy that's released each time an atom splits. According to the figures Austerlitz wrote out on the blackboard, the amount of energy from one split atom is infinitesimal, but multiplied by the number of atoms in even a gram of uranium, it's enormous.

He made no mention of how that energy might be converted into electrical current, and I think I know why. He's not building generators. He's building bombs. He'll most likely equip the steamer trunks that house them with fake electrical connectors on the exterior to quash any doubts I might have as to whether or not his fantastical "generators" might be suitable for connection to existing electrical systems. And they'll be locked, to thwart any curious impulses that would lead me to search them out in the ship's hold and look inside. In my ignorance, I'll shepherd his devices to locations in America's major cities where they'd pose a threat virtually impossible to neutralize.

I can't be sure these suppositions are true, but my God, what if they are? What am I to do?

As I ponder my situation, it's clear that this evil work must be stopped, and the responsibility is mine alone. I'm trapped here. Any attempt to back out of the agreement I entered into would no doubt result in an unfortunate—and fatal—accident for one Adam Luce. Were I somehow to obtain an audience with an individual within the army of occupation powerful enough to put a halt to this, what would I say? That an alchemist from Berlin is secretly building bombs capable of blowing up whole cities based on atomic particles unknown to science?

It's worse. I can't be sure that Portia doesn't know the true nature of Austerlitz' research, knowledge which *ipso facto* extends to Charlotte. And if it does, I can only conclude that the woman I love has never ceased to deceive me. It cannot be.

Wolfgang Austerlitz
Überlegungen, 10 April, 1924

Our predecessors were obsessed with gold, the noble metal that cannot be tarnished and the symbolical representation of a mind impervious to the distractions of the external world. But that world has changed. It has been clear to me for some time that our Work must evolve and respect the need for external manifestation, that is to say, for action.

We must now look to *Uran*[5] as the emblem of our Work. *Uran* is the most highly evolved metal known to man. It's more dense than gold, and it is so powerful that it radiates energy. Gold was the source of wealth and power for the nations of the old order. *Uran* will dominate the new, and those who can harness its power will lead the world. It is no coincidence that the *metallum primum* of the future was discovered by a German.

The Lodge must come to understand this new path. The manipulation of human chemistry, no matter what insights it may bring, must be set aside. Our new work is the chemistry of war.

Diary of Adam Luce
Joachimsthal, 11 April, 1924

Tonight was Charlotte's last here in Joachimsthal. She must accompany her sister back to Berlin, as she put it, suggesting she had a choice in the matter. It seems that Portia has temporarily assumed an important role in Austerlitz' affairs, serving as his personal secretary in those matters which he wishes to keep secret from the

KDE hierarchy. We talked, and risking all, I told her everything. Then we clung to one another as if we were fated never to meet again in this life.

Now I am once again alone. If my suspicions about uranium bombs prove out, I'm bound to act, but before I act I must see a device with my own eyes, no matter what the risk.

Diary of Adam Luce
Joachimsthal, 14 April, 1924

More than a dozen purveyors arrive at the *Kurhaus* kitchen every morning from the surrounding farms to deliver eggs, milk, butter, all manner of fresh and smoked meats, green vegetables, sacks of potatoes, onions and more, and this parade of men led me to a plan. It played out thus. I intercepted a young farmer with a horse-drawn cart full of carrots and persuaded him to sell me a crate, explaining that I wanted to play a trick on one of the girls who worked in the kitchen at the *Kurhaus* and that I would make the delivery to that destination for him.

He agreed, and when I arrived I simply followed another farmer into the door that led to the pantry. I set my crate down next to a box of onions. The other farmer left the pantry and I was alone.

I made my way to the back wall, searching in the dim light for the door I knew must be there. It was well concealed, made of the same wood as the wall itself, its existence betrayed only by a thin vertical crack. The combination lock I expected to find was hidden under a small shelf built into the door.

This was the moment of truth. Squinting to see the marks and numbers on the lock, I dialed the combination I used yesterday that had opened the uranium storage vault. Somehow I knew it would work, and it did. Thinking like Charlotte, I took this as a sign from the external world that I should proceed, and I did.

The device I was risking so much to examine rested on a metal table against the far wall. It didn't resemble a steamer case. It *was* a steamer case. I approached it and forced myself to undo the metal clasps and lift the lid without any hesitation. There was no telling how much time I had before someone would show up.

A large steel tube, held in place by metal struts, ran more than half the length of the trunk. Fitted into it on one side was a snub nosed projectile several inches in diameter; on the other, a socket to receive it. What looked to me like a firing mechanism, was mounted behind the projectile. There was also a timer with a face that resembled the stop watches one sees at athletic events here.

My heart began to pound. It appeared to me that the "bullet" could quite easily slide into the socket were the trunk to be accidentally tipped. Why, I thought, would Austerlitz risk such a catastrophe? I was overwhelmed with a wish to put as much distance between myself and that bomb as possible. It was of course a foolish thought. If detonated, the bomb would produce a crater extending beyond the borders of the village, one that would most certainly include this cabin where I'm writing now. I moved as quickly as possible to close the lid and refasten the clasps, as though those measures would somehow reduce the irrational fear that had gripped me.

I exited the lab without incident and emerged from the pantry into the fresh mountain air of a sunny morning. Then I walked straight to work. I was in no mood for breakfast.

Diary of Adam Luce
Joachimsthal, 15 April, 1924

From watching Austerlitz once again from behind the air vent I have learned that my fears about the presence of a live bomb in the *Kurhaus* are groundless. The projectile and the socket there aren't fabricated from uranium. They're made of lead. Lead and metallic uranium are virtually identical in appearance, and more to the point, they're both quite heavy. Lead is therefore the perfect stand-in for testing the bomb's firing mechanism, which is the last component that's to be completed. All that remains to be determined is the explosive compound that's to propel the projectile into its socket. The most promising candidate is to be tested in about three weeks, upon Austerlitz' return from his Berlin trip. If that test succeeds, mine will begin soon after.

I cannot allow a bomb of such destructive potential to reach American soil, but I can't think of any way to stop it. The fatal steamer trunks will be escorted to the vessel destined to carry it across the Atlantic by loyal Freikorps guards who will be immune to bribery, and whom I could certainly not overpower. Once I'm aboard the responsibility for their safe passage will be mine alone, but what could I do at that point?

I've tried to picture myself lugging a steamer trunk up from a cargo hold and somehow maneuvering it overboard during the passage to America, but that's sheer fantasy. I couldn't manage it alone, and to enlist aid in such a bizarre task would not be easy. If I could pick the lock, would I have the skill to disarm the firing mechanisms? Would it be enough to smash whatever I could, knowing the various mechanisms were out of alignment? Would such a course of action risk premature detonation aboard the ship? The fact is, I would never get that far. Knowing Austerlitz, those trunks won't be locked. They'll be welded shut.

Even if I were to succeed in sending some of Austerlitz' bombs to the bottom of the ocean, would it not be all too easy for him to build others – dozens, for all I know. Still, time would then be on my side, time to find help, someone in power who might give credence to my dubious tale. The fact is, destroying the bombs isn't enough. The builders must be eliminated from the equation as well, a necessity that's hard for me to face. Austerlitz must be killed.

✠

Diary of Adam Luce
Joachimsthal, 19 April, 1924

The plan I've managed to work out puts a friend in danger, one of the few friends I have in this life. But at least I haven't sugar-coated the risks.

I rode to Chemnitz this morning in the company of two German ladies about my mother's age and, as it always the case when I wear clothes that identify me as one of the staff, they acted as though they had the coach to themselves. Given what lies ahead for me, I wish I knew a trick that would make me truly invisible.

Upon my arrival I quickly found a public telephone and gave the operator Johnny's familiar number.

He answered in a sleepy voice, as though he hadn't had his coffee yet, but quickly brightened at the sound of my voice.

"I knew I'd hear from you sooner or later. How much money do you need, and where should I send it?"

"This isn't about money, *mein Freund*."

"If you're calling me your friend, you must be in real trouble. What's her name? Is she Jewish?"

"It's worse than that."

"What could be worse than being Jewish in southern Germany?"

I didn't respond, and my silence succeeded in bringing some gravity to our exchange.

"Okay. What's wrong?" he asked after a long pause.

"Can you come down here for two or three weeks? I can't do this alone. Actually I can't do it at all without you."

"Do what?"

I debated with myself for a long moment about how much I should share, particularly by telephone, when I couldn't gauge his reactions. To suggest that the history of the world was at stake would surely evoke skepticism, if not utter disbelief.

"Johnny, something very bad is happening down here and I think it's my responsibility to stop it if I can. But I can't do it alone."

His tone suddenly changed. "You're serious, aren't you?"

"Deadly serious."

"I can be there Monday."

"That's wonderful. But I have to tell you, this could be very dangerous."

"There's nothing worth doing that's not dangerous. You know that's how I think."

I explained the best way to get to Joachimsthal via Chemnitz, what sort of clothes to wear so he could blend in and how to find my cabin once he arrived. I was overcome with relief that he would be by my side.

"If we can do this," I said "I promise that I'll get you to America, even if I have to swear you're my brother."

I couldn't believe his response.

"I think we already are brothers."

Diary of Adam Luce

Joachimsthal, 21 April, 1924

As I sit here at my table my eyes keep straying to the make-shift bed I arranged for Johnny on the floor by the window. Once again, he has found a way to confound me. No, that's not well put. He wasn't consciously searching for a way to conjure up the unexpected. It's simply in his nature.

Being familiar with the train schedule into Chemnitz from Berlin, I estimated he would arrive around sunset. I had planned a dinner of local fare for us at the *Wolpertinger* with plenty of beer to minimize the trepidation he would certainly feel when I explained my plan to thwart Austerlitz.

He arrived almost two hours later than expected, and he was dressed to the teeth, complete with a dark green polka dot tie of fine silk. My shock must have registered on my face when I greeted him, because he quickly explained that he was staying at the *Kurhaus* and felt the need to dress so that he would avoid attracting attention.

I was speechless.

"The rooms have telephones, you know," he said. "I thought that might come in handy if we need to call for help."

I thought, *Who would we call?*

"I think we're in this alone," I said.

"Are you going to explain exactly what it is that we're in?"

I suggested we discuss it over beer and brandy, like the old days. Thankfully, we're about the same size, and I was able to provide him with a shirt and jacket suitable for the local taverns. On his suggestion we chose one of the Czech establishments, where our Berlin *sprache* would give us privacy, even among Czechs who spoke some German.

We settled on a place called *U Černého Vola*, located in a stone building not far from the dye factory that I pass daily on my way to work. and heavily frequented by the workers there. The large black cat painted on the wooden sign above the arched doorway looks down on the road with a friendly smile, and I have always had the feeling Germans would be welcome, which feeling our visit bore out.

Once we had a table we drank for awhile and gossiped about the little dramas at KDE headquarters. More than one of the serving girls gave us the eye, most likely thinking that we had more money in our pockets than the workers who were their regular customers, both for beer and other services. When I gauged the time was right, I cleared my throat, a bit over-dramatically perhaps, and set out my plan, first supplying background information that included

Austerlitz' political objectives and the existence of his chemical cabal, but excluding any references to alchemy, which I felt would seem too fantastical for even Johnny to accept.

I hesitate to commit the details of the plan to writing, but as I've already thrown caution to the winds I'll continue. Lead and metallic uranium are virtually identical in color and texture, and they're both quite dense as well, and therefore both quite heavy. The plan is to mill a projectile and socket of uranium identical in dimensions to those in the steamer trunk, and then secretly swap them to create an actual bomb that will explode when the firing mechanism is tested, destroying both itself and its creator.

When I finished, Johnny clapped me on the shoulder. "Brilliant, my friend. I didn't think you had it in you."

There wasn't a moment's doubt that he'd join me.

"I'll need to measure the dimensions of the firing mechanism. Once I have them and, of course, the uranium, there shouldn't be any problems. Everything I'll need is in the old family factory, assuming it's still standing. How much time do we have?"

"Two weeks."

"We can do it. When can I get my hands on the bomb?"

I explained its location and the danger involved were we to be caught inside the lab.

"But you said that in the morning the danger's minimal. We can use the same trick you used the last time."

Johnny's casual acceptance of the obviously great risk gave me pause.

"You're taking this so lightly. We could die."

He nodded. "I can see that. But my life is already dangerous. Too dangerous. I need to get out of Germany. So we solve this little problem, you go back home, and once you're there you use your connections to get me papers so I can join you. Deal?

I reflected that my connections were not quite as powerful as Johnny would have it, and he noted my hesitation.

"You're about to save the world from German domination! Don't tell me you can't get one Jew into New York."

"I'll find a way," I said. As always, his confidence was infectious. We shook hands, left the tavern and parted ways, I to my cabin, he to his luxury suite at the *Kurhaus*.

Diary of Adam Luce
Joachimsthal, 22 April, 1924

Can we pull this off? When Johnny asked me to explain the details of how the uranium we are to pilfer is transported to the vault and stored, it came home to me that I alone am responsible for the accuracy of the vault's inventory records. My signature is on every line of the weekly tracking sheet and in the permanent record book as well. No one else checks to verify that the output of the factory, as I've come to call the purification complex, matches the input to the vault. A missing ingot or two could go undiscovered for months. In fact, no one cares about the quantity of uranium in the vault except Austerlitz, to whom I submit written, sealed reports once weekly. Upon reflection, he has placed an enormous amount of trust in me. That stings, for now I am to betray him. But has he not equally betrayed me? I've no time to ponder all these things. The situation demands action.

The first step in our plan is to sneak Johnny into the lab so he can obtain the dimensions of the projectile and socket he's to fabricate. Tomorrow, on his suggestion, we'll begin delivering potatoes and onions to the pantry early every morning for a few days, so as to become part of the kitchen girls' morning routine, and thus avoid the suspicion that might be aroused if we were to arrive out of the blue.

We've decided the best way to remove the ingots we need from the vault is to do it boldly, in plain sight. I'll simply take Abraham with me to the vault in mid-afternoon. With his help I'll load an ingot into one of the special wheel barrows designed to carry them and head off towards the *Kurhaus* where Johnny will be waiting with a horse and carriage. He'll take the dirt road down to Chemnitz, and from there transport the uranium by truck to the family factory in Dachau. In his typical fashion, he's already arranged for a truck.

Diary of Adam Luce
Joachimsthal, 23 April, 1924

This is too easy. Charlotte would say the planets have aligned for us, but my view is that we're pushing our luck. We have indeed been trusting to luck that no one from Austerlitz' team of chemists would show up in the early hours of the morning and see one of the purification complex supervisors toting vegetables in a wheelbarrow accompanied by a complete stranger. So far our luck has held. Today Johnny hid a pair of calipers and a tape measure in one of his sacks of potatoes and spent about fifteen minutes in the lab while I stood guard outside the door to be sure he could exit without being seen.

Once we were out of sight of the *Kurhaus* he turned to me grinning ear-to-ear. "Now we're cookin' with gas," he said in English. Then, back in German, "I think today's the day we take the ingots." He was right. There was no reason to put it off. No one day was going to be better than any other.

We pulled it off without a hitch. Johnny's no doubt reached Dachau by now, while I'm left here to wait.

Diary of Adam Luce
Joachimsthal, 26 April, 1924

Johnny hasn't returned, and of course I have no way to reach him. Most likely all is well, but I can't know that with certainty. The unvarnished truth is, I can't know anything with certainty. I can't even be certain that Charlotte and Portia aren't normal twin sisters, as if the word normal could be used to characterize anything about that pair.

What's worse, I can't feel certain I will have done the right thing if I my plan succeeds. If the bomb detonates as it's meant to, one of the most brilliant intellects of our century will be extinguished, not to mention his retinue, and dozens or even hundreds of innocent peasants. Yes, hundreds of lives may well hang in the balance here, and I can't dismiss the second thoughts I'm having. Is it truly my place to make decisions like this? Would it not be wiser to let well enough alone? I could simply flee, and take my chances on the back roads of Germany. Charlotte surely has friends who could hide me once I reached Berlin. From there, Uncle Wyn's connections could get me safely home, although relying on that bastard turns my stomach.

Absent my intervention, Austerlitz' strategy would proceed to its end, effectively crippling America as a war power. It would pave the way for German hegemony in Europe and what would amount to a new Peace of Bismarck for the twentieth century, all achieved without one shot having been fired. Who am I to determine that this outcome wouldn't better serve the common good than a series of new wars, prosecuted with ever more terrible weapons?

In the end, that's a judgment I cannot make. I think it would challenge Solomon! But I do know this. I can't let myself be used once again in a scheme I do not even fully understand. If that's my sole commitment, am I bound to engineer Austerlitz' death? No. In that case I'm only bound to wash my hands of this whole endeavor, which leads back to the idea of escape.

It's too late to entertain thoughts like these. I'm not alone in this anymore. I've committed Johnny to this campaign, and he's invested as much as I am. I'm morally bound to respect the risks he took for me, not to mention his masterful metalworking.

I must admit, however, and not without a good measure of shame, that I've more than once thought through plans to warn Austerlitz if I change my mind at the last minute.

Diary of Adam Luce
Joachimsthal, 28 April, 1924

With each passing day I'm more keyed up. Only six are left before the test and I've not heard a word from Johnny. I'm having difficulty concentrating during the day to the point that even my team has noticed it. Abraham actually offered me a swig of forbidden schnapps this morning, and I accepted it. I suspect I am the only German who's ever treated these Czechs like human beings, and they've come to trust me. Well, that's an interesting slip of the pen. I just made myself a German. I'm obviously more firmly in Austerlitz' orbit than I realize, even as I seek his ruin.

Like the cold and calculating Germans in those old propaganda films, I'm obsessed with the details of arming Austerlitz' bomb with real uranium: how we'll transport the milled bullet and socket to the *Kurhaus* without attracting attention, how and when we'll enter the lab, whether or not we'll dare to turn on the lights or try to work by bursts of light from my combat flashlight, what we'll need to do if we encounter a staff chemist who happens to be working late, where we'll hide the lead components we've removed. I suppose this is my way of not confronting the essence of what I'm up to. I'm plotting a murder.

Of course, I can tell myself I'm bravely putting my life in danger to commit an act of patriotic sabotage, which is true enough, but in the end, the man who gave love and affection to Portia and Charlotte when they needed it most will be dead. Uncle Wolfie. He's been their anchor through the Great War and the chaos that's followed, and though Charlotte perceives a change and fears the worst from him, it's clear she loves him still, as does Portia. Thank God those two stayed in Berlin when Austerlitz returned down here. I'm afraid their presence here might have complicated matters beyond what I'm equipped to handle.

✠

Diary of Adam Luce
Joachimsthal, 28 April, 1924

Johnny arrived without warning in the early evening, perched on the driver's seat of a horse-drawn carriage, reins in hand, looking for all the world like a character out of a western, complete with a wide-brimmed hat. He waived and smiled as he climbed down from the carriage and tied the horse to a nearby tree. Then he walked over to me and slapped me on the back.

"We're in business, my friend. Are the wheel barrows ready to load?"

I glanced over at the carriage with its flimsy doors and high, spindly wheels and wondered at how such an innocent looking vehicle could transport such a terrible cargo. And yet it did.

"Over there," I said, nodding towards the stand of conifers uphill from my cabin.

"Then let's make the transfer. I don't want anything going wrong if my horse gets spooked and jars the replicas."

Our plan was to enter the laboratory in the dark of night. No one stays up late in this village, not even the guests of the *Kurhaus*. Johnny had estimated that the task of replacing the lead components of the test bomb with his uranium substitutes could be completed in a matter of minutes. He would depart for Berlin at dawn while I remained behind until the day of the test and, as Johnny put it, "act normal."

Around eleven o'clock we loaded the substitutes into the wheelbarrows I'd managed to borrow and, making sure to keep the uranium components far enough apart to avoid unwanted interaction, rolled them down to the *Kurhaus* by the light of the moon. The substitution went off without a hitch. Once we returned to my cabin, Johnny decided to leave at once. It seemed to me that the roads might be dangerous and night, and that he could easily get lost, but he assured me that the horse knew the roads quite well.

We shook hands and then he gave me a hug. Both of us knew we might never meet again, but he wouldn't admit it.

"I'll see you in Manhattan in a few months," he said with a jaunty smile. "Maybe sooner in Berlin, if you're not in too much of a hurry to escape the Fatherland."

He's gone now, and there's nothing for me to do but wait for Saturday when I'll take the morning carriage to Chemnitz... and never return. My small valise is already packed. A sturdy motorcycle awaits me there, for which I've paid in advance. Three more days.

Wolfgang Austerlitz
Überlegungen, 28 April, 1924

I think I've shared too much with young Luce, but I can't go back now. I've told myself that even if he knew the entire truth and tried to reveal it, he'd be met with disbelief. The variance between what we know to be true and the dogmas that are entrenched in the scientific community is what protects us when it comes to this American in our midst. Still, he's no fool, and he understands the power of uranium if not the means of unleashing it. If he suspects he's been lied to and turns against us, that's a problem. There's no doubt in my mind that he could find ways to cause us trouble. Even his death would cause trouble, and the Raven would never forgive me.

He's already in a position of trust at the purification complex, but he doesn't seem to understand how important his work is. He doesn't feel trusted. What I wish I could do is share our entire vision with him. If I had to bet, I'd say he'd be receptive, but I can't afford to take that risk. Not right now. There's too much at stake. I think the best course is to reveal just a little more about what's going on and see how he reacts.

Diary of Adam Luce
Joachimsthal, 30 April, 1924

Just when I believed that victory was ours I find myself in an impossible situation, one from which I see no escape. I can't even be sure if this diary itself will survive Saturday. It's painful to think that this journal in which I've so carefully recorded the events of the past months has been written for naught, and that it is merely destined to be vaporized. Perhaps if I calmly continue the process of writing my head will clear.

I was assembling my crew for the morning's round of inspections when I spotted Weiß come through the gates headed in my direction.

"You're needed elsewhere," he said, and with a quick nod of his head indicated that I should follow him.

"Do you have today's combination to the vault?" he asked.

I felt a surge of panic at the thought that he was here to verify the uranium inventory, which would of course reveal the theft of the two ingots. I responded as calmly as I could that I didn't yet have it, but that the calculation would take only a minute or two. We went over to the small outbuilding where the sidereal tables rested on a narrow shelf and I worked it out.

"Let's go then," he said. Herr Doktor Austerlitz is waiting."

I was completely confused. I followed him down the path that led to the *Kurhaus*, where we entered the door to the pantry. He pointed to the partially concealed combination lock on the back wall. "Open it," he said. "It has the same combination as the vault."

I did as he said, and in the lab's bright artificial light I saw Austerlitz sitting behind the utilitarian metal desk which I had observed so many times through the slats of the air vent.

"Come in, sit down," he said. His tone was one of invitation rather than command.

I sat, and heard the door close behind me.

"You can understand how eager the French and the British would be to have our secrets," he said. "Your American compatriots as well, I must add."

I nodded, wondering where in Hell this was leading.

"Some governments wouldn't hesitate to use torture to learn what they wanted to know." He paused, and for a moment I wondered if his remarks were the prelude to my own torture. "It's good practice that men who are working on a secret project know only what they need to know for their own work. Their knowledge should be like little puzzle pieces that in and of themselves are meaningless. That way, if captured they can give up nothing of value no matter what techniques their captors might use on them."

I nodded again.

"It's even better when these men are given some information that's false or misleading. This practice is unfortunate, but it must be done. That's why some of what I've told you is false."

I was dumbfounded. And then I had a chilling thought. Did he know I'd been spying on him? Was he toying with me? In fact, it was worse.

"We're testing a device this Saturday. I think it would be good for you to attend." My eyes followed his over to the steamer truck.

"Of course," I said, unable to think up any other response on the spur of the moment.

"There's one thing I need to explain," he went on. "It's not a generator. It's a small explosive device. We're having trouble slowing down the release of energy to generate useful current instead of something like a lightening strike. It may take something the size of a barn to do that. But this device is a step in the right direction.

"On Saturday, we're only testing the firing mechanism, so it will be a very small explosion. The primary explosive material has been replaced with an inert substance. We'll have motion picture cameras focused on the device that will produce a photographic record of what happens."

I could tell he was finished and I stood up.

"The existence of this little laboratory is a secret in itself," he said. "Not too well kept, but nonetheless, it shouldn't be talked about."

"I understand," I said, and then turned and headed for the door as quickly as I could, as though exiting the laboratory would somehow magically remove me from the predicament he had created for me.

"Luce," he called after me. I turned. "The carriage to the test site will be in front of the *Kurhaus* at ten o'clock.

I returned to the purification complex, but I could think of nothing but the fate that awaited me if I stepped into that carriage.

I'm not here in Germany on a suicide mission. And I'm not here to help with the Fatherland's rearmament program either, which is exactly what's going on down here, by whatever name you may call it. I need to scram, plain and simple—except it's not simple at all.

As things stand, Austerlitz suspects nothing. Were I to suddenly disappear, however, any trust he has begun to feel for me would evaporate in an instant. He'd guess that something was up, and he'd almost certainly postpone the test. Johnny's handiwork is flawless, and the fact that it's brazenly hidden in plain sight paradoxically increases the chances that it won't be detected... *if* no one is looking. But it would never stand up to the suspicious scrutiny to which my departure would give rise.

Wolfgang Austerlitz
Überlegungen, 18 November, 1923

If we can threaten the destruction of America's five largest cities, we can prevent the American *Schwein* from entering the next European war. The uranium bombs we are soon to assemble for shipment will do that. They can be hidden in any buildings constructed of wood and detonated using radio waves from a low-flying aeroplane. We'll need someone to who's technically qualified to prime them once they're in place, and to make sure the projectiles are perfectly aligned with the socket assemblies. I want to entrust that task to Luce. It's still impossible to know where his deepest loyalties lie, but realistically, what other options do I have? Any German I send would have a target painted on his back the minute he got off the boat.

Beyond deployment, the other question that remains is where to conduct a demonstration. The Americans will never believe one bomb could destroy an entire city unless they see an explosion of that magnitude with their own eyes. Perhaps an island in the North Sea. I hate the idea of wasting that much purified uranium, but it can't be helped.

Diary of Adam Luce
Joachimsthal, 3 May, 1924

Barring unforeseen circumstances, this will be my last entry journal entry. I'll not stop to write as I make my way to Berlin and thence to Hamburg, and once I'm safely on a vessel my adventure, if I may call it that, will have come to an end. It's fair to say I'm lucky to have made it this far, and I have the Czech Abraham to thank.

I called him aside in the late morning yesterday and asked him if it were true that Germans had on occasion been murdered by his countrymen because of sexual liaisons involving their sisters or cousins. At first he didn't understand me, but when I put the question in somewhat cruder language he got the gist and answered in the affirmative.

"Sometimes it's the man, sometimes the sister," he added.

Then came the delicate part. Would it be possible to fake such an event? Again, he had trouble understanding, but after several tries I managed to explain that I wanted the people connected with the mine to think I was dead. I had plenty of money to pay those that would help.

"You're our friend. You don't have to pay." I had already suspected that anyone trying to pull a fast one on the owners of a uranium mine in these mountains would be perceived as a friend. We shook hands and went back to our work.

In the early evening, per his instructions, I walked over to one of the Czech bars near the factory and took a seat at the long bar in the rear. Abraham and several male friends of his were already there, sitting around one of the large tables near the entrance, each with a large stein of pilsner. Before long a blond with strong Slavic features was sitting next to me and ordering a beer, for which I paid. She seemed to think I spoke Czech, but when it became clear that I didn't she switched to very basic German.

"You want to fuck me?" she said loudly.

"Yes," I replied in a softer voice, a bit appalled by her bravado.

"One more beer. Then we go."

I ordered another round and when we had finished she stood up and grabbed me by the shoulder like a recalcitrant farm animal. "We go."

We made our way to the door and out into the street. The air was cool, the night sky dark and full of stars. She walked me to an alley that led away from the main street and then, to my shock, ripped open the white blouse she was wearing and put one of my hands on her exposed breast. Then she pressed her lips to mine.

I tried to pull back but she restrained me. "People must see," she said.

By then, Abraham and his friends were crossing the street in our direction. Two of them grabbed my arms while Abraham pulled the girl away from me and slapped her face. The two men held me helpless while a third landed several punches to my gut. I must say, they didn't feel like fakes. Then I was dragged further into the alley and released. Abraham handed me the small canvas bag I had packed with basics, and I put a hundred rentenmark note in his hand, explaining it was for a few more rounds of beer and to replace the poor girl's blouse. I also handed him my old jacket, which was to be doused with pig's blood and left near the site of our scuffle to create the impression of a stabbing, at least for a few hours. Then I headed down the alley and found my way to the back road that led to the next small village to the south.

I walked down its deserted main street in near darkness and then continued on at a steady pace for about three hours until I reached Karlovy Vary, a spa town whose renown rivals that of Joachimsthal. Knowing I would need my best energy for the trip ahead, I found a park and slept until dawn on a wooden bench that, in my state, felt as soft as a bed.

The small risk of sleeping under the open sky proved worth it. When the morning sun awoke me I felt refreshed. I continued on the road that led southeast. Once outside the town I managed to hitch a ride with a farmer who was on his way to the large Saturday market in Chemnitz, and here I am.

The test of the bomb took place about five minutes ago, if it indeed took place. Knowing the urgency of the project and the German obsession with schedules, I think it did.

At Sea, 6 May, 1924

Grasping the rail of the Lituania and staring forward into the monochrome gray sky that hung over the North Sea, Adam Luce felt his stomach lurch, and smiled. The gloomy skies and rough weather were a small price to pay for his freedom – indeed, for his life.

His last hours with Charlotte already felt like a distant dream. Their lovemaking, their release from the locked glass vessel by hooded figures who had arrived on horseback, the dangerous final hours as he rode in darkness to the harbor, the nervous waiting while the crew completed final preparations for the large ship's transatlantic crossing, all leading to this moment... like a chemical reaction whose ultimate result was inevitable, determined as it was by the immutable laws of nature. But there was a chemistry of stasis and one of transformation. His was the latter.

In his valise was a folded copy of the *Hamburger Abendblatt* he had picked up at kiosk prior to boarding the steamer that was to take him home. A small article on the newspaper's front page described a mysterious explosion that had occurred in the Erzgebirge not far from the famous *Radium Kurhaus* spa. There were no known deaths, but given the size of the crater, the explosion's force would have been such as to vaporize any individuals or structures in its proximity.

Recollecting that article he thought, *It's over*. He knew he would never return to Germany. It was as if the explosion had not only vaporized its victims, but all the events of the past six months as well. He had never felt so free and so ready for the future.

Margaret had accepted his telegrammed apologies and pleas for forgiveness. She was no doubt at that very moment making her preparations for the trip from Bryn Mawr to Manhattan. A new man would walk down the Lituania's gangplank to embrace her. In his mind, Adam had already composed a letter to his former professor enquiring about the potential for taking a position in the chemistry department at Yale. He already knew he would be accepted. That salary, along with the royalties from the text books he was already formulating in his mind, would be more than adequate to keep Margaret happy and support a family. As for *The Furnace*, he would keep it hidden, like his memories of Berlin, and let its secrets die with him.

Amerika

Yale University, August 17, 1936

As Adam Luce grasped the heavy brass handle of the faculty club door, he realized his palms were sweating.

This won't do, he thought. *Redgrave will read weakness into a damp handshake. Weakness and... uncertainty*. There was no room for either in Roosevelt's brain trust. Taking no risks, he detoured to the men's room to wash his hands rather than going straight to the lounge where Redgrave awaited him.

Staring into the mirror, he thought, *This is ridiculous! I'm acting like a freshman.*

The reflection he saw was of a tall, bespectacled college professor wearing a gray tweed coat that was very close to the color of his prematurely graying hair, a man to whom students and colleagues alike listened with close attention whenever he spoke. Hardly a freshman. His work on elementary particles had won him international recognition, and a tenured position in record time.

He had a wife, a son and a daughter, and they all looked like they belonged on a magazine cover. He also had a lot of money. And he had been close enough to death to know how little money and the other externals of life really mattered. Still, in this little game he didn't have the strong hand. So be it. He straightened his tie, squared his shoulders and then, as an afterthought, toweled his heavily scarred hands a second time.

Bill Redgrave rose from a deep leather chair in the far corner of the lounge as Adam entered. Late afternoon sunlight shown through the translucent curtains behind him, so that Adam saw the man's large, athletic frame, but was unable to read his expression.

Adam thought: *He planned that.* He crossed the room, passing a table where three faculty wives were planning something that involved typewritten lists, and another where a young history professor he had met at some faculty party or other read a thick book with a red cover. No one else was in the club this Saturday afternoon. As Adam had expected.

Redgrave grinned as they shook hands, a toothy, politician's grin, somewhat marred by nicotine stains. Of course, Redgrave wasn't the kind of politician who was in the public eye.

"Great to see you, Adam. It's been – how many? – four years? Too long, in any case. Too long."

A waiter approached their table and Adam ordered a scotch. Redgrave already had a half-empty martini in front of him. "By the way," he said. I've got a cab coming over to take me to the train. It leaves at five-forty-five."

Adam translated. *You've got an hour of my time. This had better be good.* He began carefully.

"How were you received by the forum today, Bill?"

Again, the too-hearty grin. "Well, they didn't throw tomatoes. And I'll tell you this, Adam. I'll take a group of Establishment academics any day over the New York Union Club. They're too damned conservative."

"The isolationist movement is gaining then?"

Redgrave raised an eyebrow. Adam continued, inching towards his purpose. "We're not really in touch with the rest of the nation here at Yale, Bill, despite our propaganda. We don't sense the mood out there. You do."

"The mood out there, Adam, is screw Europe, screw Chamberlain, and screw anybody else, unless they can pay net thirty days in American dollars." Redgrave signaled the waiter for another martini. Adam wondered, *Is this his third? His fourth?*

"It's tough out there, my man." Redgrave gestured vaguely with his hand, as though *out there* were only a few yards beyond the walls of this comfortable, stuffy club. "Damned tough."

Adam thought, *He's drunk!* He said, "Look, Bill, what I have to say is important. And complex. I'm presuming upon our family connections because I think it's a matter of grave importance to the national security, maybe even to the survival of the human species." *There,* he thought, *it's out.*

"I'm a chemistry professor, Bill. I'm not exactly a Nobel Prize winner, at least not yet, but I know what I'm talking about because..." he hesitated, "because of my time before I came back to Yale." He searched for a reaction to this Berlin reference in Redgrave's impenetrable blue eyes and found none. "If you'd prefer to discuss this in Washington, I'll gladly come. I thought an informal—"

Redgrave raised his hand and cut Adam off. His eyes had suddenly gone icy, and for the first time Adam saw the Redgrave who had access to FDR on a weekly basis. Under the searchlight of his attention, Adam words that could influence this busy, intoxicated senior advisor to the President.

"Bill," he said finally, "Do you think war is inevitable?"

Redgrave hesitated an instant before replying. "Yes, I think war is inevitable."

"I don't mean in Europe. I mean war in general. As a phenomenon of human society."

"That doesn't change my answer," said Redgrave. For a moment, Adam had the uncanny sensation that he was talking to a human calculating machine that could weigh in an instant the consequences of any response, and answer accordingly. His plan suddenly seemed naïve. How did he think he could possibly influence this man, much less the United States government?

"What I want to talk to you about, Bill, is weapons. Not actual weapons, but weapons that could theoretically be built."

Redgrave betrayed no reaction whatsoever. Adam pushed on, reaching into his coat pocket for a pencil he had brought along for this purpose. He held its eraser between thumb and index finger, drawing Redgrave's attention to the small cylinder of pink rubber.

"Did you know that there's enough energy in this eraser to blow up half of Manhattan?"

"No, I didn't know that. Is it true?"

"Theoretically. We're talking about theory, Bill."

"Get to the point, Adam."

Adam had finished his scotch, and he felt his emotions rising under its influence. He yanked on the eraser, pulled it out of its metal socket and put it in the palm of Redgrave's big hand.

"You're a Bolshevik agent. I've just given you a bomb that will destroy half a dozen skyscrapers and several thousand people, and you can carry it in your pocket."

"You're serious, aren't you?"

"I've exaggerated a little. The real thing would have a core about the size of a grapefruit. The whole bomb might weigh fifty pounds. So we're talking about a small suitcase. But it would probably destroy most of Manhattan."

"How far away is this development?"

Adam retrieved the eraser and twisted it back into its socket. "Fifty years, if nobody tries hard. With a concerted effort, two or three."

Redgrave swallowed the rest of his martini in a gulp.

"It wouldn't be simple," Adam continued. "You'd need a team of very bright technical people, and precision machinists. You'd need to do some chemistry on a scale that's never been done before – except maybe at I.G. Farben in Germany. You'd need to take some personnel risks."

Redgrave regarded him evenly, weighing his response. "Adam, is this work... underway?" He leaned forward. "Are *you* working on this thing?"

"Should I be?"

"What the Hell kind of question is that?"

Adam surveyed the room. A short, husky man with red hair was sitting at the bar drinking a beer. The wives had gone home to cook dinner for the families. "When I realized what was possible, my first thought was that the country who had a uranium bomb –"

"A uranium bomb?"

"This bomb I'm talking about would be made with uranium. Anyway, I thought that whoever had it would rule the world."

"You did, huh?"

"And I thought we should spare no effort to make sure that country was America. But then I had another thought"

"Well?" Redgrave seemed impatient now.

"I thought, what if there's another war, and *both* sides develop this capability? The thing is, this type of weapon has certain after-effects that can't be reversed." He took a deep breath. "It could mean the end of civilization."

Redgrave sat back in his chair and lit a Lucky Strike. "Adam," he said finally, "You know what I think you should do?"

"What?"

Redgrave took a deep drag on the cigarette. "Get a side job writing fantasy for the pulps. They pay damned good money for stuff like this."

✠

Adam stood alone in front of the faculty club, shielding his eyes against the sinking sun as they followed Redgrave's faded yellow taxi until the road carried it out of sight. In mid-August, the scent of Autumn was already in the air. His wife, Margaret, was in New York on another one of her endless shopping expeditions, so instead of heading home he let his feet carry him through the deserted campus to his office in Sterling Hall.

He hadn't really expected to get through to Redgrave. The man was too oriented towards the practicalities of the present day. Redgrave had no sympathy for speculation that had the ring of science fiction. He had been a long shot from the beginning.

The letter that had launched his failed mission with Redgrave was still carefully folded in the inside pocket of his jacket. *Next to his heart.* The information in the letter, he reflected, might change the lives of everyone at Yale. Of everyone in the world. The sender had cruelly scented the single translucent sheet with her lavender perfume. No, he corrected himself, not cruelly. Lovingly. There was no date. Only one sentence, written in her familiar loose script.

Es ist noch mal angefangen. Ich liebe dich.

Charlotte

It has begun again. I love you. Charlotte.

From the moment the letter had arrived in his faculty mail slot, he had kept it on his person constantly, hiding it at night among his sweaters in a drawer where Margaret would never look.

It has begun again. Everyone involved in the project was dead – vaporized – of that he was certain. But of course, it was impossible to kill an idea.

The brain trust needed to know about this, and to reach them, he needed help in high places. He thought of his old friend Johnny out in Hollywood. He had high-level connections, but not the right kind for this. There was only one hope.

He sat down at his old oak desk, found a sheet of Yale stationery in one of the drawers and picked up his pen, a Waterman Margaret had bought him for Christmas two years ago.

My Dear Zsvilárd,

I hope you remember me. We met in Berlin some years ago, where we shared some experiences at the clubs which are, I would venture, no longer part of our lives. I am confident, however, that the same does not hold true for our pursuit of science.

I remember several interesting talks we had on the subject of elementary particles, and also on the new theories of your friend Einstein. It is he who is the subject of this letter.

An individual with intimate links to the German scientific community recently informed me that Einstein's theories have given rise to a research project that would utilize them in the development of advanced munitions. It's my opinion that individuals at the highest levels of the United States government should know of this threat. Given your relationship with Einstein, I believe you could successfully encourage him to be the messenger.

Let me be more specific....

Author's Note

This is a work of fiction. However, this much is true: In 1921 there was a massive explosion at the I.G. Farben facility in Oppau, Germany that created a crater larger than a football field and blew out windows eight kilometers distant. The plant's designer, Fritz Haber, a chemical genius best remembered for the invention of artificial fertilizer, cryptically stated at the time that an investigation might reveal "new and terrible forces." In fact, the cause of the explosion was never satisfactorily determined. But *The London Daily Mirror* didn't hesitate to speculate that it was a failed attempt by German scientists to produce what the newspaper dubbed "an atomic bomb."[6]

---

[1] KDE is an acronym for *Kohlenteer Derivat Entwicklung*, or "coal tar derivative development" in English. The key component of the aspirin molecule is a coal tar derivative.

[2] Überlegungen: reflections, contemplations

[3] *Grefreiter* is equivalent to the rank of Corporal in the U.S. Army

[4] Acetylsalicylic acid, chemical name for aspirin.

[5] Uranium

[6] Source: Diarmuid Jeffreys, Hell's Cartel: IG Farben and the Making of Hitler's War Machine

About the Author

Michael Stevens is a freelance writer whose clients include some of the largest corporations in the world. A serious amateur musician and linguist, he is fluent in several European languages, including German, which he speaks with a slight Berliner accent. He lives with his wife in Berkeley, California.

About the Author

CPSIA information can be obtained
at www.ICGtesting.com
Printed in the USA
BVHW072013251122
652769BV00007B/360